Annie Bags

The Lady in Rags

Laurence Joseph Murphy

ISBN 978-0-9923046-1-4

Annie Bags; The Lady in Rags is also available as an ebook

.

Published by
THUNDERBOLT PUBLISHING

Acknowledgments

I offer my sincere thanks to my brother Mr John Murphy, BLS. (Hons). University of Adelaide, who edited the manuscript, asked vital questions, challenged the historical accuracy in certain sections and made suggestions that have enriched it in general detail.

My appreciation also goes to other friends and relatives who have encouraged me by admitting to shedding tears for Annie as they read of the events that compelled her to take the drastic action that changed her life, and made me all the more conscious that her sad tale was worthy of the telling.

Dedication

To my wife Anne (nee. Annie Grey) whose tolerance and support has been my strength as I walked this unforgettable path with the other Annie.

And to that other Annie
Annie Ferdinand.

Introduction

Old time North Queensland residents who were children in the years between the two World Wars and even long after those conflicts were over, still have recollections of being scolded by their mothers with a commonly used expression at the time, *'you can't go to school dressed like that; you look like Annie Bags.'* Many have admitted that, although familiar with the saying, they were never aware Annie had been a real person and was not just a figment of their mother's vivid imagination. I can assure those who have heard of her, but who doubted her existence, that she was indeed a remarkable woman whose name was Annie Ferdinand.

This is a work of fiction that is informally based on Annie Ferdinand's life and many of the events described actually took place. A number of fictional characters have been introduced, however, in order to provide substance to the narrative as it may have unfolded, but several of these characters have also been created by the author from fragments of information about real life individuals who are thought to have played a role in Annie's past and who, subsequently, had a major effect on her life.

The non-fictional characters whose names are mentioned throughout the narrative have been personified, as far as possible, as history has recorded them and their exploits are factual and chronologically correct.

With the passage of time Annie Bags has faded from the recollections of many, but she remains a legendary figure in the folklore of Northern Queensland, Australia.

Chapter 1: London, England 1879

A young woman hurried along a cobbled street in London's East End. She picked her way carefully, her attention fixed on the narrow footpath that was still littered with the rotting detritus of the weekend markets, and she held her full-length day dress just above ankle height with one elegantly gloved hand. She wore her long dark hair tied up in a bun and pinned with brightly coloured hairpins in the style much favoured in London and the great cities of the continent. Her deep-set, soft blue eyes and high cheekbones gave her a somewhat regal appearance, an illusion further accentuated by the graceful manner in which she carried her lithe frame.

Her pace slowed as she passed a narrow alley separating two buildings. She'd noticed a beggar huddled in its shelter, for it was a dismal winter afternoon and a blustering cold wind whistled around the chimneys and rattled the windowpanes of the high brick tenements that lined either side of the road. She selected a pear from the shallow wickerwork fruit basket that hung over her arm and placed it in the trembling hand that the vagrant held out to her. Then, with a heavy heart, she resumed her brisk pace, shivering beneath the woollen shawl that was drawn tightly around her slender shoulders.

A four-wheeled wagon laden with empty fruit and vegetable boxes lurched around the corner at the end of the street. It clattered towards her over the uneven cobbles, pulled along by a plodding Clydesdale horse that looked like it was nearing the end of its working day and longing for the feed and warm stable that would be its reward.

The greengrocer's delivery boy, a rotund little fellow in his early twenties with a pock-marked face and rounded shoulders, had been crouched on his seat aboard the wagon, looking every bit as weary as his horse did. When he saw the young woman, however, he straightened his shoulders and managed to conjure up a wide grin.

"I didn't expect to see you today, Miss Ferdinand!" He said, doffing his cap. "It's a bit cold for you to be out walkin' so late in the afternoon, don't you think?" He tugged on the reins and the old horse stopped obediently, his big shaggy head drooping and his long-lashed brown eyes half closed.

The woman stopped too and responded with a smile. "Yes it is, Harry, but I will soon be home and my papa will have a good fire going in the hearth." She glanced at the empty boxes piled on the wagon behind him. "And so will you and old Jack, I think. You have completed your deliveries for today by the look of your cart."

"Aye, that we 'ave, miss." His eyes strayed to the fruit basket she carried. "I could pick up those groceries for you and deliver them to your door, Miss Ferdinand. It'd be no trouble at all. Save you the walk in the bitter cold, it would."

"Yes I know that you would and I thank you, but I had to do some other chores and I do enjoy the walk to the shop, Harry," she said. "I really do. It gives me a good excuse to get out and about in the fresh air instead of worrying…"

She stopped mid-sentence and a frown creased her brow, but it was replaced almost immediately by another pleasant smile. Harry didn't seem to notice.

"Well, take care then, miss. I'd offer you a lift, but if I tried to turn old Jack around now I think he'd kick both of us in the shins."

She looked at the big, old horse. He was as gentle as a lamb, and she usually gave him a pat on the neck when she saw him standing patiently outside the Greengrocer's shop, but now he'd turned his head sideways to stare at her, apparently annoyed to have had to make this unscheduled stop. He was beginning to stamp one great white hoof on the cobbles. "Yes, I think so too," she said, "You'd better get him home right away. Thank you nevertheless for your kind offer, Harry."

Harry grinned again and replaced his cap at a jaunty angle on his head. "Come on then, Jack, giddy-up old boy; feedbag's awaitin' you an' me both." The old horse needed no further prompting and she watched as the wagon clattered slowly along the road until it disappeared out of sight.

She liked Harry, but more importantly, she felt in her heart that she could *trust* him and although some would argue that a woman of twenty-eight years should *know* instinctively who to put her trust in, she knew that she was not worldly wise enough yet to be sure of her intuitions. In fact, her papa still constantly warned her of the danger of conversing too freely with the young men of this great city who, he said, were not averse to taking swift advantage of vulnerable young ladies if the opportunity arose. She sighed. Papa was right of course, just as he always was, and it was her safety and happiness that had been his greatest concern ever since they had lost Mama.

Harry had always been a pleasant, courteous young man, however, and like most women she could sense that he was attracted to her. The little signs were all too obvious; the change in his voice, his keenness to please her, the nervous fidgeting with the reins and the short awkward silences following each exchange between them. She sighed, feeling his pain and knowing that, without a doubt, Harry was just as lonely as she was. But there was little point in dwelling on that aspect of her life, knowing that she must concentrate all her efforts in supporting her papa in this, his time of need.

She had commenced to turn down a side alley when a man's voice from close behind startled her. "Excuse me my lady, but *surely* you are not going to venture into that alley on your own, are you?"

She froze for a moment, and then turned to look into the eyes of a fresh-faced, red-haired youth. He had the look of a gentleman, well dressed and respectable in a grey tweed overcoat that was open at the neck, revealing a white, high-collared afternoon shirt. The anxious look in his green eyes convinced her at once that he had a genuine concern for her welfare and, although her papa's dire warning was still fresh in her mind, she waited while he scanned the alley, where long shadows were forming as the weak February sun continued its rapid descent in the western sky.

"This is not the most pleasant part of London in which to be taking a stroll," he said, turning to face her again. "If you keep to this road and turn into the wide avenue at the end, however, you will eventually arrive at beautiful gardens and pathways lined with rose bushes, where a great number of ladies promenade at this time of the late afternoon."

She studied the young man in amused silence for a moment. "I'm grateful for the concern you display for my welfare, sir but the wide avenue of which you speak will not take me to my home, whereas, this alley will. You see, I live in this *unpleasant* part of London."

The young gentleman looked surprised, but quickly regained his composure and a wide grin lit up his freckled face. "In that case it is obvious that I have been sadly misled and it is not as unpleasant as I had always imagined, although I must say, tales of murder and mayhem that have been perpetrated in this district abound in the drawing rooms of the West End. Would you be so kind as to allow me to accompany you? It would give me peace of mind, - with regard to your personal safety, of course."

She studied his face for a moment, turned once more towards the alley and then stopped, looking sideways at him from beneath long dark eyelashes. "If you are to be believed and this is really such an unpleasant part of London, may I be so bold as to ask you for an explanation of your presence in the East End, sir? Your appearance and cultured accent suggest to me that you may be more familiar with those West End drawing rooms of which you speak, than these alleyways?"

"An excellent observation and a fair question," the young man said. "The explanation is quite simple, although I sincerely hope that, in its simplicity, it will not raise further doubts or suspicions in your mind." He clasped his hands behind his back and stared at the ground at his feet in the manner that she suspected might be adopted by a mischievous child who had been caught with his hand in the sweet jar. "I do, quite shamefully, admit that I was observing you from a distance when I saw you in conversation with the grocer's boy. You see, I wondered where you might be going."

Her eyes widened. "You were observing me?" she said sharply. "That explanation can hardly be regarded as a simple one. Frankly sir, how can I be certain that I would be safer walking down this alley with you than walking alone? Why, indeed, would you be interested in the destination of someone who is a complete stranger to you, if not for some nefarious purpose that I dare not even contemplate?"

"Oh no," he protested. "That is not the way of it; let me assure you, please. It is not often that one sees a lady of your obvious quality walking in any part of London without a chaperone, let alone walking in this sort of district, so of course my curiosity was aroused and I also had the time on my hands to investigate." The young man held out his hands palms upward and he had such a contrite look on his face that she couldn't help but smile.

"Chaperones are a little out of fashion now, don't you think, sir? They are certainly becoming so on the Continent anyway, although with gentlemen such as you following ladies not known to you, I should not be surprised if they are still a necessity in the West End of London."

He stood in silence looking somewhat crestfallen, and she hastily made a decision. "Sir, you may accompany me if you wish, but you must take your leave of me immediately if I request it. My papa will be anxious and may be standing at our front porch awaiting my arrival. He does so whenever I am later than expected and dallying here with you has only contributed to my lateness."

"I should not like to risk the resentment of the father that you speak of with such respect," the youth said. "Perhaps, in retrospect, I have been much too presumptuous in my approach and should have found an alternative method of making your acquaintance."

She shook her head. "No, no," she said, her expression contrite. "Please, do not be misled by my careless words. My papa is not a tyrant who must be feared and avoided. On the contrary, he is gentle and fair. I should explain, however, that he is a notable and proud Prussian *Graf*, - a Count in your language, who was dispossessed of his grafschaft, or family estate, during the war with France. Although that conflict was concluded over eight years ago, on satisfactory terms for many Prussians, some territories are still being disputed through the legal system and it has cost my papa dearly. He would be humiliated to receive a stranger, whom in our former circumstances he would regard as an equal, in the humble lodgings in which we have been forced to reside as a temporary arrangement until the issue has been resolved and we can return home to our estates."

"Ah, I see," the young man said, "It was obvious to me, of course, that you had a trace of an accent, but I was unsure as to whence it originated. You speak excellent English, if I may say so."

"Many Prussians speak English capably," she said, "It was already popular when your Queen Victoria married our beloved Prince Albert but became even more so after your young Princess Royal, Victoria, married our Crown Prince Friedrich Wilhelm twenty years ago. She was a popular choice, particularly amongst the fashionable younger set, and that stimulated the desire to learn her language. My papa speaks English too but finds it somewhat awkward when he is trying to make a point about something. He often reverts to our native tongue whenever he feels that he cannot express himself adequately."

The youth had raised his eyebrows. "I admit to having been completely ignorant of your nation's interest in our language until now," he said.

She continued her gentle reproach with an impish smile. "Of course you were, sir. It is well known in Prussia that, even though you English are our neighbours and closest Allies, many of you are so preoccupied with the perceived importance of your own language that you disdain to learn that of any other realm."

"Yes! I must agree with you wholeheartedly and can offer no credible defence to that accusation, but please, rather than make myself sound foolish by attempting to speak what little I know of your native tongue, would you allow me to introduce myself in English, if I may be so bold?"

They waited in silence on the narrow footpath as a horse-drawn carriage approached. The sound of the metal rimmed wheels clanging on the cobbles made further conversation impossible. After it had passed, she laughed. "You must certainly introduce yourself, sir." she said, as they turned into the alley, "As you implied, I should not walk through this awful part of London with a *complete* stranger. My papa would be furious."

"You mock me," he said, "and I again admit that to speak to you without first being introduced was quite insufferable. I am James Pottingley." He paused, but her face offered no signs of recognition of his name, so he resumed his introduction. "My father is Lord Pottingley. As you supposed, we live in a mansion in the West End called Topsham Manor and my father is a Member of Parliament, - but I can see that you are not familiar with our family name."

She shook her head. "Your father must be a very important man, sir, and I hope I have not offended you by my ignorance, but I am not acquainted with many people in London, although I do teach piano to some students, - the sons and daughters of respected West Enders. Papa and I will only remain here, you see, until his grafschaft, - his estate, is restored to us. In Prussia I should be known as Countess Anna Maria Ferdinand, but I have never felt comfortable with such a cumbersome title. My papa and my friends call me Annie and that is my preference."

"Well then, with your permission, so too will I. I'm very pleased to make your acquaintance, Annie. London can certainly be a lonely place if you don't know anyone, particularly in winter when most of us spend a great deal of our time in the warmth of our homes with family and close friends." He looked up at the high dark walls of the tenements where several thin slivers of yellow light escaping from the edges of the windows were the only suggestion of life beyond them. "I've often wondered, as I've passed the shuttered windows of the houses in every part of London, if those who are fortunate enough to have a roof over their heads, know, or indeed even care about the poor souls who are left out in the cold to fend for themselves."

She stole a glance at him and a wave of geniality swept over her, for these were the very sentiments that she herself shared. *'He is not only handsome, but also kind hearted',* she thought.

James interrupted her thoughts. "Annie, you would do me the greatest honour, if you would allow me to become your friend and escort for the remainder of your visit to our great city." He said it with such enthusiasm that any remaining doubts she had sustained about his sincerity were cast aside immediately.

"I believe I would appreciate that experience, Mr Pottingley, - ah, James," she said, a deep flush colouring her cheeks. "I really do need a *friend* right now." At once, she regretted that admission, for it occurred to her that James, as charming as he seemed to be right now, might soon come to the conclusion that a lonely foreign woman who freely confessed to a craving for a new friendship might become more of a burden than a companion.

His response eased her mind somewhat. "Then consider it done, Annie. I'll be the *best* friend you've ever had and I'll show you how fine a city London is." He stroked his chin. "Now, let me see. Where can I start?"

"Perhaps we could take a stroll in the rose gardens at the end of the avenue, James," she suggested.

They walked side by side along the alley in silence for several minutes before he turned to face her. "Annie," he said, "we've only just met, but already I have a confession to make to you; you see, I don't think there are any rose gardens in this part of London. What I said was merely a way of breaking the ice, so to speak; a way of making conversation with you. I hope you will find it in your heart to forgive my indiscretion as trivial."

She didn't look at him directly but a hint of a smile played on her lips. "Yes, I was already aware of that slight untruth, James. I do love to stroll in the beautiful gardens of your great city, but I have walked in that direction several times before today and have found none." She paused for a moment. "And I also do not know of any rose that will bloom in mid-winter. Do you?"

He grimaced and his face reddened. "Ah, - no. I suppose not," he said.

"I will forgive you on this one occasion, James, as your deception was so transparent and I wilfully played along with you, but I sincerely trust that if our friendship is to continue, you will promise to be truthful with me, as you will soon realise that honesty is so very important to me."

He placed his hand over his heart in a gesture of oath. "I do make that promise to you my lady. I am such an obvious amateur at deceit and so easily found to be so, that I may as well be truthful, but in my defence I must add, that the reason I am not a good liar is because I am so unused to it."

He moved a little closer to her as the footpath narrowed even more and their arms brushed lightly together. Annie felt a shiver of anticipation run through her body and hoped that it didn't show in her face.

The weeks turned into months and, by the time summer approached, their friendship had blossomed to the extent that Annie felt that they had become quite inseparable. James took her to the theatre. Gilbert and Sullivan's *H.M.S. Pinafore* was playing at the Opera Comique, and they discovered that they both enjoyed the classical extravaganzas that were presented regularly in the Royal Albert Hall. Like many other couples, they strolled for hours in the warm summer sunshine along the pathways of Hyde Park and over London Bridge. They enjoyed leisurely walks among the myriad fountains in the gardens of the Crystal Palace on Sydenham Hill and sometimes, to get away from the weekend crowds, they took a carriage ride along narrow country lanes, with the lush green meadows of the upper Thames valley on either side, stopping to lay out a picnic lunch on a rug in the shade of one of the many ancient yew trees that lined the river.

Annie was tremendously happy. James was so attentive and so keen to please her in every way possible. She had never met anyone quite like him and felt that, at last, she had found someone who could fill the great void in her life. He made her laugh so easily and, as time went by, she began to notice many little things about his character that charmed her even more. He'd run his fingers through his tousled mop of red hair and frown in frustration when a planned outing didn't go so well, or had to be cancelled for some reason. Moments later, however, his green eyes would light up and he'd be talking excitedly about some other adventure, while she listened on in amusement and tried in vain to match his fervour. Walking together, their arms linked, he would suddenly dart off to pluck a rosebud for her. A rosebud was the symbol of purity and innocence in England, he told her, and she was the very first woman that he'd thought worthy of the tribute.

Their first kiss came at the Royal Albert Hall after an emotional performance by the acclaimed 'high priestess of music', the virtuoso pianist and composer, Clara Schumann-Weick. As one, the crowd had risen to its feet in a standing ovation, applauding and calling out 'Bravo,' and 'Encore'. Annie's face shone with an inner glow and there were tears in her eyes as she turned towards James, who was energetically joining in the applause. She leaned closer to him so that he could hear her words over the clamour and whispered, "That was one of Mama's favourites."

James stopped applauding and looked at her tenderly for a moment and then, instinctively, he reached for her and brushed her lips with his, much to the dismay of the elderly couple who had been seated behind them. The lady produced a silk handkerchief and sniffed loudly into it in embarrassment, while her husband coughed politely and adjusted his collar in discomfort at the unacceptable public display of affection that they had just witnessed.

Towards the end of summer Annie's contentment suffered a setback. James failed to keep an appointment with her. At first she suspected that it was a simple misunderstanding between them of the plans they had made, but after four days without any word she began to feel a little uneasy; it was so uncharacteristic of him. After a week had passed she became quite alarmed. His return, however, was as sudden as his departure had been, and was accompanied by flowers and profuse apologies. He had been called away on urgent business, he said; so urgent in fact, that he had been unable to find the time to arrange for a message to be delivered to her.

Annie had no idea of the nature of James's business affairs, and she knew that it would have been much too impolite of her to question him on the matter. The ladies of this great city, she'd learned, never entered into discussions on subjects that were clearly the domain of gentlemen and which were generally only spoken of in the privacy of their exclusive gentlemen's clubs.

James was absent several more times in the following months, however, and Annie sensed a change in his demeanour on his return from each of these business ventures. He would be unusually lethargic and morose, unwilling to enter into conversation about some newspaper current affairs article that would, on other occasions, have provoked a lively discussion between the two of them. It distressed her to see such a change in him, but after several days in that state of indolence, he would return to his former self, with his boundless energy and constant laughter, and she resolved to say nothing to him about her concerns. It was also vexatious that he had never invited her to Topsham Manor to meet his parents. He'd told her a little about them and about his brother, Charles, but she had gained the distinct impression that he preferred to distance himself from his family. She understood that Lord Pottingley was a very busy man, and that even James had limited access to him when the House of Lords was in session. She began to wonder if James was deliberately avoiding the prospect of introducing her to his mother and brother who, she was sure, were often at home at the manor. And although she tried to dismiss it from her mind the niggling doubt persisted that perhaps *they* did not want to meet *her*; that perhaps his family thought she was not a suitable companion for James. He, on the other hand, had already been introduced to her papa, and to her great delight, had made such a favourable impression that he had already been approved as a worthy suitor.

It was on a fine autumn day, as they rested on a wrought iron bench in Hyde Park - watching cheeky squirrels dart up and down the trunks of the giant elms and across the thick carpet of yellow and brown leaves, - that she decided to broach the subject that had been bothering her. She turned to look at him and there was apprehension in her voice. "I should very much like to have the opportunity to be introduced to your family, James," she said. She hesitated and averted her eyes before adding, "Or do you suspect perhaps that I may not meet with their approval?"

His face took on a stony expression and he sat, slumped, with his elbows on his knees, staring at the ground in front of him. "I had anticipated that you would request a meeting with them soon," he said. "My dear Annie, it is quite the opposite. You would, without any doubt, meet with my mother's approval and that is all that matters to me, but you may find my father and my brother so disagreeably arrogant that you will consider it prudent to excuse yourself from having any further association with me." He paused, and his shoulders sank further. "That, of course, would be devastating for me because I love you so much."

She placed her hand on his forearm. "I would *never* willingly excuse myself from your company James, because I love you too and there is nothing that your family could say or do that would bring my love for you to falter."

He continued to stare at the ground, but took her hand in his. "You see, Annie, my father is an abrasive man whom I hardly ever encounter in my daily life, and I have often wondered how I have lived for so long under the shelter of his roof and yet know so little about him. My brother Charles is also a very cold and aloof person like my father; he has always been courteous to me, but singularly distant in his demeanour towards me, and whenever I am in his presence it is never a jovial occasion as it should be between brothers."

"And what of your mother, James? You do not speak of her often, but when you do it is with so much affection."

"Ah, - Mother," he said. "She now is a different story. She has always tried so hard to be both mother and father to me. She is my rock and I do love her - of course I do." He sighed. "Annie, I know I should not put this meeting off any longer. Needless to say, I would be proud to introduce you to the whole world as my own true lady, but I do not look forward to introducing you to my family in these circumstances. I *shall* arrange for you to meet with my mother at the very least, but I cannot with any certainty, vouch that my father or my brother will make themselves available."

Annie was apprehensive when James arrived to take her to Topsham Manor. He had arranged for a single-horse, light cabriolet to pick them up and he too seemed tense, she thought, as they sat in the cabriolet while the cab driver adjusted a new clockwork device which he said he had recently installed. The man explained in painstaking detail and with obvious pride that the machine, which he said was known as a taximeter, would click over and sequentially display a new number with every revolution of the carriage wheels, and this would allow him to calculate the correct tax he could charge for the length of the journey. Customers were much happier with the new metered taxi cabs than they were with the older hansom cabs, for which the driver could estimate whatever tax he thought was due to him for the time it took to complete the journey, often resulting in bitter disputes over the fare. The driver took his place on the sprung seat behind and above the canopy and immediately opened the small trapdoor near the rear of the roof. Its purpose was to allow passengers to communicate directions to him but it was put to good use for the remainder of the journey by the driver, who continued his monologue as the horse trotted along at a good pace. James looked irritable, Annie thought, but whether it was due to the long-windedness of the driver or the prospect of what lay ahead of them was difficult to guess.

She felt a weight fall from her own shoulders, though, when the cabriolet passed between two high stone pillars, each crowned with heraldic lions and supporting ornate wrought iron gates, which had been thrown open as if in welcome. And her impression of hospitality was further enhanced when she looked up at the arch that bridged the gap between the pillars and saw the inscription that had been worked into the intricate wrought iron lacework.

'Intrare et exire in pace amicitiam'

She instantly recognised its meaning for she had been taught Latin by her tutors as a child. *'Enter in peace and depart in friendship.'* The cabriolet continued along a winding paved driveway and, over the laurel bushes and rhododendrons that bordered either side, she caught her first glimpse of Topsham Manor. Her eyes were still fastened in admiration on this imposing mansion, its many gables girdled with ivy that crept over and partly concealed the warm, mellow glow of old brickwork, when the cab was pulled up in front of a set of broad stone steps. A footman in powder and livery had already opened the massive oak door and he descended the steps to greet them.

"Good afternoon, Master James," he said, in a practised, resonant monotone.

"Afternoon, Parsons." James jumped from the cab. "Be a good chap and see to my guest, will you?"

The footman bowed. "Very good, sir." He walked around to the other door of the cabriolet, opened it and let down the folding step. "Good afternoon madam," he said gravely, bowing again as Annie alighted from the vehicle.

James paid the cab driver and dismissed him. He took Annie's arm as they ascended the staircase and led her between the massive entrance columns into a long marble tiled hallway, with a wide Persian rug that ran its entire length, and she gasped in admiration as she looked up at the white-and-gold embossed dome of the cathedral ceiling, from the centre of which, hung an enormous three-tiered crystal chandelier. *'I think this may be far grander even than the Schloss of our Kaiser'*, she thought.

The footman had closed the massive door behind him and followed them at a respectful distance.

"Is father home, by any chance?" James asked, as the footman took their coats.

Annie thought she detected a faint sigh of relief from him when Parsons replied. "No sir, he is not, and Master Charles commenced his daily walk to the Kensington Gentlemen's Club…" He produced a silver watch on a chain from the fob pocket of his waistcoat. "…not more than fifteen minutes ago. I'm sure he will be sorry to have missed you."

"Yes I'm sure he will," James said, his voice humourless.

"Lady Pottingley is in the library and wished to be notified immediately of your arrival, sir. If you have no further instructions I shall go and inform her that you and your guest await her in the drawing room."

"That will be fine, Parsons."

The footman bowed and strode away down the hall and James shook his head and ran his fingers through his hair in annoyance as Annie had seen him do previously. "I'm quite certain that Charles, at *least*, would have known of your impending visit," he said.

Annie knew that he felt hurt and she tried to console him. "Do not be distressed on my behalf, please James," she said. "It is your mother to whom I primarily wish to be acquainted and your brother may have had important business to attend to." As an afterthought she added. "Just as you too have sometimes had to attend to your business at a moment's notice."

There followed an awkward silence as James gazed at her blankly for what seemed an eternity and she felt that perhaps she had been impolite in mentioning his business affairs, but then he laughed suddenly. "Oh yes, quite so; Charles may very well have had urgent business to attend to at his Gentleman's Club."

The impression that Annie gained from her visit to Topsham Manor was that Lady Pottingley seemed to be a sad-faced, but gracious woman. At first she suspected that the crow's feet lines around her eyes and at the corners of her mouth were merely an indication of advancing age, or perhaps the onset of infirmity. James had mentioned that she suffered from migraine headaches, the pain of which often left her weak and bedridden for several days at a time. By the end of the afternoon, however, when they took their leave of her, she had decided that there was something else that disturbed her about Lady Pottingley. It could have been the forlorn expression on her face, or perhaps the way in which she clung to her son's hand when they said goodbye. It seemed to Annie that she looked as if she was afraid to let him go; as if she foresaw a time when she and James might be torn apart. A terrible thought entered her mind, but if Lady Pottingley suspected that Annie would cause her to be separated from James, she had carried herself through what *must* have been a dreadful ordeal in an extraordinary manner.

The young couple decided to walk the three miles back to the East End as it was still early in the evening and the weather was favourable. James was quite subdued, Annie thought, and she didn't feel that it would be fitting to press him into conversation. Perhaps he too felt a little perplexed by his mother's odd demeanour.

A week later, however, he seemed to be more at ease as he walked her home after attending the theatre. "Did you find my mother to be a person with whom you could become acquainted easily?" he asked her.

Annie laughed. "Of course I did James," she said. "Lady Pottingley appears to be a fine and gracious person and it was obvious to me that she loves you dearly, as I expected she would. I just wish that my own mama had not been taken into God's care when I was so very young." She sighed deeply. "I *am* fortunate, nevertheless, that my papa has cherished her memory over the years since his great loss and that he expresses and shares his enduring love and devotion for my mama with me to this day."

They stood together at the front porch of the run-down house that Annie shared with her father. It was in a narrow street amidst a double line of dull, flat-faced tenements. Rain had been falling lightly and the wet cobbles gleamed in the yellow, flickering light of the gas lantern hanging from a bracket on the wall nearby.

"When I was a little girl growing up on my papa's estate in Prussia," she said, "I had a dream that one day I too would meet a man who would care for me as my papa cared for my mama. I dreamt that he would love and protect me for as long as I lived and remember me tenderly if it chanced that I passed from this life before he did. I love *you*, James, and I believe that my future lies entirely with you, but I am so afraid of what may be my own failings in the years ahead. I shall plead with you to assure me that you truly love me. I yearn for that reassurance, just as my mama did. I know that you have said that you love me James, but do you truly believe that your love for me will last forever?"

He drew her near until his lips were close to her ear. "Yes, I do, Annie, and I will always love you while there is still breath in my body," he said. "I *will* love you, and I *will* reassure you of my love every day of our lives if you will allow me to. I *do* respect your father and I defer humbly to the undying love for your dear mother that he has continued to demonstrate to this day. I can only hope most fervently that your expectations will be fully realised and that you will not compare me too harshly with the admirable personage that he is."

He took a step backward as if about to take his leave of her, but she held both of his hands in hers and looked earnestly into his eyes. "My papa has had to go to Berlin to take care of some urgent business," she whispered. "Please stay with me tonight, James. I *hate* to be alone: - I've always hated being alone."

He didn't resist as she gently pulled him towards the door. "I promise you that you will *never* be alone again my beautiful Annie," he said, and as she looked up at him his face and his red hair seemed to be surrounded by a halo. She understood, of course, that it was an aura created by the mist in the yellow circle of gaslight behind and above him, but it was so appropriate to the way she felt in that instant that *surely* it was a sign, for even his green eyes shone with a radiance that was indeed heavenly.

'Oh Mama, have you guided me towards the man who will love me as Papa has always loved you? I do believe you have sent me this omen. Look at his face Mama. Does it not glow with his love for me?'

Chapter 2: Trouble in Whitechapel

"Hey, innkeeper old chap, get us another round of drinks, if you please, and do hurry up about it before my friends and I die of thirst." The drunken young man swayed unsteadily on his feet and then fell backwards into his chair. The buttons of his waistcoat were undone, as was the high collar of his white afternoon shirt, which was stained and wet, and his overcoat, carelessly thrown over the back of a chair several hours before, lay in a sodden heap on the floor.

The proprietor approached the table where the youth and half a dozen other young men, all in a similar state of insobriety, were gathered. A couple of them had fallen into a stupor, spreadeagled in their chairs with heads tilted back and mouths hanging open and the others, their arms flung over each other's shoulders, swayed from side to side in absurd unison as they laughed and sang in drunken revelry.

"No more drinks tonight for you, sir," the landlord said in a calm but firm voice. "You haven't paid for the last two rounds yet and it's past closing time. The Peelers will be around soon to check that I've closed the doors and I'll be in trouble if you're still here."

"Peelers?" the youth sneered. He dragged himself out of the chair and stood up, leaning askew on unsteady legs as he gripped the edge of the table for support. "Did you say *Peelers,* old chap?" He managed to raise one hand in a feeble gesture to silence his friends, who stopped carousing one by one at his command and fixed their bleary eyes on the hotelier.

"I believe this insolent little innkeeper has just insulted Sir Robert Peel's fine London Metropolitan Police Force." He pointed his finger accusingly at the landlord and his voice rose menacingly. "Which was set up, I might add, to protect the likes of you, little man, from the thieves and murderers who frequent this abominable neighbourhood. Peelers indeed, sir. How impertinent of you."

A couple of his cronies shook their heads in feigned disgust and he smirked, relishing the fact that, as their unofficial leader he could say and do as he pleased and still rely on their absolute support. He turned to them "What do *you* chaps think then? Are we entitled to an apology from this disrespectful little… scoundrel?"

The others raised their empty mugs. "Aye, aye, an apology," one of them snarled. "We demand an apology, little scoundrel."

The leader glared at the publican, his eyes cold and menacing. "Sir Robert Peel was my great uncle Bobby - God rest his soul," he said through gritted teeth. "In the West End we call his dedicated officers 'London Bobbies' in his honour."

A couple of the other youths cast doubtful glances in his direction, but he was oblivious to them. He wagged his finger at the landlord. "You are an impudent little wretch and we have decided that you may only excuse your dishonourable reference to my kinsman by…" He slapped his hand on the table and burst into raucous laughter, "… by getting us another round of drinks: On the house, of course."

The others howled their approval and applauded by banging their mugs on the table.

"Go on now, be a good little innkeeper and do as I say." His voice became low and threatening again. "So help me old chap, if you don't comply with our request, we will consider it our moral duty to teach you a lesson you will remember on how to behave towards gentlemen who visit your despicable establishment from the West End."

The publican was frightened by the young man's thinly veiled threats, but he was adamant. "If Sir Robert Peel really *was* your great uncle, sir, then you must know that his London Metropolitan Police Force has put strict limits on the opening hours of despicable establishments like mine in order to curb the violence that you have just spoken of. Now, sir, it *is* past midnight and I really must ask that you and your friends leave or…"

The youth drew his large frame fully upright so that he stood over the innkeeper. "…Or what, old chap? Do you mean to say that you are going to throw us out in the street?"

An elderly man, who had been dozing by the edge of the fireplace, leaned forward in his chair and squinted across the room. He took an old clay tobacco pipe from the corner of his mouth and pointed it with a trembling hand at the group. "Steady on now young fella'," he said, stifling a shallow, wheezing cough, "that's not the way you should be speaking to your elders now, is it?"

"Shut up, old tramp," the leader said, without taking his eyes off the hapless landlord. "Come on chaps, I'm tiring of this little man's company. Let's teach the uncivil rascal a lesson he won't forget."

The innkeeper's face suddenly became a mask of fear as he realised that the youth was deadly serious and he backed away as the drunken young men advanced on him, knocking over tables and chairs and stumbling about in their haste.

"Over to the canal with him," someone said.

"Yes, the canal," another cried, sniggering as they pinned the man's arms and dragged him towards the door.

Only one youth in the group protested. Not quite as intoxicated as the others, perhaps, a red-haired young man stood in the doorway, blocking it. "This has gone far enough, Wilson," he snapped. "Let him go and let's get out of here."

"Hah! Not until he's paid the penalty for his insolence," Wilson's eyes were glazed, his nostrils flared and his voice trembled with excitement.

The red-haired young man stood his ground. "You've already frightened him out of his wits, man," he said. "For God's sake, what more do you want of him?"

"Step aside or you'll join him in the canal," Wilson bellowed. He was much the larger of the two and easily elbowed the red-haired youth out of his way. He cried out as he reeled backwards and fell sprawling over an upturned chair.

"You're a madman, Wilson, and I'll have no part in this," he yelled. Scrambling to his feet, he bundled someone aside and lunged forward, managing to get a grip on the innkeeper's leg, but it was all too brief, for the mob had reached the door. A couple of them had already squeezed through the narrow opening and were pulling on the unfortunate victim's arms from the outside while the others fought, with howls of delight, against his flailing legs from inside. Wilson took up the rear, bellowing words of encouragement, but just before he too passed out into the street he reached out and grabbed the red-haired youth by the shirt, tumbling him out through the doorway as well.

"Come on. You're in this with the rest of us," he hissed.

Once out in the open, however, the youth managed to break free of Wilson's grasp. He crouched, fists clenched and glared first at Wilson then at the yelling mob with the writhing, screaming innkeeper in their midst. Wilson lunged towards him again. "I warned you Pottsy," he yelled. "You're next in the canal. We're coming back for you."

"You're going to pay dearly for this, Wilson," the red-haired youth said, backing away from him. "You've gone too far this time." But he knew there was nothing else he could do to help the unfortunate man; there were too many against him and with his own welfare in serious jeopardy the youth shook his head and ran his fingers through his hair in frustration, turned away, and disappeared into the darkness.

The innkeeper was a diminutive man and would not have been a match for Wilson on his own. Against all of them together he had no hope of escape. A low stone wall, topped by a steel railing, separated the narrow footpath from the dark waters of the canal and the innkeeper had somehow managed to get his hands around the uppermost handrail. He clung to it in abject terror and desperation, his knuckles white and his arms rigid. "I can't swim," he sobbed in anguish. "Please don't do this to me. You can have all the rum you want. Let me go. Please don't throw me in."

Wilson's laugh was full of derision. "It's too late for begging, old man. You should have thought of the consequences of being rude to your customers over there in the inn. Help me heave him over chaps. He'll soon learn to swim, won't he?"

Two of the others, one on each side, prised the innkeeper's fingers from the railing while Wilson grabbed both of his legs at the ankles and heaved upwards. The terrified man uttered a long piercing scream as he somersaulted over the railing and then there was a loud splash, followed by silence as his body hit the cold, murky water and sank out of sight.

The youths lined up along the railing, peering down at the bubbles rising to the surface amid widening circles of ripples. Wilson stood between his two principal supporters and slapped their shoulders. "Come on, old man, let's see you swim," he roared with exhilaration, but the other two had stopped laughing. They, a little less drunk perhaps, stared at each other in mute bewilderment, their befuddled brains beginning to understand the enormity of what they had just accomplished.

"He's not swimming," someone cried out in a voice full of panic. "Surely he must come up for air soon."

"I think he knocked his head on the parapet of the wall as he went over," another answered. "My God, I'll wager you've drowned him, Wilson."

Wilson peered anxiously into the dark water and then at the mob who had gone silent. "We're all in this together, - *aren't* we?" he whined, as he glanced fearfully from one to the other, but his leadership had dissolved entirely in an instant and each of his erstwhile cronies now stared at him accusingly, their ashen faces laying the responsibility on his shoulders alone for the serious predicament they now found themselves in. But Wilson hadn't risen to be unofficial leader among them without a tussle of wits, and his voice took on an air of defiance. "If I go down because of this *accident* you're all going down with me," he said, "but then it wasn't *us* who threw him in, was it lads? It was Pottsy. Yes Pottsy did it, - and we tried to stop him. Right lads?"

Before any of the others could reply the shrill note of a police whistle echoed eerily from further along the road beside the canal. Wilson was the first to react. "Quickly chaps, let's scarper out of here. It's the Bobbies." He pushed off from the railing and began to sprint away from the sound, but then he abruptly changed course when another whistle answered the first from that direction. He cannoned into someone who'd been following him and threw him aside, cursing in his haste to get away. "Out of my way you fool," he yelled. "Spread out lads; it's our best chance."

By the time the first two officers arrived on the scene the group had melted into the maze of narrow, cobbled alleyways and the silence that greeted the officers was broken only by the laboured breathing of the old man from the inn who had hobbled slowly across the road and now stood staring over the railing in utter disbelief.

"What's 'appened 'ere now sir? We 'eard a lot of screamin' an' shoutin' a few minutes ago. Sounded like summ'un bein' murdered. Wot's down there, in the canal, that's got yer attention?"

"Oh my Lord, they've done for little George the innkeeper. They pitched him in; drowned him they have," the old man moaned, "Poor old George. He never did anybody any harm in his whole life. Oh my Lord, but he didn't deserve this."

Two more policemen arrived on the scene and one, a senior officer, took charge. He despatched a constable to wake the warden, who lived in a cottage next to the lock, so that a rowboat could be launched to scour the canal, but they all knew that it was too late to save the landlord; he'd been in the water far too long and they now had a murder on their hands. All they could do now was recover the body for identification and arrange an autopsy to discover the cause of death. Scotland Yard would have to be called in to examine the crime scene. He sent a second constable to notify the duty detective, while a third was instructed to guard the site until the detective arrived on the scene.

The officer gently led the elderly man; whose name he learned was Tom, back across the road to the inn with a burly arm around his frail shoulders. He ushered him inside and, carefully avoiding the overturned chairs and the hats and scarves that were strewn about in the vicinity of the initial assault, sat him down near the hearth. But despite the warmth emanating from the low fire, the old man continued to shiver. The officer stepped behind the bar and poured old Tom a stiff mug of brandy; he didn't think the innkeeper would have minded. With the mug cupped between his trembling hands, Tom raised it to his lips and sighed gratefully as the liquor worked its way down his dry throat.

The officer pulled up a chair and settled down opposite the old man. "Take your time, sir," he said. "I'm sure the detective will be on his way here soon. Did you see what happened?"

The old man nodded.

"Right then; try to keep in mind everything you saw and heard, because whoever did this will soon be swinging from the gallows at Newgate, without a doubt."

"And I hope they hang every single one of them," old Tom muttered, staring grimly into the hearth. "I've known George since he was a boy. He was a good boy and he grew up to be a good man too. Those young bullies think that they can get away with whatever they like in Whitechapel, just because they live side by side with royalty in the West End. We're not all beggars and thieves you know. A lot of good honest hard-working people live here too."

He looked up at the police officer but his eyes were still glazed with shock "Things have got out of hand now, ever since Parliament banned public floggings and executions about ten years back. It was a good way of keeping thugs like them in line. They knew they'd get a public flogging at the very least, and if it went as far as it has tonight, a cheering mob would be at Newgate to watch them swinging on the end of a rope. I've seen quite a few of them you know; my Lord I have; their bloated tongues all purple, sticking out from the side of their mouths and their own muck staining their britches."

The officer shook his head. "It certainly was a strong deterrent, Tom, but…"

The old man continued as though he hadn't heard. "What a pity the government pensioned off old Bill Calcraft. He's done the floggings and hangings all over the country for nearly half a century. Bill was a great showman. He would've had those bullies crying like babies watching him step up on to the platform, swishing his birch rod and the crowd going wild. It was like they were at a circus."

"I remember Mr Calcraft," the officer said. "I was taken to see one of those floggings when I was a boy. My father said it would be a good lesson for me. As you said though, a lot more just went along to enjoy the spectacle of seeing someone else suffer. Human nature I suppose. Incidentally Tom, it would be a bit too late to bring back Mr Calcraft. I read in the newspaper he died just a few months ago."

Tom shook his head. "I hadn't heard about that. What a shame. Nowadays the young thugs don't have the respect for their elders that we did, and what worries me is that some of those bullies will, most likely, be running the country in a few years' time if you don't put them away." His rheumy old eyes swam with tears. "Find them and string them up for George's sake, Officer, and for the sake of his wife and the little ones he's left behind. Whatever will become of them now? They'll probably finish up in the poorhouse, I suppose."

Chapter 3: Lady Pottingley's Revelation

"I do believe something has to be done before James is the ruination of us. He and those so-called friends of his are nothing short of a bunch of drunken bullies with far too much free time on their hands."

Lady Pottingley carefully laid her embroidery down on a small side table and rested her head against the high backrest of her rocking chair. She closed her tired eyes and waited until her elder son, Charles, paused in his tirade. At thirty, Charles was six years older than his brother James. He had excelled in his studies at Oxford and had continued his achievements with great success in his business affairs.

"I find it difficult to give any credence to your suspicions, Charles," she said without looking at him. "James is just somewhat hot-headed and rebellious at the moment. I'm quite sure that his displays of defiance will pass, given a little time and patience." She picked up her work again and peered at it through her spectacles, shaking her head slightly as she plied her hook and evidently not entirely satisfied with her previous stitch.

Charles stood at the empty fireplace with an elbow on the mantelpiece and a foot on the polished brass hearth guard rail. It was purely out of habit for it was a warm August day and the bay windows had been thrown wide open to let in the fragrances from the extensive gardens that surrounded Topsham Manor. He could hear the contented whistling of the old gardener as he went about his work, and the buzzing of the bees as they pollinated the sweet scented Devon violets, purple chrysanthemums and white carnations that the old man had planted in the beds below the window.

Charles thought briefly about lighting his pipe, one of the few concessions that he allowed himself in an otherwise strict adherence to the austere family values that had been handed down to him over countless generations. He knew, however, that Lady Pottingley did not approve of his smoking, particularly in the drawing room, and even at thirty, his mother's approval was of prime importance to him. James, on the other hand, he thought grimly, seemed to be hell-bent on estranging both of their parents with his reckless behaviour.

At times he was reasonable, almost bearable even, and he had actually spoken civilly to Charles in light-hearted conversation on several occasions when he was sober, but that was a rare occurrence indeed these days. It was much more common for him to spend his considerable 'free' time with his cronies, mostly ne'er-do-wells 'sent down' from Oxford as James had been himself, and they would engage in bouts of drunken revelry, sometimes for days at a time. Charles, with the family reputation always at the forefront of his thoughts, had quite often been obliged to send a coach to some unsavoury little public house in the eastern quarter of London, to retrieve his sodden brother from a filthy gutter, or to extricate him from some dangerous situation into which he had managed to get himself involved in.

Up until quite recently, Charles had managed to keep the increasing gravity of James's excesses from their parents to some extent, but he knew that their father had been hearing rumours through his parliamentary associates and had asked Charles some awkward questions, which he had been hard put to answer in a forthright and honest manner.

"Ah, Mother," he said, "I feel that I have to speak with Father about James and his appalling behaviour." He realised at once that the tone of his voice must perhaps seem a trifle condescending, but that was how family matters were *always* handled and he held two fingers up to his lips in a gesture that signified that he'd concluded speaking on the subject, "I shall say no more on the matter for, as you are aware, it is men's business. Consequently, you need not concern yourself with any of it and I shall inform you of my discussion with Father in due course."

Lady Pottingley sighed and seemed about to turn her attention once more to her needlework, but Charles noticed that her hands were trembling. She looked up at him and spoke, softly and deliberately. "My dear Charles," she said, "it is very painful and embarrassing for me to speak to you, my son, about such an indelicate subject as that to which I feel I must in this circumstance."

Charles frowned. His mother had never before spoken to him of anything even remotely indelicate in the whole of his life. What on earth could this be about? He waited in stunned silence for her to continue.

Lady Pottingley took a deep breath, as if to summon much-needed strength. "Charles! Your father has not loved me for more than twenty-four years," she said at last.

Charles stared at her, his face turning red in embarrassment. "That is preposterous. How can you even utter such thoughtless words, Mother?" he protested. "Father provides for your every need. I know this to be true because I manage all of the household expenses, as you very well know."

Lady Pottingley glanced up at her elder son once more and then lowered her eyes again quickly, seeking the safety of her embroidery to avoid his shocked expression, but in that fleeting moment there had been so much sadness in her countenance that Charles could not have failed to notice. In that instant he regretted his choice of words and tone of voice, and he gritted his teeth in self-reproach.

"Yes, indeed you do my son, and your father *has* provided a wonderful home for me, Charles," she said. "And he has afforded me every luxury I have ever needed to live the most comfortable of lives. I am sure you will agree too, that he has been a generous father to both you and James. I would like you to listen to what I have to say, nonetheless, because it is important to me that you understand why I believe James is so different and why he resists conforming to our social expectations.

As you have so rightly pointed out, our home and our affluence are testimony to your father's care and attention. I would never dispute that and I assure myself that he still loves me in his own way. But what I am saying to you is that your father has not loved me in a physical way in all of those years. You see Charles; he only ever wanted us to have one child. He made that very clear to me even before we were married, but being very much in love and being so young and somewhat naive, I gave it little thought. I believed that my love could influence him and that, given time, I would convert him to my way of thinking. It is a mistake that I have learned, with the wisdom of age, to be common amongst women. It has often been quoted that a woman will marry a man, believing that she will change him and he seldom ever does, and that conversely, a man will marry a woman, assuming that she will never change and she very often does. Cynical as it may sound; I now believe that to be quite the truth of it."

Charles produced a silk handkerchief and mopped his brow. This was not a revelation that one expected from one's mother and he wasn't sure that it was something he needed to hear despite her request for his attention. In fact, it was becoming rather distasteful.

'This is almost improper.'

Lady Pottingley's face brightened a little and she managed a wry smile. "We had six wonderful years together after you came along, Charles, years in which my love for your father continued to grow. He was so attentive to both of us and I am certain that we lost the services of a number of your nannies because they felt intimidated by your father's presence in the nursery on far too many occasions. I am equally certain that those early years shaped your character too and that, when a lady of your choice happens along, you will be as tender and attentive as your father was at that time.

I was so happy when I found out that I was with child a second time and I could not wait to inform your father. I believed that he would be as overjoyed as I was, but I was wrong, so very wrong, and the birth of your brother, James, marked the beginning of a long period of misery in my life which continues to this day."

Charles shook his head in disbelief as his mother's words sank in. *'Mother has been miserable for most of my life and I have never even noticed it. What an unconscionable fool I have been!'*

"Charles, your father simply stopped loving me from that time onwards. He barely acknowledged James's existence from the beginning and gradually withdrew himself from our little family. He attributed his many absences to the pressure of business placed upon him by external sources and offered his apologies on each occasion, but always claimed that he was powerless to do anything to change the state of affairs."

Charles listened to his mother's confession in abject bewilderment, for a *confession* was what it amounted to, and he was beginning to feel that it was something she had wanted to talk about for a long time but had been unable to; he let her continue uninterrupted.

"The House of Lords had recently accepted non-landed gentry and your father was progressing quite rapidly towards a seat in Parliament at the time. Consequently, James did not have the benefit of your father's love and guidance as was bestowed on you, Charles. Certainly not in his formative years when, as I said, I firmly believe a child's character is shaped. James had no mentor to guide him and no role model to tell him right from wrong. Your father had abandoned him and he may as well have been an orphan, except for the additional love that I gave him to try to make up for your father's neglect."

Lady Pottingley placed her embroidery on her lap and looked up at her elder son once more. The lines around her eyes, which were moist with tears, seemed deeper than usual to Charles: Her face was flushed and she became more agitated.

"I could have done everything I knew James required on my own, Charles; I could have fulfilled that guiding role. I could have set my younger son on the right path, but society would have frowned on my efforts as gross interference in what has long been regarded as a father's role and I would have been branded a manipulative mother. Your father would then have been considered a weakling; a man unable to take charge of his own household and who, therefore, could not be expected to take any significant part in the running of our country and empire. The result is that I have been forced to stand by helplessly and watch as my family slowly disintegrates around me. Believe me, Charles, one day people will look back on today's society, with our ridiculous restraints and our sanctimonious attitudes to almost everything. They will laugh at us; they will laugh at our prejudices and our mistaken morality and they will wonder how their grandparents managed to fumble their way through the eccentricities of their self-imposed social restrictions, yet still produce individuals who have grown up to be normal human beings. All that is left for me to do, as your mother, is to hope and pray that both of my sons fall into that category. I know that you have become a good citizen, Charles, and I do seriously believe that James will eventually become one too. It comes as no great surprise to me, however, to learn that he has rebelled at this particular time in his life. As a matter of fact, I fully expected this to happen, but whatever trouble he brings upon himself, or indeed on all of us Charles, I can assure you that we all, your father and I, and you also, must hold ourselves at least partly accountable for his actions."

Charles strode to the window and looked out pensively over the gardens. "My dear Mother," he said at length, "It never occurred to me that you and Father…" He stopped in mid-sentence, unable to put words to the thoughts that were churning around in his mind, but Lady Pottingley intervened.

"…No, and you never would have known, Charles," she said. "I would never have told you about this, had it not been for the fact that I desperately want you to understand why James has turned out the way you say he has, and to ask - no, to beg you, - to show compassion towards your brother in his time of turmoil"

Charles looked askance at his mother. She had always been a tower of strength to him in the past, but now he was seeing her in a very different light. Now she seemed very vulnerable - a small, ageing woman, slumped in her chair, bereft of any hope of ever again feeling the warm touch of a loving hand on her cheek or a strong arm about her shoulders. He wanted to take her in his arms and hug her, but he felt that such a display of emotion would surely have been unacceptable between an adult son and his mother. It occurred to him, with dismay, that he could not ever remember seeing his father show the slightest hint of affection towards his mother and he had foolishly assumed that this was because it was the manner in which all members of a refined society behaved in public.

'If Father has indeed shaped my character, as Mother believes, then what hope do I have of ever being able to openly show affection towards any woman and perhaps one day, find my own true love?'

He walked over to his mother, bent over and kissed her lightly on the forehead.

Lady Pottingley looked up and smiled wistfully. Her eyes were still moist, but they glowed with love when she spoke, and it seemed to Charles that she must have read his innermost thoughts, for her words reflected them.

"Thank you, Charles," she said. She placed her hand lightly over his. "You have always been my pride and joy and I'm certain you will find someone with whom to share the rest of your life in love and happiness. As for your father, I know that he will do whatever is necessary to ensure that James is discharged from any trouble in which he finds himself, and he will do it in such a way that James will be absolved of any wrongdoing, but I can also assure you that it will not be done out of any sense of devotion towards James, and it will not even be done out of guilt over the past neglect of his paternal responsibility. It will simply be done for the preservation of his and our family's reputation."

Charles winced, remembering that the preservation of his own and the family's reputation was the first thought that had entered his own mind.

'Perhaps I am more like Father, than even Mother appreciates, and if I am, God help me.'

Chapter 4: Interview at Scotland Yard

Charles Pottingley strode along Whitehall towards Trafalgar Square. He turned into Whitehall Place and located the entrance to the Metropolitan Police Headquarters building in Great Scotland Yard. He'd never had a reason to visit this building before, but he knew from his student days that it had been aptly named. Scottish royalty and noblemen had habitually lodged here when they visited London, but that was long before the Act of Union had united the two kingdoms, of course. Charles felt apprehensive because he had no idea why he had been asked, or rather, *instructed* by his father to attend a meeting at this location on his behalf and to report back to him without delay with the details of whatever took place. Lord Pottingley had declared that a prior engagement demanded his attention, but a glance at his appointment book revealed that it was more likely that his father was simply reluctant to be observed entering the Metropolitan Police Headquarters. After all, he thought with a cynical smile, it might do his reputation untold harm if his parliamentary colleagues became aware that he'd been summoned here for an urgent discussion regarding the escapades of a family member.

Great Scotland Yard was one of those dingy, yet imposing buildings, dun coloured and flat faced, with the intensely respectable and solid air that aptly demonstrates the workmanship of the Georgian builder. It hardly seemed large enough, however, to accommodate the four police commissioners and all of their inspectors and officers.

Charles's initial impression was confirmed when he was shown into a small, musty-smelling office. It was sparsely furnished with an ancient writing desk taking up most of the centre space, the walls behind and on either side concealed by shelves from floor to ceiling, each piled high with brown folders, which he assumed held case files.

The man who occupied the chair behind the desk was a fleshy faced, heavily jowled individual, moustached, with short hair shot with grey and small bright eyes that gave the impression of being capable of assessing the microscopic details of a crime scene in a single penetrating glance. The girth of his mid-section was prodigious and told a sad tale of many years of inactivity, possibly spent sitting behind that same ancient desk, ever since his time as a junior detective on the streets of London.

"I am Detective Inspector Harold Haines. Please be seated, sir," he said, indicating a high backed wooden chair opposite to his own that was the only other piece of furniture in the room.

Charles extended a hand across the table and was mildly surprised as the detective's firm grip belied the pasty softness of his features. "Charles Pottingley, Detective Inspector," he said.

"Would you care for some tea, sir?"

Charles declined the detective's offer and sat rigidly on the edge of the chair, waiting expectantly. The frown on his face must have revealed his anxiety for the detective resumed his business-like manner immediately.

"You're a busy man I know, Mr Pottingley and so am I, so I'll try not to keep you too long."

"Thank you, Inspector Haines. I'm obviously intrigued by the purpose of my visit here; an urgent matter, I was informed."

"Yes, unfortunately it is, sir. It's unusual for me to get involved in this type of investigation now, but rank has its privileges, as I'm sure you would be well aware."

"It probably does, Inspector, but Lord Pottingley may know more about that than I would. I am his elder son."

"Ah, yes of course," the detective said. "I had assumed that you must have been His Lordship's son, otherwise he would have been suspected of discovering the fabled fountain of youth." His laugh was deep and hollow, an indication to any businessman of Charles's calibre that the man probably resented having to deal with the nobility and perhaps even felt a little intimidated by his presence.

He smiled politely at the detective's quip, but his amusement was directed more towards the jelly like wobble of the inspector's vast abdomen, rather than at what had been said. "My father is a very busy man and has another important engagement, Inspector. If I can be of assistance to you, however…"

"…Quite so, Mr Pottingley; quite so." The slow, deliberate way in which he pronounced the words and the equally deliberate nodding of his bullet-like head left Charles in no doubt that the inspector understood very well why it was he and not his father who had kept the appointment.

"As I said, sir; it's unusual for me to get involved in particular cases of this nature, but if I had ordered one of my detectives to handle this case, and with the diplomacy that it may require, it may have been alleged that he was attempting to pervert the course of justice."

Charles was genuinely intrigued. "How odd, Inspector! I was of the opinion that nothing the Metropolitan Police did in the line of duty could be perceived as perverting the course of justice. You have already somewhat transformed my judgement of your vocation to the pursuit of justice by insinuating that rank may have certain advantages. Is this one of those situations?"

Haines was quick to reply. "No sir, it is not, and you would be doing Scotland Yard an injustice if you persisted in that notion. We pursue every case on its merits and this one is no exception, but because we are investigating some young men from very prominent and influential families on some serious charges we have had to tread very carefully in prosecuting them. That's why I've asked you, or rather, I *had* asked your father to come in for a chat today."

Charles was beginning to feel alarmed. "Serious charges, indeed? This *is* about my brother James, Detective Inspector Haines; is it not?" he said.

"I'm afraid so sir," Haines replied.

"What has he been up to now, Inspector?" Charles shook his head in exasperation. "Drunk and disorderly again, I suppose."

The inspector's smile had evaporated and his bright little eyes narrowed. "No sir. Not just drunk and disorderly. If that had been the case I would never have bothered to summon your father to this meeting. No, no, it's much more serious than that - much more serious, let me assure you, Mr Pottingley. Someone is going to *hang* on account of this little caper."

Charles felt his mouth go dry and his heart began to thump in his chest. "Good heavens, Inspector; whatever has he got himself into now?" he managed to ask, in a voice that was hoarse with anxiety.

The inspector studied his ashen face for a moment and then held up a plump hand to calm him. "Please compose yourself, sir. It may not be quite as damaging for your brother as I may have led you to believe. You may have read about the recent drowning murder of the proprietor of a tavern in a Whitechapel canal?"

Charles shook his head.

"Ah then, that's not surprising," Haines said. "It barely made the news, after all."

Charles drew in a deep breath and exhaled slowly as he waited nervously for the inspector to continue. *'Good God; that's where James and his drunken cronies gather.'*

"Briefly sir, these are the facts," Haines said. "We've been investigating the tragic incident in which a number of young men have, allegedly, thrown the proprietor of a tavern into a canal. It seems that he refused them credit, or some such other trifling excuse. The unfortunate man didn't survive and the pathologist who examined the corpse has concluded that his neck was broken on the parapet of the canal wall as he was pitched over it. He was a kind man with a young family, and the attack was quite unprovoked."

Charles flinched as he thought about the victim's last moments and of his brother's possible involvement. "How terrible, Inspector. And you say you have established the identities of the perpetrators. I assume then that there were witnesses to this cowardly act, sir?"

"We do have one witness, Mr Pottingley, whom we consider to be quite reliable. His description of the attackers led us straight to a particular group of young men. We'd been keeping an eye on them for some time, although obviously not close enough. They'd been frequenting the bars and taverns in the docks area on a regular basis of late, generally being a public nuisance and revelling, we believe, under the illusion that they were superior to the locals and could do whatever they pleased with impunity. They were always patently conspicuous by their mode of dress and their cultured accents as belonging to some wealthy families in the West End."

'Oh no; what have you done, James?' Charles nodded solemnly as he tried desperately to stop himself from crying aloud. "They would be the scions of some of our prominent and influential people, without a doubt, Detective."

"Precisely, sir," the detective agreed. "And that's why we have to be sure that this prosecution is watertight before it goes public, because it will cause a minor sensation when some of the names come out. There will be a lot of bitterness in the East End too if we fail to achieve a satisfactory outcome. Our reputation at Scotland Yard has been built on fair justice for everyone regardless of social status and if we lose the respect of the East Enders it will be a long, long time before we regain it."

"I understand, Inspector. Please forgive me for, despite my previous unsympathetic remarks, the integrity of the Metropolitan Police has always been unquestionable, but you must surely have an ulterior motive in inviting one of those prominent West Enders to discuss this matter with you."

"Yes, of course I do, Mr Pottingley. We have interviewed your brother James and, naturally enough, he has denied that he had anything to do with the matter, as did all of the other young men who were interviewed."

"But, I must then assume that you give some credence to whatever it is that James has told you, or I would not be sitting here speaking with you today." Unruly as James was, Charles found it difficult to believe that he would willingly indulge in that kind of extreme behaviour but, nevertheless, he had obviously got himself into a predicament that must inevitably, and perhaps disastrously, affect the whole Pottingley family. *'Including you my dear mother; you who have loved and protected him for so long and so diligently.'*

"Your assumption is correct, of course," the inspector said. "We know he was in that particular tavern with the other youths involved in the murder, Mr. Pottingley, but we have very good reason to believe he wasn't involved in the actual attack. One of the others, a youth named Wilson, whom our witness has identified as the instigator of the assault, has already been arrested and charged, but is intent on transferring the majority of the culpability for the outrage on to any one of the others. Your brother has been targeted by him as the chief perpetrator of the attack, but our witness has said that a red-haired youth tried to stop Wilson and had, in fact, physically challenged him before the landlord was dragged from the inn. James was the only red-headed person present and we believe that Wilson, who is quite a strong man, may have forced him to leave the tavern with him and the rest of the mob. James's version of the events has been supported by our witness, but Wilson has denied all of it, of course, and has been backed up by several of the other youths who are also very seriously involved."

"James is being set up as the sacrificial lamb, Inspector Haines?" Charles said.

Haines nodded briefly. "There are no lambs amongst that mob, Mr. Pottingley, but yes, I suppose it's one way of describing it. Unfortunately, our witness doesn't know what happened to the red-haired youth after the scoundrels left the inn and this poses a problem for us. You see, he is an elderly local man from the East End. His faculties are quite good but his general health is poor and we believe he could be easily intimidated and confused by the type of barristers that the families of these ruffians can afford to retain. We have enough evidence to convict Wilson and his friends, but if they all stick to the account which they have had time to concoct, James, whom we believe to be guilty of drunkenness but innocent of the actual murder, may go down with them. He may even, as you say, be the sacrificial lamb who pays the ultimate penalty while Wilson and his primary associates regain their freedom in a few years hence." The inspector put a hand to his lips and coughed into it politely. "Of course if we couldn't *find* James it could be a different story…"

Charles raised his eyebrows. "…If James wasn't here, it would make a difference?"

The inspector nodded. "It *could* make a difference Mr. Pottingley. If the primary accused has vanished, the other suspects quite often panic and start to put blame on each other to minimise the role they themselves have played in the sorry affair. That can then lead to the truth eventually being extracted from the tangled web of accusations and counter-accusations that are thrown around in fright."

"But what can be done to make this happen, Inspector Haines?" Charles was intrigued by the inspector's novel approach to his brother's possible salvation from the gallows.

"Influential suspects have been known to abscond to the furthest corners of the empire when faced with bringing discredit to a family's reputation," Haines said. "Their family at home may conceivably encourage them to live in exile until such time as it's deemed appropriate for them to regain their place in society. They are usually provided with a remittance, or allowance, to provide for their basic necessities and frankly, to prevent them from returning home too soon, so they've come to be known as 'remittance men'. I suggest with all due respect, sir, that you and your father seriously consider this as an option."

Haines shook hands with Charles as he took his leave. "I hope you have come to understand now, sir, why I decided to conduct this interview personally as I see it as the only opportune way to prevent an injustice from occurring. I cannot hide my disdain for the manner in which certain highbrows from the West End conduct themselves when confronted with the fact that their little darlings are flawed and need to be severely disciplined, but as I said to you previously, we pursue each case on its merits and the rank of the perpetrator, whether high or low, has no bearing on our pursuit of justice for everyone within our authority."

Charles smiled gratefully. "I will never again doubt the veracity of that statement, Inspector and I'll wager the solution you have proposed in order to obtain that justice is not in Sir Robert Peel's police instruction manual that you, no doubt, have read from cover to cover. But I *do* applaud you and thank you most sincerely for your insight in dealing with this matter in such a novel way. I will take your proposal to my father and I am certain that he will acknowledge the wisdom of it and act promptly to execute the necessary arrangements."

"I trust that our conversation here today will remain confidential and I advise you to keep that word *'execute'* well within your current considerations, Mr Pottingley," the inspector quipped. Charles laughed with him, quite genuinely this time; but it was with relief rather than humour.

He turned to leave, but on an impulse stopped and wheeled around to face the detective. "Inspector Haines, I believe you mentioned that the deceased Innkeeper was a family man with young children." He reached into his waistcoat pocket and produced a chequebook. "Would you be so kind as to deliver this to the poor man's wife? I would prefer it if she was unaware that the benefactor was a highbrow from the West End, of course."

Haines nodded his agreement. "That's understandable, sir. These people may be poor, but if the widow thought for one minute that it was blood money to keep someone from the West End out of trouble she would quickly throw it back in my face. Thank you - and you can trust me to handle the matter sensitively."

"I have no reservation whatsoever about that, Inspector."

Charles strode back through Whitehall with his mind in turmoil. His worst fears had come to fruition. Should James be charged and convicted, it would be a devastating blow to the reputation of the Pottingley family. It would undoubtedly lead to the forced resignation of Lord Pottingley from The House of Lords, and to Charles being avoided at, or even excluded from his cherished membership of Kensington Gentlemen's Club. That thought was almost too much to bear as he had practically no social existence outside of his club.

There were somewhere in the order of 400 other gentlemen's clubs in London, but they all had waiting lists that were so long that a child had to be registered for membership at birth to be eligible for acceptance at twenty-one years of age. Charles had been fortunate, due mainly to the pedigree of his family, to be admitted to membership of possibly the most sought after club in the country. To lose that status would be to lose his only link to London society and to the business contacts that formed a sizeable portion of his member associates. Frankly, as the inspector had said, there were no other options that were open to them and the matter had to be resolved quickly. *There isn't any other way to handle this awkward situation, Mother. It must be done immediately. James has to get out of England and become a remittance man in a faraway corner of the empire, for his sake as much as for ours!'*

A few days later, Lord Pottingley summoned his two sons to attend an urgent meeting with him in the library at Topsham Manor. Charles, as required, had already briefed his father on the facts associated with the incident at Whitechapel, the allegations made against James by Wilson and supported by his cronies, and the solution that had been recommended as the saviour of James, - and ultimately the family reputation, - by Detective Inspector Haines. It was a suggestion that Lord Pottingley considered to be of the greatest merit.

Charles had also spoken to James, who had told him that he had tried, in vain, to stop Wilson and the others from persisting with their drunken assault on the innkeeper when they had emerged from the tavern, but he had realised he could do no more and left the scene. He had simply hoped that the others, some of whom he said were decent enough men, could convince Wilson to discontinue his intended course of action. He was mortified by the outcome and partly laid the blame on his own disgraceful behaviour when he learned that the innkeeper had been murdered.

Charles, on hearing his brother's frank admission and of his shame at being involved in the murder of an innocent man, now regretted his haste in passing on the inspector's recommendation to his father and began to worry about how his mother would react when she was told of the proposed arrangement. Lord Pottingley was resolute, however, and presented James with an ultimatum. If he chose to stay in London, he would be cut off from all family connections. He would have no allowance and no inheritance and, with no assistance to fight his case, would either end up in prison, or at worst on the gallows. If he did the honourable thing by his family, however, and embarked on a prolonged journey to the colonies at the earliest opportunity, he would be provided with a liveable remittance that would be delivered to him on a monthly basis. The arrangement would be strictly administered by an associate of his father who lived in Melbourne, in the Colony of Victoria in south-eastern Australia. In other words, he would become a *remittance man*.

James, prudently, chose the latter option. Urgent preparations were made and within two weeks the steamship SS Victoria sailed out of Portsmouth bound for Australia. On it, a much chastened and subdued Mr James Pottingley occupied one of the saloon cabins on the upper deck.

Chapter 5: Wilhelm Ferdinand

"There, there, hush meine liebe." Wilhelm Ferdinand drew his only daughter into his arms as they sat together on a worn divan in their humble lodgings in London's East End. "Tears will not return the jungen mann to you any the sooner. Herr Pottingley has been away on business before, nein?"

"Ja, Papa, but not for so long. It is now over two weeks and I have not heard from him."

"It is the way of men, Annie. Ve must conduct our business as ve see fit and your duty is to be patient. Give him a little time."

"I worry that he has abandoned me, Papa."

"Ach, mein kind: you are so much your mama's tochter. She too was convinced in her own mind that I had abandoned her every time I had to go away. But I always returned, ja? I always returned, Annie, because I loved her. I loved your mama so much that I would have fought the entire French Legion, if it had been necessary, just to make certain I could return home to her. If Herr Pottingley truly loves you he will also do whatever he can to return to you as I did with your mama, - if, of course it is within his power to do so."

She relaxed with her head on his shoulder. "You are so wise in such matters and always a great comfort to me, Papa," she said. "Tell me about Mama."

Wilhelm patted his daughter's cheek with his free hand. "Ach, what can I tell you that I have not told to you hundert times before, meine tochter?"

"Tell me once more Papa, *please*. I love to hear how much you loved Mama from your own lips. Was Mama *really* so beautiful?"

She felt her father take a deep breath and then exhale slowly. "Hah! Wundershon frau! Ja, your mama was the most beautiful of all. Die jungen manner, how you say…?"

"…Young men, Papa."

"Ja, the joung men, they all of them were jealous and tried to catch her eyes when I was not there, but your mama's eyes were for your papa only." His chest heaved and Annie could tell he was bursting with pride. "Mama loved me and I loved her in return and to this day our love endures. Ja, to this day and forever after this day when we are reunited im Paradies."

"You will be reunited with Mama in paradise, dear Papa, I know it in my heart. But did Mama ever believe it when you told her she was beautiful?"

"Nein, Annie." Wilhelm shook his head and sighed. "Your mama *never* would believe she was beautiful, mein kind. To those who knew her, but not so well, and even to many of our freunden, on the outside she seemed to be eine frau with a strong enough character, but inside," he tapped his chest, "in her heart, she was a fragile flower bending with the breeze that, in her conviction, constantly blew against her. When that breeze became such a strong wind that her resolve began to fail, she tried so much to stand against it, for the sake of you, her little tochter, and for your papa too, with all of the courage she possessed."

"But it was not enough, Papa?"

"Nein, Annie, your mama could not understand what made her feel so bitter towards herself, and your papa could only reassure her constantly that she was much loved and appreciated, but it was to no avail. One day the few remaining petals of her confidence were stripped away in the storm that raged in her mind and your mama, - when she should have been in the full bloom of motherhood, - my fragile flower wilted and died before my eyes with you, mein kind, in her arms."

Annie brushed away a tear from her eye. "I was too young to understand, of course, Papa, but even small children can have a perception that something is amiss and not quite the way it should be. A sadness in the tone of someone's voice, a certain wretched look in their eyes or the stoop of their shoulders where before there was none: I began to harbour doubts that you loved me, because each time you held me close you would look at me in such a miserable way that I knew you were still grieving for Mama. I became convinced in my own little mind that you secretly held me responsible for the void in your life, and I constantly craved reassurance from you that it was not so. Over time I have come to realise that my fears were unfounded. I know now that your love for me is unconditional and genuine, as you know my love is also for you Papa. But the memories of those uncertain times in my childhood return sometimes to haunt me and I am filled with doubts about my own state of mind, even though I try to banish them from my consciousness."

"And I meine leibe, was so deep in my sorrow that I often had the selfish reflections of joining your mama im Paradies, and it is true, I did look at you with a heavy heart, but it was not with any regret or blame to you for my own loss. Nein! That was never so." Wilhelm shook his head and sighed deeply. "Nein, Annie. My heart was heavy because I knew my little tochter would never again hear her mama's sweet voice. When I was forced by circumstances to leave you for long periods during our nation's Wars of Unification, I arranged for the very best of nannies to care for your every need. I employed educators who taught you languages and the arts, the piano, sewing and embroidery, but I knew in my heart that nothing I provided you, not even the very best nannies and educators I could find in all of Prussia, could ever replace the desolation of never knowing your mama's soft touch, never knowing the feeling of her arms around you when you needed love and comforting, and most of all, not having her feminine companionship to guide you as you grew into womanhood. When I looked at you I saw meine kind, my sad little tochter with only her faithful dog for companionship."

"Oh yes papa. How well I remember my dear Albert. You had been to Alcace on business and you brought him home for me. He was just a puppy. You refused to allow my tutors to help me train him, but insisted that you and I should ourselves teach him. I remember the many hours we three spent together then and it became one of the happiest times of my young life."

"Ja Annie, and that was also the period when *you* began to draw *me* from the depths of my own depression. I told your mama in my dreams that I could not join her until I was certain that I could leave you, my conscience clear with the knowledge that your happiness was assured."

Annie felt a tear roll down her cheek and she sighed, the memories of those happy times with her papa and the Alsacian puppy Albert disappearing into the mists of time as she reflected again on her current situation. "My happiness will be assured only if James returns to me Papa, just as you returned to Mama so many times."

Wilhelm cupped her chin in his hand and turned her face towards his own. He kissed her gently on the forehead. "Ja, Annie, mein tochter; that is natural enough and I believe that you will find that happiness, but you must have the strong will to do so. You must not give up and you must forever try to be strong on the inside like your papa; not just on the outside like your poor mama."

Chapter 6: A Plea for Help

"Welcome back, Mr Pottingley." Joseph John Hathaway, or simply 'Old Joe', as the members of Kensington Gentlemen's Club knew him, had been the valet for as many years as anyone could remember. Charles was immensely fond of the old chap, who always raised his spirits and made him feel welcome, even in the dismal weather they were now experiencing in London with the early onset of winter. Joe was always impeccably dressed, no matter what time of day one entered the club, with his cutaway morning coat and collarless white waistcoat, and Charles often wondered in idle moments if the old man actually lived in a secret room in the basement of the club and perhaps even had a family hidden away there somewhere.

"We have missed your company these past two months, sir," Joe said, "and the other members have left messages of condolence and regret for you with regard to your recent very sad loss."

"Thank you, Joe," he said, feeling the dull ache in his heart return. It certainly had been a bitter two months and he wished so much that he'd handled things differently. It was too late for that now, of course, - much too late. He'd assumed that his father had brought his mother up to date with the whole sordid affair of his brother's involvement in the innkeeper's murder, a duty that he'd felt was not his to appropriate on his father's behalf. He'd been terribly mistaken in that supposition, for it was only after James had been rushed off on a ship to Australia that he learned, to his utter mortification, that Lord Pottingley had shirked his duty and left it to him to inform his mother about what had happened and why it had been necessary for his brother to be dispatched with such haste.

Lady Pottingley had been bewildered at first and then shocked that James had been bundled off without even being able to say goodbye to her, but Charles had stopped short of criticising his father's spineless avoidance of his obligation to discuss the matter with her, despite knowing full well that she would have fiercely opposed the decree. He was to regret his silence, for his feeble justification that Lord Pottingley had expressly forbidden James to have any further contact with any family member had fallen on deaf ears and, indeed, had implicated him even more in the treachery. With tears running freely down her lined face she had cried, in a voice charged with the passion of a mother's tragic loss, "Charles, both you and your father will regret this *final* betrayal of me; each of you in your own way, for the rest of your lives."

The word 'final' had not even registered in his mind amid the enormity of the shame he'd felt. He'd remained silent, slumped in his chair as his mother left the room and slowly made her way up the wide staircase to her bedroom. A small solitary figure, she had looked back at him and their eyes had locked just before she passed out of sight. And the memory of that last fleeting glance, he knew, *would* stay with him forever for he had caught a glimpse of something in his mother's eyes that shook him to the core. At the very least it had been displeasure and, - he dared not think of it, - perhaps even loathing.

The maid found her the following morning when she didn't come down for breakfast at her usual time. She was surrounded by empty bottles of the opiate Chlorodyne, which many people kept for the relief of insomnia, but judging by the quantity, the doctor believed that she had almost certainly been hoarding them for quite a long time, perhaps with that very purpose in mind.

Charles managed a smile, but his eyes gave away the deep hurt that remained with him. "I decided that I needed to get away, Joe. Too much stress you see. I took a train over to Devon to stay with my mother's family in Plymouth. Better to grieve together with family than alone, don't you think? I am sorry, I really should have let you all know, but it was organised by others as I was in no condition to make decisions for myself." He rubbed his cold hands together and looked around the empty foyer. "I know I'm a little early today, but I received your note and came as quickly as I could."

The old valet helped Charles to remove his overcoat and scarf and placed his hat in the hatstand behind the solid oak counter in the foyer. "It is a little early sir," he said, "but I was hoping you'd come in while it's still quiet. There's a little business that requires your attention, if it's not going to be too taxing for you after all you've been through lately."

"One must get on with life, I suppose, Joe. I need to get back into my business affairs; keep busy you know; all part of the healing process, so I've been told."

"Yes sir. I'm sure." Joe was sympathetic. "In anticipation of your return, however, I've ensured that your slippers have been warmed before the fire and placed under your usual chair and I have laid out your morning coat, should you require it. He reached into the pocket of his waistcoat and produced a gold fob watch. "It's not officially evening yet sir, so you may dispense with tails for the moment. May I bring you your usual refreshment?"

"Yes, thank you. It's so good to be back here. I feel more relaxed already."

"I have a letter for you, Mr Pottingley,"

"For me?" Charles said, raising an eyebrow. "I don't know why anyone would write to me here at the club. Are you quite certain it is for me?"

"I am certain sir. It was not long after you last graced us with your presence, Mr Pottingley, that a young lady came to the foyer asking for you. Perhaps that's not so unusual in some of the other less reputable establishments I might add, but as you know, it is quite extraordinary in a genuine gentlemen's club such as ours. She appeared to be a young lady of some refinement and seemed to be quite distressed, so I admitted her to the first lounge anyway, which was empty of members at the time. Pretty young lady she was too sir, except for the dark rings around her eyes. She looked as if she'd been doing her fair share of crying. I told her that I wasn't sure where you'd gone, or when you'd be in attendance again. She then asked if I knew the whereabouts of your brother James and when I told her you had mentioned that he would be away on business for a considerable time, she started crying again. It was heart-wrenching to see her, Mr Pottingley. I didn't know quite what to make of the situation. I gave her a glass of water and she just sat there for a time, weeping and daubing her eyes every so often with a little lace handkerchief. After a while she seemed to compose herself. She drew a deep breath and straightened her back as if she was gathering her strength, got to her feet, thanked me very much and left."

"And she gave you a letter for me?"

"No sir, not at that time, but she did come back the following week, asking for you again. When I said you still hadn't been in attendance she looked disappointed, but she didn't shed tears on this occasion, although it was quite obvious that she had been crying extensively before her arrival." Joe moved behind the counter and peered up at the row upon row of numbered pigeonholes, some with letters and periodicals sticking out, ready to be claimed by their owners. "Let me see, your membership number is forty-eight, right sir?" He didn't have to ask. Joe had every member's personal number stored in his memory. "The young lady pleaded with me to pass this letter on to you personally, when you finally came in. When I asked her why she didn't drop it in the letter box at Topsham Manor, which would have been just as easy for her, she said she didn't want to post it to the Manor, because she was not sure that you would get it, for some reason."

Charles frowned." I can't think of any reason why I wouldn't be able to receive it at Topsham Manor; this all seems rather strange." He shook his head in bewilderment, took the scented envelope and retreated to his usual comfortable armchair in a corner of the lounge near the fireplace.

A few minutes later Joe approached once more carrying a small silver tray. He placed it on the malachite table next to Charles's elbow. It contained a silver letter opener and his usual glass of rich port. He picked up the glass and held it up against the light, watching with the eye of a connoisseur, the tiny scales of beeswing floating enticingly in its rich, ruby depths. The fire in the hearth, as it spurted, threw fitful light on his pale clear-cut features as he raised the glass to his lips, tilted it and then replaced it on the tray. "Whatever can this be all about?" he muttered, as he sliced open the envelope and unfolded the letter that it contained.

Dear Mr Charles Pottingley,

I am writing this letter to you with the faintest hope that you will take pity on me, for I surely must be among the most forlorn of all God's creatures. The cause of my anguish is your brother James who, without a word of goodbye, has disappeared from my life and my love.

Oh, please reassure me that I have not been so foolish as to have given my heart to a man who could not list among his virtues the common decency of personally informing me of his intended prolonged absence. Has he abandoned me in a cruel and pitiless fashion, knowing as he must, that my humble heart would be broken by such a callous and unmanly act?

I think of him, and grieve over him constantly, and I wonder at the possibilities surrounding his sudden withdrawal. Is it because of his love for me that his family has removed him to a far place and away from my influence? If that is so then let me please assure you that I am from a noble Prussian family and will be independently wealthy when my father regains his estates. I will never be a burden on your family's assets.

I have felt so secure and confident in the belief that James loved me as much as I love him. What great calamity can have befallen him? Has he wantonly deserted me? I do not know where to turn, but to you for guidance. If you feel even the slightest sympathy for my plight, I beg you to reunite me with James, for I will never love another man and whatever time God shall allow me to remain on this earth will be lived in wretched loneliness, devoid of happiness until I will gratefully surrender to the call of my Saviour.

In my desperate hopelessness, I have placed my address on the envelope enclosed with this letter.

I will remain forever
Your humble servant,
Annie Ferdinand.

Charles reread the letter and when he had finished, he rested his head against the thickly upholstered back of his armchair. He closed his eyes and in his mind, conjured up an image of her; a young woman, grief-stricken, alone and abandoned to her fate by his *brother*.

He thought of the hopelessness he'd seen written on his mother's face, even after the passage of more than twenty years of an unhappy marriage to his father; her impassioned plea to him to have compassion on his brother; her reminder that James was not solely responsible for his waywardness, and the heartbreaking consequences of his failure to recognise the extent of her love for him. Now this young woman's future seemed destined to be as bleak as his mother's past must have been, perhaps with the same dire result.

'But why hasn't James mentioned her to me? Perhaps he thought that it would make no difference anyway and that I would still pursue the same course of action, regardless of his and her feelings. Would it have made a difference? Would I have risked the ruination of our family's reputation by refusing to plant the detective's solution to the problem in my father's mind? In my defence, it is a question that defies a fair answer. I did not have all of the facts accessible to me at the time that I made such a critical decision and of course, once I had presented the plan the execution of it was taken out of my hands.

I am confident that if James had informed me of his love for Miss Ferdinand I would have been compassionate enough not to have mentioned the detective's solution to my father and would have tried some other tactic instead to save the family reputation. I would, quite possibly, have assisted them to elope together, which would have been just as effective as the current situation.

Of one thing I am quite certain; that the extent of James's love for this poor lady and of her love for him would have made no difference to my father. He would have regarded it as just another of his dalliances and - good God; I have to consider that, if my mother was correct in her assessment of my character, there is still the possibility that I am deceiving myself and that I may have taken the same inflexible line as my father.'

More doubts began to surface in Charles' mind.

'Did James, in some roundabout manner actually tell me of his love for her and I have simply put it out of my mind? I really don't know. I do remember that he spoke fondly of a young woman, but that

was after a night out when he was almost incoherent and the effects of the rum that he had consumed had loosened his tongue. But no! I can recall that it was later, after I had managed to get him into his cot and he had fallen into a drunken sleep that, I'm almost certain, I heard him call her name. Yes! I'm quite sure of it now. It was Annie that I heard him call out on several occasions. One thing is without any misgiving, though; if James didn't mention her because he simply didn't care for her and thought she would eventually just forget about him and get on with her life, then he has assuredly misjudged the lady.'

He opened his eyes, sat upright and beckoned to a waiter. "Would you please furnish me with a pen and ink and some writing paper? I shall sit over there, at that writing bureau near the window."

The waiter returned with the items and Charles thanked him and began to formulate a reply to Miss Ferdinand's letter.

My Dear Miss Ferdinand

It is with the utmost remorse that I write to you, for I have only in the last few minutes read your heartfelt letter, having just returned to the city after a lengthy visit to a relative in the West Country. What can I possibly say that will lessen your anguish and perhaps persuade you that you have not been deceived by a pretender to your affection? I can only declare that I have become convinced in my own mind that James must have held you in great esteem, for I believe that I have heard him call out your name on several occasions in his private room, whilst he was in troubled sleep.

Regrettably, I must divulge an aspect of my brother's character of which I am certain you have not been aware in the past, in order to explain his sudden and unexpected departure and to excuse his apparent desertion of you.

James and I did not share a close relationship when we were children and in our adult years we seem to have drifted even further apart. Consequently, it came as a great shock to me the first time I saw him so severely affected by alcohol that he was incapable of standing up and had to be carried to his room. That was several years ago and since then I believe he has tried quite desperately to escape the grip that the demon drink has had on him, but whenever his resolve fails him he embarks on drinking binges, often for days at a time, with a group of degenerate friends with similar traits to his own. He may have explained his previous absences as attending to private men's business affairs, a convenient excuse in this day and age, I'm ashamed to admit, among men who have something to hide from their families and friends.

Sadly, I must inform you that the most recent of these excursions culminated in foolish and rough behaviour by a group of young men which resulted in the tragic death of an innocent innkeeper. James was identified as a member of that group and by association, was implicated in the crime. I need not elaborate on that issue, except to assure you that, if James had not taken up the opportunity to remove himself from England at little more than a moment's notice, he would not be free to spend any more pleasant hours in your company than he is able to at this particular time.

Although I have been convinced of his innocence in any direct involvement in the crime, and the evidence against him is contingent on the sworn statements of the real culprits, who have implicated him in order to conceal the extent of their own heinous conduct, had he not fled immediately, he would by now be incarcerated in Newgate Prison and would possibly be sentenced to, either remain there for a very long time, or to be hanged for a crime he is not responsible for. I have, indeed, read quite recently that the main culprit and leader of the group responsible, a man named Wilson, is to be executed next month, and two of his accomplices have each received prison terms of twenty years. James would surely have received at least a similar sentence to the latter pair.

I sincerely hope that I have succeeded in easing your pain to some degree and also, I hope I have dispelled any doubts that you have had, as to your own part in this sorry affair. I can assure you with the utmost conviction that the state of your family's fortune has never been the subject of discussion by any member of our household.

If you should require any further information, it will give me the greatest satisfaction to assist you in this unfortunate matter, by whatever means it is humanly possible.

I am

At your service,

Charles Pottingley esq.

Charles carefully copied the address written on the front of the envelope she had provided into his diary and put it in the pocket of his waistcoat. He placed the letter in the envelope, called the waiter and requested that it be sent by the next day's post.

A week before Christmas, old Joe couldn't hide his excitement when Charles entered the foyer of the Kensington Club.

"Another letter for you, Mr Pottingley. It's from Berlin this time. Would you believe that? Looks like it has some kind of a royal crest or something. It might be from the Crown Prince, or even President von

Bismarck himself." He held the envelope close to his face, squinting at the crest in the top right corner. "No, it's got a scent like the last one had. It's from *your* lady friend."

Charles laughed. "I don't think I'm on Crown Prince Frederick's mailing list, Joe, or on Otto von Bismarck's either for that matter, and the lady you refer to is not *mine,* but I'm unlikely to find out soon unless you give it to me."

Joe handed over the letter with a suspicious grin and Charles, after ordering his usual rich port, took his seat in the corner of the lounge. The letter was indeed postmarked Berlin and it had an embossed family crest on the envelope, under which he could just make out the word, 'Ferdinand'. He neatly sliced the envelope and unfolded the letter.

Dear Mr Charles Pottingley

I received your most welcome letter with the unbridled joy of a child, and I cannot find the words to adequately express my gratitude to you. I had almost given up hope of ever hearing from you, but now my spirits are higher than they have ever been since I last saw my beloved James.

My father has regained possession of part of his grafschaft and consequently we have been compelled to return to Berlin for legal reasons, but I assure you, Mr Pottingley, that I will return to London as soon as I am free to do so, with the most fervent hope that we may meet to discuss the possible arrangements that might be made for my reunification with James.

Thank you so much for your kind thoughts and your offer of assistance. I shall be forever in your debt if I can only have the opportunity to look into his eyes and profess my unconditional love for him once more. It matters not what crime he has been accused of, because I shall never believe that such a gentle and considerate man could ever indulge in any deliberate action that would cause even the slightest harm to any of God's creatures on earth.

Once more I thank you, for the hope and belief in all things good that you have, by your correspondence, returned to my life.

I am,

your most humble friend,

Annie Ferdinand.

Chapter 7: A Meeting Arranged

The winter had been harsh and the snow that had blanketed much of south-east England in January had turned to brown slush under the hooves of the horses and the wheels of the carriages that plied the streets of London.

True to her word, Annie contacted Charles again in early February and a meeting was arranged. The carriage passed between the familiar entrance pillars and below the arch bearing the inscription in Latin that translated as 'Enter in peace and depart in friendship,' and she wondered if, indeed, this visit would be as peaceful and fulfilling as the previous one? As for departing in friendship; that now seemed an unlikely dream, and as the carriage continued along the winding driveway to the ivy-girdled manor, she felt the aching wretchedness return in full.

The ever polite footman, Parsons, in his powder and livery, greeted her with a stiff, low bow and ushered her up the steps into the long central hall. "Mr Charles awaits your arrival, ma'am. He has asked me to escort you to the drawing room, if you would kindly accompany me please." Annie followed the footman down the hall, her mind still occupied by thoughts of her previous visit. He stopped in front of the ornate door and adjusted his waistcoat before pushing it open.

"Miss Ferdinand has arrived, sir," he announced in his customary monotone. He stood aside and bowed his head as she entered the room, elegant in a fashionable black day dress with a square neckline, and long sleeves that flared slightly at the wrists. A black velvet ribbon was clasped high around her slender neck and her long dark hair was drawn up in a stylish coiffure.

Charles, who had been standing by the window, strode towards her and Annie noticed, to her surprise, that he appeared to be a little flushed. "Thank you Mr Parsons. Please do make yourself comfortable, Miss Ferdinand," he said. He indicated a pair of carved oak chairs, upholstered in plush, deep green velvet. "It is quite delightful to make your acquaintance at last."

"Mr Pottingley," she said. "It is gracious of you to receive me. I hope that I will not take up too much of your time."

"No! Not at all, Miss Ferdinand," he managed to mumble. "You have been in my thoughts a great deal over the last few months." He coughed politely. "I mean, of course, with regard to your concern in locating my, ah…my brother." His words trailed off.

Charles waited until Annie was seated and then sat down opposite her, with a low polished oak table between them. "Now then,

Miss Ferdinand," he said, rubbing his hands together, "would you care for a cup of tea? We have it imported directly from India, you know. It's not the contaminated brew that some scoundrels have been importing; quite the opposite in fact. A rather palatable beverage, if I may say so. You do like tea, I suppose…?"

"…Mr Pottingley," Annie said gently, "may I call you Charles?"

"Why, yes of course, please do," he said with a sigh. "I do ramble on, don't I? It's a nervous reaction I suppose. I've never been very accomplished when it comes to speaking to people, - ladies in particular, - especially, ah…, beautiful ones."

Annie studied her host. His hair was fair, not ginger, and he had no freckles, but he had the same jawline and the same kind eyes as James, although his were grey and not green. She felt the familiar misery once more clutch at her heart and winced, but Charles had failed to notice; he had abruptly stopped speaking and his eyes were downcast. She remembered the same downcast expression from her first meeting with James.

"Charles," she said.

He looked up self-consciously and met her gaze, "Yes, Miss Ferdinand,"

"Thank you for the compliment." She smiled. "Yes, I would like a cup of your Indian tea and, please call me Annie, if you will."

Charles rang a bell and a housemaid appeared, pushing a small ornate cart containing an elegant silver tea service with two porcelain cups and saucers, all evidently prepared in advance in readiness for the expected request, and while the servant went about setting the table, they began a mundane conversation regarding the weather and other news of the day.

Several times during their conversation, Annie felt that it was time to broach the subject that was the reason for her visit, but she faltered on each occasion, unable to begin the discussion that she suspected may very well culminate in the bitter realisation that her dream of a lifetime of happiness had been cruelly shattered and it was unlikely that she would ever see James again. At last, however, she worked up enough courage to put her fears into words.

"I had dreaded making contact with you or your father about what had become of James, Charles," she confided, "but I had previously been fortunate in meeting your mother over afternoon tea. She impressed me as being of a very sympathetic disposition and I thought she would understand my predicament so I wrote to her, but I have, as yet, received no reply…" She stopped speaking when she noticed the look of pain that had suddenly clouded his eyes.

"Charles! Is there something wrong? Your mother…?"

He nodded, quickly covering his eyes with his hand. "…Mother is not with us now, Annie, and I have not felt up to the task of attending to her personal correspondence at this time."

"Oh Charles, how very selfish of me to intrude on you in your grief," she said. "You poor man: had I known of this sad affair, I would not have bothered you with my own troubles as they are clearly insignificant in comparison to what you must have been through recently." She stood up, walked around behind his chair and placed her hand on his shoulder, although she suspected that it was something an upper-class Englishwoman would never do. Charles, with his hand still covering his face, flinched at first and she thought that he might pull away, but then he looked up at her with an expression that she understood to be a mixture of wonder and gratitude, placed his hand over hers and patted it lightly. She held his gaze briefly and in that moment, felt that a bond had been struck between them, for she could see the loneliness in his eyes and saw in them a sad reflection of her own isolation. She sat down again and looked at the man opposite her with a new respect; he was not at all the kind of man she had expected to have to contend with.

"No," he said. "It's not selfish of you at all, Annie. On the contrary, it's a relief for me to be able to talk with someone, instead of constantly brooding over it in my mind. You see, I really have no-one in whom to confide, or even to share commonplace small talk with, now that mother is gone. I didn't realise just what an important part of my life she was and how much she filled my days with love. She always had time to listen to me and, good heavens, how I must have bored her at times, with my chatter about such uninteresting subjects as the stock market." He swept the room with his arm. "This is a big, empty house now and a very lonely place to be on one's own."

Annie listened to him with tears moistening her eyes. "I'm sure she would not have been bored at all, Charles. I gained the impression that she loved *all* of her family very much."

"Yes, she did," he said. He looked at her in such a poignant way that she waited, knowing that he needed to talk about his mother; to put into words what he had been bottling up inside.

"I had only recently learned the full extent of her love for us all and the dreadful consequences that it had exerted on her life. Unfortunately, it was all too late," Charles shook his head sadly. "The ship had sailed, literally, and it was much too late to stop it." He went on to tell her of the anguish that he now knew his mother had gone through over so many years at the hands of his father.

Annie nodded. "James portrayed your father as an imposing man of some authority and you, Charles, as somewhat cold and aloof. I believe him to be very much in awe of both of you. That is why I was afraid of being rebuffed and humiliated by you."

"That revelation is a surprise to me," Charles said. "I must agree that James is certainly in awe of Father, as I am, and there are many other people besides who would readily admit to the same respect and admiration for my father's work and for his charisma, but I find it inconceivable that he would place me in the same league as Lord Pottingley." He hesitated before adding, "James and I are so different."

"You *are* very different and I am able to appreciate that now that we have met. You seem to be so calm and cautious in your manner while James, on the other hand, is quite ebullient and unrestrained. It has become apparent to me now though, after conversing with you for this very short time, that James was mistaken in describing you as a cold and aloof person."

Charles grimaced. "James and I have never been close in our whole lives, as I believe I mentioned in my letter. I do regret that now, but it's much too late for self-recrimination. Perhaps he hasn't been mistaken, Annie. Your perception of my character before our meeting today was based on the impression that my younger brother has obviously conveyed to you. I have to accept that, at least to him, and perhaps to many other people, I have, and will always, be judged as a cold and aloof man without me even being aware of it." He smiled, but his voice was grim. "Those words, I would venture, are yours alone and the terms that James may have employed would be quite improper for you to repeat."

"That is not so, Charles," she admonished him. "Those were his actual words, but although I love James dearly, I would be a foolish person indeed if I failed to recognise that the description of your character that he communicated to me was an inaccurate assessment by someone who simply did not understand you."

"Thank you, my dear Annie. I am comforted by your reassuring words. I have been plagued by guilt and regret even before I received your impassioned plea for my assistance. My mother's disclosure of her misery and her subsequent sad demise has completely transformed my understanding of how fragile relationships can become and that sometimes are already existent between two people no matter how close they feel they may be, and this has left me often sleepless and distraught over my role in your heartbreak. I had already resolved in my mind to assist you in any way I could, to assuage your grief in these unfortunate circumstances, as well as to try to convince you of the futility of prolonging the agony, so to speak. But now that we have met my impartiality has crumbled. You are no longer a faceless name at the close of a letter, someone whom I must advise, with summary regret, to move on with life and forget about my brother. No, I am now irresistibly drawn to you as a friend and as such, could not dismiss you so callously. I hope and pray that you may regard me in the same way.”

Annie’s relief was written in her eyes. “Your sentiments of friendship are reciprocated, Charles. I began to feel at ease when I first entered this drawing room today and perceived you for the first time, and just to know that I have a friend such as you to listen to my woes has brought a warmth to my heart that I have not felt in many months. My dear Charles, if it is destined that I am never to look upon the face of my love ever again, I will find comfort and solace in the friendship that you have offered me today, and I shall accept it gratefully.”

Annie closed her eyes for a moment, clasped her hands together as if in prayer and sighed, bracing her nerves against the expected disappointment of hearing the worst news possible. At last she opened her eyes and broached the subject which she now knew from their conversation that Charles, as much as she, must have been dreading. “Charles, do you have any information that may help me to contact James?” she asked, in a thin voice.

Charles nodded, his expression grave. “Yes I have a little information, but I must warn you, Annie, it is not much on which to pin our hopes. I am unsure of how current it may be, or even if it is sufficient to be able to contact James in any case.”

“I would be so grateful if you would tell me as much as you can, please?”

“James has been forced to travel to the furthest part of the empire, Annie - to Australia in fact.” He paused briefly. Her eyes had widened and then seemed to glaze over as a shadow of pain passed across them and Charles glanced down at his fidgeting hands to avoid further contact. “He has been allocated an adequate amount of money, which he has been receiving regularly, through a trust fund that my father has set up to help him adjust to his new situation. It is administered by an associate of my father, but because of this gentleman’s influence in Australian politics, Father will not divulge his name – even to me. The reason for such secrecy, he has told me, is so that the gentleman cannot be implicated by association if James embarks on any criminal activities in Australia. I am extremely doubtful that such a situation would eventuate, but Father is as unyielding as the gates to the Tower of London. I have found out, quite by chance however, that the last forwarding address the gentleman has been given for James was from a town called Ballarat, in the Australian colony of Victoria."

While he had been speaking Annie's shocked look had changed to one of grim determination. "Then *that*, my dear Charles is where I must go," she said, in an unwavering voice.

Charles stared at her in astonishment. "Annie, please think about what you are saying, for heaven's sake," he said. "You can't go running off to the furthest corner of the British Empire just like that. It's halfway across the world."

"And why can't I, Charles? That is what your father has forced James to do, is it not?"

"Well yes, of course, but dear God; there are Aborigines there who spear horses and even people too if they stray away from the settled areas. I've heard that outside of the big cities, which are few in number, no woman can travel alone for fear of her life, - and it is so hot, even more so than India, that if she were to take her bonnet off for only a few minutes her skin would begin to peel off and…"

"Oh, Charles, it's not at all like that," she laughed. "Those are fairy tales. I have been fortunate enough to have read a recent account of life in the colonies by a respected Prussian scholar and if what he has written is accurate, then much of the violence that did erupt from time to time over the last ninety years of European settlement was the result of the forced removal of the Aboriginal people from their tribal lands. I can assure you with complete confidence that I am not going to try to take anyone's land from them. I shall find James and look into his eyes and only then will I know if he still loves me."

Charles looked deflated. "But Annie, even if the violence of the conquest of the native population is in the past it's still a dangerous place for a young woman to go on her own. It isn't that long ago that it was a dumping ground for all sorts of criminals and misfits. Who knows what kind of misfortune you may bring upon yourself by wandering around alone in such a remote and wild part of the British Empire?" He shifted uncomfortably in his seat and grimaced, and she knew that it had occurred to him, as it had to her, that it was precisely one of those criminals and misfits that she was intent on finding - *his brother James*.

Chapter 8: A Father's Comfort

"Ach, meine liebe, des jungen mannes ist verschwunden."

"Ja, Papa, he is gone, as you say, but it is not by his own doing. He is gone for the convenience of others. I have spoken with his elder brother, whose name is Charles. He is a nice man and he too believes, as I do, that James loves me. He has pledged to try to help me be reunited with him."

"Aber, Australien mein kind: it is half the world away. How can you possibly find someone in such a massive land?"

"It is true what you say, Papa. Australia is as big as all the countries in Europe together, but only half a million people live there. They live mainly around the eastern coastline because the interior of the continent is so arid. And Charles has provided me with the information that I am certain will help me to locate him."

"And when you do finden ihn, Annie, meine liebe, how do you know he will still liebe dich? You have placed so much belief and trust in James; could not he *and* his brother Charles be scharlatane?"

A frown creased her forehead. "I do not know the answer to that question, Papa, but I have to find out and it must come from James alone. He must look into my eyes and tell me he does not love me, just as he once told me he did."

Willhelm Ferdinand gently took his daughter in his arms. "Ach, you are so much like your mama. You trust all men to speak the truth to you." He shook his head. "Nein, Es ist nicht wahr. Some men are so devious in the pursuit of their own pleasure that the words they utter mean nichts. They will tell you only what they believe you want to hear, mein kind. You must consider it is possible that you have become the victim of a scharlatan, but I will nicht verbieten sie. You would not forgive me if I did so. You have my blessing, Annie. Find der junge mann and tell him that he is willcommen in meinem haus."

Annie threw her arms around her father's neck. "Danke, Papa. I would never leave without your blessing, but I knew you would not forbid me to go. I shall find der junge mann, James, and tell him he is welcome in our home."

Chapter 9: A Voyage to Australia

Annie's resolve was unwavering! "My dear Charles," she said. "My papa and I have been through the volatile aftermath of the Franco-Prussian War and my family is recognised in my homeland for its proud and brave heritage. I believe in my heart that I possess the fortitude to withstand any hardships that I may encounter in Australia, or anywhere else for that matter."

She looked at Charles defiantly, but there was also tenderness in her gaze. "I must find and speak with James personally. How could I live for the remainder of my life alone and with nothing more than my memories of him, knowing that I had given up my dream so easily? Please try to understand, for no matter what the consequences are for me in the end I *must* see this through. I must do whatever I can to find James or I will never again be able to live with peace of mind."

"I do understand, Annie, please believe me, I really do," Charles said, "but if anything were to happen to you my dear, I would forever hold myself personally responsible. I could never excuse my own negligence for having provided the information that has made it so imperative that you pursue what I think may be a reckless adventure."

"Nothing is likely to happen to me, Charles," she insisted, "but if by some unforeseen circumstance anything does, then you must forget about me and get on with your life. You must release yourself from any guilt and be secure in the knowledge that you did your best from the outset to persuade this unreasonable and distracted woman to abandon her foolhardy mission."

"No, no, Annie. I could never do what you are asking of me." His face was a mask of distress. "You are in my thoughts daily and I doubt that I could ever forget you. It is simply out of the question, but since our first meeting I *have* given a great deal of consideration to this quest that you are so intent on embarking on and I suppose it isn't quite as hazardous as I foolishly tried to misrepresent to you. I unreservedly acknowledge that my preference would be for you to banish any thoughts of travelling to such an outlandish place as Australia and to remain in a civilised region like London or Berlin. But I realise, of course, that any further argument is futile, because it is quite obvious that nothing I can say will have the slightest impact on your motivation and you will do whatever you feel is necessary to accomplish your goal."

He paused briefly and his drawn smile belied the worried look in his eyes. "Annie, my concern for your welfare is probably unfounded as Australia, according to The Times, certainly seems to be progressing at a rapid pace. There is even a telegraph line, laid under the ocean that connects the larger cities in the colonies directly with London. I've read too, that an enormous quantity of gold has been discovered in various regions across the continent of Australia and *that* is apparently what is driving its prosperity. There are gold mining towns and communities springing up all over the country and the town of Ballarat, which is the name I was given for James' possible location, seems to be one of the most productive sites. If James has indeed settled himself in that town then, considering his adventurous nature, it would be no surprise to me to discover that he is trying his luck at prospecting for gold."

Annie laughed. "Yes, I too can imagine that he would Charles, and I shall certainly let you know if you are correct in that assumption," she said.

But Charles remained solemn. "I regret that my business commitments will not allow me to accompany you so that I can personally oversee your safe passage, Annie, and in any case James would probably consider an unannounced visit by me to be a further interference in his affairs. I beg leave of you, however, to allow me to arrange for you to embark on the SS Victoria, which is the very same ship that conveyed James to Australia. Its commander is Captain Jeremy Treloar from Plymouth. He is a family friend and I know he will ensure that your journey is both safe and comfortable."

"Charles," she said, "you have been so kind to me, considering that we have not long met, and your generosity is much appreciated, but I *have* previously told you that I would never be a burden on your family's assets and I intend to stand by my word. I have earned a little money from teaching piano and although my earnings were meant to supplement my father's legal expenses he has assured me he does not require further input from me and I have his blessing to find James and tell him he is welcome in our home. My father has not been able to realise fully his former financial position at this stage and it is his explicit desire that I delay any thoughts of returning to Berlin until he is certain that our legal struggle with the French has been completely resolved. That, I understand, may be still some time off, so it will give me the time that I believe I will need to find James." She smiled, but her troubled eyes told of other emotions, of pain and heartache that lay smouldering just below the surface.

"I *insist* on covering the necessary expenses for your voyage at the very least, Annie." Charles was adamant. "After all it is because of my family's unconscionable behaviour that you are in this predicament and I shall greet with great joy, the day that I hear of your reunion with James."

"But Charles…," Annie began.

"…Yes, I *know* you are a proud, independent woman Annie," Charles continued before she could mount any further challenge to his offer. "But I would be most honoured to provide any assistance you require to gain the happy ending you desire." His tone became one of resignation and he smiled weakly again. "I know it may be difficult to find one of our familiar red post boxes in the Antipodes, but do promise me that you will write whenever possible, even if it is just a few lines to let me know of your progress."

"I shall certainly write to you, Charles," she said. "I promise I will."

Charles met with Annie at every opportunity in the following weeks as they made the necessary preparations for the voyage, but as the SS Victoria's sailing date approached he became increasingly despondent. On the morning of her departure, however, he managed to present a particularly calm appearance until Annie, her eyes brimming with tears, took his hands in hers to bid him farewell. It was then that the full extent of his fondness for her surfaced in his mind and a dreadful feeling of humiliation almost overcame him. He scolded himself bitterly, for he knew, in that moment of madness, that he had wished she would *not* find James and would come back to London to be with him.

'No, no. That can never be.' He was appalled that such a disgraceful thought had crossed his mind. Annie was so devoted to his brother that she was prepared to risk her life, embarking on a perilous adventure to find him, in the hope that she could persuade him to come back from the place to which he, Charles, had been instrumental in removing him. No, there was absolutely no possibility that she would ever see in him anything other than a remorseful benefactor on whom she could depend for support whenever, or if ever, it became necessary. *'I should be grateful for that small blessing at least,'* he thought ruefully.

Annie stood at the rail of the upper deck with the other first-class passengers as the gangplank was drawn up and final preparations were made for the ship's departure, and Charles began to feel a little apprehensive as he looked up at her for possibly the last time. The exuberant air of anticipation that had swept her along over the past few weeks towards this moment was nowhere to be seen. It was difficult to tell from where he stood, of course, and he acceded that he could have been mistaken, but she looked quite pale and subdued; a small, fragile figure waving to him with, what he imagined to be, resignation on her face. It was the kind of look that he believed he'd seen on his mother's face as she walked up the stairs for the very last time. At least, that's what he had decided to believe in, for it was much too distressing to think of that unhappy event as something more unbearable. And were the circumstances so very much different now?

'Will I ever see Annie again?'

The steamship cast its moorings and its warning siren sounded three short blasts as it slid away from the dock and into the channel. Long after it had passed out of sight and everyone else had dispersed to their carriages or to the train, Charles remained. He stood alone, immersed in his thoughts, letting the pain of this second loss wash over him and then, staring down into the sullen grey water without really seeing it, his shoulders heaved as he leant over his cane and shed silent tears of regret.

Chapter 10: An Expected Letter

Charles once again approached the ornate front entrance to the Kensington Gentlemen's Club and rang the bell. It was a fine and pleasant early summer evening in June, and he had walked the short distance to the club from Topsham Manor. But his mood was not in keeping with the weather; in fact he felt quite melancholy, a state of mind in which he had quite often found himself during the last several weeks. He had not received any word from Annie since she had left at the end of March and he was beginning to wonder if everything had gone to plan, although he refused to dwell on the possibility that anything sinister could have occurred that would prevent her from writing.

Joe, as usual, opened the door and admitted him. "Ah, good evening Mr Pottingley." His voice reflected the excitement that showed on his face. "Come on in sir: I've been waiting for you to arrive. May I take your coat? There now, sir, can I get you your usual refreshment?"

Charles managed to maintain his air of upper-class reservation and slipped out of his coat. He handed it to Joe as nonchalantly as he could, but his mood had changed in an instant, for it was obvious that what he had been waiting for had finally arrived.

The old valet handed him an envelope. " I know you've been waiting ever so patiently for this, Mr Pottingley," Joe grinned. "It's from Australia."

Charles heaved a sigh of relief. He had indeed been waiting for this letter and he could barely control the emotion he felt as he held the precious document in his hand.

'Joe, my old friend, you really have no idea how impatient I've been these past couple of months.' He thanked the valet, trying not to appear unduly hasty, and ordered his usual rich port before retiring to his armchair in the corner of the lounge.

His fingers fumbled with the letter opener. The three months that he'd had to wait had consumed his mind for so many hours each day and had been almost more than he could bear at times. He had known, of course, that it would have taken some six weeks for Annie to travel to Australia and a further six weeks for mail to be delivered from Australia to London so the time lapse was inevitable, but that hadn't made it any easier. He took a sip of port, unfolded the letter and began to read.

15th April 1880, Wallaroo, South Australia
My Dear Charles,

My first correspondence to you has been written, as you would have noted from the postmark, from a town named Wallaroo in the colony of South Australia and the first thing I must do is thank you once more for your friendship and benevolence and your interest in my welfare.

When I last saw you standing on the dock as the ship began to move out into the channel, I felt that everything you had said to try to dissuade me from undertaking this journey rang perfectly true. If I could have disembarked there and then, I would have admitted that you were right and I was being a foolish woman. With your friendship to comfort me I think I may have been able to struggle through until James returned to England of his own free will.

It is done now. I am in Australia and I shall make the best of it. My journey was long, but mostly pleasant to say the least. After we left England, we proceeded south through the Bay of Biscay, where the Atlantic swell caused many passengers to become more than a little distressed. Fortunately I was not affected too much and, in fact, weathered it like a sailor, according to your friend, Captain Treloar.

I was invited, along with some of the other first class passengers, to dine at the captain's table on several occasions. It was fascinating to learn that the convict ships, at the beginning of this century, took from four to seven months, depending on the weather conditions, to sail to Australia from England, having to call in at Rio De Janeiro in Brazil for supplies and then follow the trade winds across the southern Atlantic to Capetown, South Africa and then go around the Cape of Good Hope at the southern tip of Africa.

Only a decade ago the Suez Canal was opened, as I am sure you would know, so we were able to sail between the Pillars of Hercules at Gibraltar, cross the calm Mediterranean Sea, and then enter the canal at the Egyptian, Port Said.

What a majestic sight that was. We sailed between high white sand banks that rose up on either side of the canal, each topped by a wide, flat road and along its length we could clearly see white-robed Arabs leading long caravans of burdened camels, each beast fastened to the tail of the one in front of it.

From the canal we entered the Red Sea at Suez and then proceeded into the Indian Ocean and I marvelled at how far we had advanced in less than a century of seafaring. I shall refrain from complaining, therefore, about the six weeks that it has taken to complete my journey thus far.

I will mention, however, a dreadful storm which we were forced to endure in the middle of the Indian Ocean. It came upon our ship so suddenly and with such ferocity that I, along with my fellow passengers, feared for our lives.

We were ordered to our cabins as the wind howled through the rigging and our ship was tossed about dangerously for what seemed an eternity. When at last the wind dropped and was replaced by a strange and eerie calm, those of us in first class came out of our cabins once more and gathered together on the deck. Some of the unfortunate passengers travelling in 'steerage' class had even managed to come up from below decks to find out what was happening. This was generally allowed only for a short designated period each day and at the stern end of the ship, of course, but the sailors were much too busy to take any notice. I must therefore again thank you for attending to my welfare by allowing me to travel first class as I would otherwise have had to endure the conditions of the steerage. Many of us stood in a huddle with pallid, frightened faces and others, equally pale, weaved about holding their sides and looking very ill, as the ship silently heaved from one side to the other in a heavy swell.

We soon began to congratulate each other. It seemed as though we had survived and the threat of death by drowning had passed, but we were surprised to hear the captain continue to shout orders to the crew as if the storm had not yet abated. I could not understand why his tone was so urgent, considering how calm it had become.

We soon became aware, however, that the wind was beginning to pick up once more and we were again ordered to return to our cabins. We then had to endure the lashing rain and howling wind a second time, but from the opposite direction.

My suspicion that the captain and his crew were alert to the return of the wind was confirmed as he later explained to me. He said that this type of storm is variously called a cyclone or a hurricane. The winds circulate constantly and furiously in a clockwise direction in the southern hemisphere. In the northern hemisphere they circulate in an anti-clockwise direction and there is a calm centre to this enormous eddy that is called the 'eye'. We must have sailed right through the eye of that storm.

Our first port of call in Australia was the town of Fremantle, which serves as the port for Perth, the capital city of the colony of Western Australia. I have learned that this is the town that was the destination of the last shipload of convicts to be transported to Australia a mere twenty-two years ago. The prison, a monstrous building, is capable of holding a thousand men, but at the present time is host to only about sixty. Perhaps this is an indication of the continuing civilisation of the colony and gives me confidence that the eastern colonies will be even more so, considering that they have been free of convicts for much longer.

After unloading some passengers and cargo we sailed along the southern coast of Australia through what is known as the Great Australian Bight. The captain told us that the coastline of the Bight was made up of massive, unscaleable cliffs some seven hundred miles long that were being continually eroded as the huge breakers of the Southern Ocean pounded them mercilessly. Beyond that, he said, lay a barren treeless plain called the Nullarbor.

Our captain has proved to be a man with superior knowledge and a humorous disposition. I shall relate an incident that typifies his artful ways.

One of the other passengers, a pompous individual, surmised that 'Nullarbor' may have been a term by which the Aboriginal inhabitants referred to the area and asked the captain in a haughty manner if he might explain its meaning. He was, I think, hoping to embarrass him, but our captain was one step ahead and turned the tables on the unfortunate man by enquiring of him if he had ever been taught Latin at school. When the man testified that he had, the captain admonished him light-heartedly for not realising that 'Null Arbor' translates literally from Latin as, 'no trees', hence, the desert beyond those imposing cliffs is a treeless plain. The poor man was embarrassed, of course, but to his credit, once he realised that his ruse had been foiled he joined readily in the merriment that some of us who were also versed in Latin were already enjoying.

We have been entertained with many more anecdotes, (our captain calls them 'yarns') that have made the journey quite pleasant so please be assured, dear Charles, that I am safe and well and in good spirits. Captain Treloar and his crew have been wonderfully attentive to my needs and to those of the other passengers as well.

I am looking forward with great excitement to the prospect of beginning my search for James when we arrive at our ship's next destination, the city of Melbourne, where I shall be disembarking.

I shall write to you again at the earliest opportunity, at which time I hope to be able to provide you with the good news that I know you will be content to hear.

Until then I shall remain,
your faithful friend and humble servant,
Annie Ferdinand.

Chapter 11: Wallaroo, South Australia

"What a beautiful afternoon, Captain Treloar," Annie said. She had come up beside the commander as he stood, resplendent in his gold braided white uniform with his pipe in one hand, leaning over the deck railing.

"Oh! Aye it is a mighty fine afternoon," he said, turning quickly and doffing his white peaked hat in greeting.

"I'm sorry, did I startle you?"

"No! No, of course not, don't apologise, please. Your step is ever so light and I'm afraid I was away in a world of my own."

"A penny for your thoughts then, sir." Annie leaned on the railing beside him.

The captain laughed. "Ah well Miss Ferdinand," he said, "I was doing some reminiscing about my early life and contemplating what might lie ahead for me in the future. You see, this is my last watch as a ship's master and I'm going to jump ship and retire at the end of this voyage."

"Oh, how nice for you." Annie said. "And will you retire to London perhaps, or to a small seaside village somewhere in England?"

He shook his head. "Neither one nor the other. I've arranged to leave the 'Victoria' in the hands of another master at Sydney and I may then travel overland back to Melbourne where I have some unfinished business to which I must attend. The time is at hand for me to mark a new beginning." He held his pipe to the side of his mouth, puffed on it and then smiled serenely into the distance. "Yes indeed, all being well, a new beginning, Miss Ferdinand."

Annie looked down at several of the male passengers who were helping the crew to unload boxes and chests on to the jetty, and then at a group of women and children who had moved a little distance away and were conversing in subdued whispers as they gazed around at their new surroundings. "Those poor families look so bewildered," she said, with a hint of pity in her voice. "Don't you feel sad for them?"

The captain glanced at her with a frown and then shook his head. "No! Certainly not, and neither should you, Miss Ferdinand," he said. "Those people don't know it yet, but they'll realise soon enough that they've been very fortunate. They're Cornish miners who've been handpicked to come out and work the copper mines, here at Wallaroo and at Moonta, just down the coast there a couple of miles. The men will all be strong individuals who can work a full day in the mines and their wives will be hard workers too, quite accustomed to looking after them and their children in the roughest of conditions. But the conditions here, they'll shortly find out, are very much better than where they've come from."

He pointed to a row of neat whitewashed cottages perched on a hill, half a mile south of the town proper. "That's where they'll live; in cottages specially built for them, and when they have more children, the mine management will have extra rooms added at the back of the cottages as they need them. They'll have access to a school and a hospital too."

Annie could sense the pride in the captain's voice. "You really *do* care about these people, don't you, Captain?" she said.

He nodded and puffed on his pipe. "Yes, of course I do. They're my own kinsmen, Miss Ferdinand, and I'd retire here if I didn't have *that* other business in Melbourne to look forward to. If that doesn't work out the way I'd like it to then I certainly will come back here."

Annie cast a sideways glance at him, the hint of a smile caressing the corners of her lips. "And could there perhaps be a lady involved in your final decision, Captain?"

The commander grinned, and his already ruddy complexion seemed a little more coloured. "There could be, Miss Ferdinand, - aye, there could be at that."

He looked down again at the crowd on the jetty. "It won't be all hard work for them here, you know," he assured her. "We Cornish people know how to enjoy ourselves and just to ensure that they don't get too homesick the miner's welfare management group organise a regular Cornish gala fête. They call it 'Kernawak Lowender', which in our own language means, 'Cornish happiness'. They play their pipes and whistles, dance around a maypole and drink quarts of 'Scrumpy', their traditional cyder, which they brew themselves." He grinned. "The first thing the settlers have all done on their arrival is to plant apple trees in their gardens. There are hundreds of them now. You would probably know 'Scrumpy' as apple wine."

"Ah yes, of course, Apfel Wein" Annie nodded. "It is brewed in certain parts of Prussia too where there is an abundance of apple trees."

"It's brewed in *every* country where there is an abundance of apple trees," the captain said. "These settlers keep honey bees too, so they can brew their mead and they make a good beer called 'Swanky'. Believe me, Miss Ferdinand, they will get along very well in their new homeland."

Annie laughed. "You make it sound so appealing, but you must forgive my ignorance Captain. I was not aware that the Cornish people had their very own language. I thought they had only a quaint dialect of English"

"Aye! What you hear nowadays is a dialect, of course, and the old Celtic language hasn't been spoken regularly for over a hundred years, but we still retain some of it as a small way of clinging to our traditions. It's a way of maintaining a separate identity from the Anglo-Saxon English, just like the Irish, Welsh and Scots." He paused, listening to the melodies the men sang as they worked below. "Those songs have been handed down to them over many centuries. Some of them don't even know what it is they are singing, but they stick to the traditions like their fathers did before them. The copper mines in Cornwall have all but closed down so the mines here at Wallaroo are their salvation and their future, as they are for the economy of South Australia. This colony was almost bankrupt before the discovery of copper here a decade ago."

"And what about the name Wallaroo, Captain? I have been thinking about it since our arrival in the port, but I was fearful of asking you publicly for an explanation so that I may be spared the humiliation of being the subject of your humour. I hope you are not going to tell me it is another Latin word, for I cannot think of any Latin word that I can relate it to?"

The captain didn't look directly at her, but the crafty smirk he tried in vain to hide told Annie that he'd enjoyed deflating the ego of the pompous passenger with his 'Nullarbor – no trees' lesson in Latin.

"No Miss Ferdinand, it's not Latin," he replied, "but if I'm to be honest with you I must be a little impolite." He hesitated. "If you do not wish me to proceed then…"

"…My dear Captain Treloar!" she said, feigning exasperation. "You have whetted my appetite and now you venture to ask if I wish to partake of the food for thought that you offer me. Please go on sir or I shall be left wondering about it for the rest of my life."

"Well then," the captain said. "You see, when the first of the exploration parties came in contact with the local tribe of natives the white men pointed to the ground and asked them what their name for the area was. The Aborigines then pointed to the ground too and repeated the words 'wadla waru' several times. The white men decided, most generously, that if that's what the natives called it, then that's the name that they would adopt for the town they hoped to establish. However, after that, every time they repeated the name the Aborigines would roll around on the ground laughing. Much later, when they had learned to communicate with the tribe they realised that the Aborigines had, in fact, been telling them that there was plenty of food here for everyone."

"I'm intrigued, Captain," Annie said, "but I find nothing impolite in what you have told me so far."

Captain Treloar averted his gaze towards the town and coughed politely. "Wadla waru actually means 'Wallaby urine' Miss Ferdinand. The Aborigines thought the exploration party was out hunting for food as they were and were merely telling them, in friendship, that there was plenty of food for all of them because they could smell the wallabies' urine. The name of the town was quickly changed to Walla Waroo and has only been shortened to Wallaroo in recent times."

Chapter 12: The *Working Girl* Problem

18th May 1880
Ballarat, Victoria, Australia.
My dear Charles

I shall continue my narrative where I left it in my first letter to you from Wallaroo in South Australia and I hope you will deem my letter worthy of your attention.

The 'Victoria' departed Wallaroo and sailed along the southern coast of Australia in favourable light winds and so after another three days we anchored off a narrow channel between two headlands. Captain Treloar announced to the passengers that we had to wait for 'slack water', which he explained was a short period at the turn of the tide when there was no movement of the tidal stream. The strong current that flows in either direction at other times is the result of the narrowness of the channel and the vastness of the large sheltered bay beyond it, which he called Port Phillip Bay. In the calm weather we were treated to the spectacle of a pod of dolphins frolicking exuberantly around us, and when we eventually entered the bay, they followed, leaping out of the sea until their whole bodies were visible and then diving as if to impress us with their cleverness. As we crossed the bay and came close to shore we could see penguins nestling amongst the rocks and scores of graceful black and white pelicans, some soaring above and others languidly bobbing in the water, occasionally plunging to come up with an unwary fish in their long yellow bills. On 29 March, the ship berthed at my destination, a place called Sandridge, which our captain said was soon to be renamed Port Melbourne.

Captain Treloar was most attentive to my needs and on his recommendation I immediately found very decent and clean lodgings. Mrs O'Hara, who was the proprietor, was fastidious. Her guests, who were without exception, ladies, were continually fussed over and she went about ensuring that everyone was happy with the service she was providing. Her one strict decree was that no gentlemen visitors were allowed in the quarters occupied by the ladies as this would have cast suspicion on the nature of her tenancy, although friends, both male and female, were welcomed in the sitting room where a piano had been installed for their pleasure. These arrangements suited me perfectly, of course, and if I had not been consumed by my eagerness to begin my search I could well have remained there indefinitely as Melbourne gives the impression of being a beautiful bustling city.

My spirits were elevated as I set about arranging the necessary transport to Ballarat, which I had been informed, was some seventy-

five miles distant. It was at this point, however, that I encountered my first very serious problem. There is a coach company operating out of Melbourne curiously named Cobb and Co. This company provides a daily service between Melbourne and Ballarat and many other destinations besides. Their advertisements assure the traveller that their coaches are as comfortably appointed as any you will see on a London street and also, oddly, that the wheel springs have been specially strengthened to cope with the rough tracks that pass for roads in Australia. Alas, I was not to test the authenticity of this assertion for several reasons. These coaches are very popular and are always booked well in advance, the booking agent told me, but even if any of his coaches had been completely empty he could not have provided me with a seat unless I could state the exact nature of my business in Ballarat. The municipal authority in that city had ordered his company to only allow passage to single females who had demonstrated a legitimate reason for travelling to their city. Naturally I found this absurd in the extreme. I could not understand why such an archaic law was allowed to be enacted, even by your British standards, in this remote part of the empire.

The explanation that the agent offered for this prohibition was equally confusing. He told me that the Ballarat Divisional Board was trying to clean up the image of the goldfields and that there were already far too many working girls in their city. My confusion was brought about because I had no idea what the term 'working girls' really signified and I wondered, naively, how their divisional board supposed that preventing domestic servants and washerwomen from travelling to Ballarat could possibly serve to clean up the image of their city, - rather the opposite one would have thought. So, my dear Charles, it was to my consternation that when I explained that the purpose of my visit to Ballarat was to search for a red-haired man, the Booking Clerk became somewhat flustered. He was quite affronted that I should be so candid about what he believed to be my very dubious motive, for he steadfastly refused to reverse his decision or to speak of it any further and bade me a curt farewell. I tried several other carriers, but they either had no coaches going to Ballarat or were fully booked for weeks ahead, or at least, so I was informed.

Mrs O'Hara burst into laughter when I recounted my experience and asked her about the surplus of working women to be found in Ballarat. My embarrassment must have been at least equal to that suffered by the booking agent for Cobb and Co. when I learned the truth of the matter. Charles, I thought I had mastered your English language reasonably well, but it is obvious that I still have a lot to learn, - at least the Australian colloquial speech continues to cause me some problems, as I am sure you can tell from my exchange with the agent. There are so many words and phrases that may be interpreted in several different ways. Why there is a need, in the apparent interests of colonial respectability, to call a prostitute a 'working girl' I cannot imagine. It seems that my education in this new land is only beginning.

As the opportunity to travel to Ballarat by coach was closed to me, I became all the more desperate to get there. I was miserable, believing that I was so close to my goal and yet still so far away that I may as well have been in London. My desperation called for desperate measures. I decided that if no carrier would take me to Ballarat then the only recourse left open to me was to walk there. Having travelled so many thousands of miles to get there, seventy-five miles to my final destination did not, after all, seem an insurmountable distance at the time.

I confessed my predicament to Mrs O'Hara amidst a torrent of tears and she, bless her heart, was most sympathetic. She was such a comfort to me and seeing how determined I was to get there, she even suggested that it would be as well for me, for my own protection, to dress like a man, and a destitute man at that. She said it was quite a common occurrence for prospectors who had been unlucky on their claims to walk from one gold mining town to the next. They usually pushed a wheelbarrow or some kind of handcart containing their picks, shovels and all their other possessions, with nothing to keep them going except hope that their next claim would make them rich. Mrs O'Hara's opinion was, and I had complete faith in her judgement, that this subterfuge would enable me to pass unmolested and unchallenged by the highwaymen who have been the curse of the travelling public in Australia for the better part of this century. They are known as 'bushrangers' here. She told me that a notorious bushranger had been executed just four months ago, in January of this year. He was a man who went by the romantic name of Captain Moonlight, but whose real name was Andrew Scott, and he conducted his nefarious enterprises near the small settlements along the very road that I was about to travel. She must have perceived my look of alarm for she went on to say that, although he probably was not the last, there are few of these rogues still abroad on the roads, at least in this area. She did feel it necessary to warn me, however, that a 'new chum', the Australian term for an unseasoned traveller, conspicuous with his shiny new wheelbarrow and unused pick and shovel would still be a prime target for any opportunist brigand who happened upon him on a lonely 'outback bush track', as Mrs O'Hara calls it. You will notice, Charles that I am beginning to compile a modest Australian vocabulary. With that danger firmly in mind this wonderful woman procured the necessary items for me, all in quite poor, but useable condition. At the same time she had in her possession, some old, but clean small man's clothing that, from the manner in which she clutched it to her bosom before handing it to me suggested that it may have belonged to a person whom she had cherished dearly. Out of respect I did not ask and she offered no explanation for her willingness to part with, to a virtual stranger, those reminders of someone whom I felt sure had been lost to her. Her unspoken words, however, accompanied by that gesture of devotion made me realise once again that my quest to find James would, if successful, be worth any hardship that I was about to face.

Charles, I am sure you can imagine how comical I must have looked after I had put on those clothes. My long hair was tied up in a tight bun and hidden under a shapeless wide-brimmed hat. I wore a faded red miner's shirt and long baggy pants tied with a piece of rope at my waist. My feet were encased in old leather boots that, despite being heavy, were surprisingly comfortable, although I had to wear two pairs of heavy woollen men's stockings to make them fit. Mrs O'Hara was enthusiastic about our efforts and with much merriment between us, declared that she had not had such entertainment for many years. It was wonderful to see her face light up with laughter. You don't look like a 'new chum' at all, she told me. You look like a seasoned 'digger'. Just don't let anyone see your beautiful hands or you will surely be found out. She need not have worried about that as the next part of my adventure was to prove.

The possessions that I did not immediately require I left in the care of this remarkable lady and I took with me only the basic necessities and one complete set of my best daytime wear for my anticipated meeting with James. I felt confident that when we were reunited we would return together and relieve Mrs O'Hara of the burden of storing my several chests and bags.

Charles, the next ten days of my life were so physically and mentally taxing that I find it difficult even to recall many of the details of my trek to Ballarat. I am loath to admit that there were even times during the journey when I was so exhausted that I could not remember why I was trudging along that road at all. It was a strange feeling, knowing that I must reach Ballarat, but not being able to recall why it was imperative that I be there. Eventually however, with a great deal of concentration, an image of my beloved James would materialise in my mind as if he was emerging from a swirling mist, grinning cheekily and beckoning to me. That gave me renewed strength and purpose to keep going. I sincerely hope, however, that I shall never be obliged to endure such an experience again in my lifetime.

My first day out on the highway had been pleasantly cool and ideal for walking, and it reminded my wandering mind of a pleasant summer day stroll in England with James by my side, the sentiment giving me even more motivation to reach my destination so that I could again feel his strong arm linked in mine, but as evening fell and the light steadily diminished, so too did the number of fellow travellers that I encountered and I became gloomily aware that I had not met anyone going in either direction for quite some time. I was completely alone in this strange land of lengthening shadows and a kind of vague anxiety began to impose on my senses. I quickly realised that nightfall in Australia is not as it is in England or Prussia in the summertime, during which there are pleasant, lingering twilights that allow for leisurely rambles long after the sun has set. It was April, of course, and heading into Australia's winter, but because the day felt so balmy I was misled into believing that I had several more hours in which I could travel before I had to find shelter. But no, it was not to be. The sun seemed to tumble from the sky and it became dark very quickly. But oh! Charles, as soon as the sun's light disappeared completely from the sky, the heavens glowed with the breathtakingly glorious sight of millions of tiny points of light, ablaze in the soft white ribbon of the Milky Way. There must have been a hundred, no, a thousand times the number of stars we witness in the skies over Europe. The sheer magnificence of the clear night sky made me reflect on just how insignificant we humans are and how trivial our difficulties are too, including my own mission in finding my beloved James.

But despite the beauty of the spectacular canopy above, I had not prepared myself for the gloomy silence that closed in on me from all sides and my apprehension quickly increased. I sensed that many eyes were watching me from concealed places. My heart began to flutter and I quivered in dread as I strained to see what my other senses told me was there, hidden amongst the trees. I decided at length that I would feel more at ease if I was not so exposed on the road and so I went a little way into a thicket and sat down on a carpet of dead leaves, with my back against a large tree and the shovel in my hands for protection against whoever or whatever it was that had unnerved me. I suppose it was a kind of hysteria that gripped me then because I giggled quite uncontrollably at the thought of how absurd it would be to swing my weapon about in the darkness at my invisible adversary. I spent a very uncomfortable night listening to the rustlings of many animals or reptiles, both on the ground and in the trees above my head. I had no idea, of course, as to what species they belonged and whether or not they were dangerous, and I was constantly petrified by fear. Mrs O'Hara had said that some of the world's most poisonous snakes are to be found in this country and, although I appreciated that she had given me the information in good faith I wished she had left me in blissful ignorance and had never mentioned it. To make matters worse, I was forced to move several times in the darkness to get away from hordes of biting ants.

When I did eventually reach my destination I found that my fears had been largely unfounded and that the nocturnal rustling that I had heard above my head was most likely to be harmless native tree dwelling marsupials that are called possums, while that on the ground was undoubtedly the scampering about of rabbits. I saw many, many rabbits on my journey and was intrigued by their similarity to our own European variety. I was informed later that they were, in fact, the very same. It seem that about twenty years ago a gentleman named Thomas Austin had twelve pairs shipped to Victoria to serve as game in his sport of shooting. The rabbits found that they loved their new life here and bred so prolifically that there are now an estimated twenty million of them in Victoria alone and they have become a pest of tremendous proportions. They have eaten out large tracts of land and many farmers have been forced to abandon the farms they have worked so hard to establish. Mr Austin is obviously not a great success at small game hunting and I am thankful that he did not envisage himself as a hunter of large game animals and populate the country with lions and tigers, otherwise, I surmise I would not have made it this far.

I was relieved to see the first glow of dawn light up the eastern sky on the morning of my second day on the road and, although tired from lack of sleep I was keen to continue my journey. Mrs O'Hara had insisted on packing a large number of homemade biscuits and a flask of water in my wheelbarrow, so I broke my fast on these. I discarded the pick and shovel, having convinced myself that they were unnecessary for the verification of my disguise. In truth, they were becoming such a burden that I knew in my heart I would not be able to physically complete my journey if I persevered with them.

Unsettled by the discomfort of the first night, I weighed up the relative dangers of sleeping in the open with unfriendly snakes and insects against the possibility of being discovered to be a woman in disguise trying to slip into Ballarat unnoticed and I decided that the latter was the least harmful. From then on I managed to find adequate shelter at the end of each day at one of the many rough boarding houses in the small settlements along the way. I was vigilant, of course, in checking that the establishment I had selected was not a house of ill repute and that I could have a small room to myself for an extra fee. They were commonly manned by disinterested attendants who only seemed to show signs of being aware of my presence at the sound of coins being placed on the desk at their stations. Not one of them gave me a second glance so I felt that either my disguise was working admirably or I really was beginning to look like a tired and destitute miner with the dust of the road on my face.

I wondered, with a vanity I tried hard to suppress, just how much they would have engaged with me if they had looked a little more closely and realised that I had shoulder-length hair tied up tightly under my baggy felt hat. I am embarrassed to admit, dear Charles, that after each of these encounters, having deceived the clerks so easily, I was intoxicated with delight at my success and exulted in it when I was safely within the privacy of my simple quarters. I slept well each night, totally exhausted, and each morning made a habit of bathing early and leaving at first light before any of the other patrons were up and about, refreshed to some extent and a little closer to my goal.

Each day heralded a new challenge that I knew I must overcome. I began to grow fatigued more rapidly as my strength deteriorated and found that, in order to keep going, it was necessary to concentrate on placing one weary foot in front of the other. As I came closer to Ballarat the country became more undulating and I found myself engaged in a tiring struggle to push my wheelbarrow up and over a hill, only to find there was another, and still another beyond that. I lost count of the number of days that I had been walking and I watched the sun's slow progress across the sky in a kind of trance, knowing only that when it was positioned just a little way above the western horizon I would have to consider where I was going to rest that night.

Whoever it was who had constructed the road had, just as in Europe, thoughtfully placed wooden markers every five miles along its entire length and had carved into each the letter B with a number below it that told me the number of miles that I still had to walk to reach Ballarat. Each time I passed one of these it gave me a small thrill of achievement and I felt a corresponding surge in my strength. On the final day of my journey and with only four miles to my destination, I hid the wheelbarrow in a thicket of trees and carried my belongings over my shoulder in a grain sack that I had found. This was a great relief as my arms were aching dreadfully and the blisters on my hands had made it almost unbearable to grip the handles. When I reached the outskirts of Ballarat I felt that I almost had a spring in my step, such was the feeling of elation that overcame me at my success. I changed into my day dress in a public bathing house, managing to avoid the probing eyes of the attendant long enough to make my escape and then, rather boldly, I convinced the proprietor of a good hotel that I had arrived by Cobb and Co. coach that very morning. I was careful to conceal my damaged hands and broken fingernails while I signed the register.

Lies and deceit are becoming so much a part of my everyday life Charles, that, when at night I pray for guidance in my search I cringe at just how far I have deviated from the old-fashioned course of truthfulness that my papa taught me and that I have always tried to follow. I can only salve my troubled conscience with the firm conviction that it is all in a good cause and that my sorry saga is nearing what I hope to be a happy conclusion.

I have already embarked on several excursions in the five days since my arrival in the city and I am surprised that Ballarat is much larger than I had imagined it to be. It is quite a magnificent city and, I have been told by a proud resident, compares in size and population to Melbourne. The wealth of its citizens and their confidence in the future of their city is evident in the magnitude of the public buildings, the generous public recreational areas, and the opulence of its commercial establishments and private houses. It is difficult for me to comprehend that less than thirty years ago, before gold was discovered nearby, this area supported only a population of cattle.

Charles, I feel that my recuperation from the trauma of my arduous journey has been sufficient for me to resume my search tomorrow. The sheer size of Ballarat may, of course, delay my reunion with James, but if he is still here I am confident that I shall find him.

I know that you will understand that I cannot provide you with a return address at this time, but be assured, Charles, that I shall inform you of my progress at the earliest opportunity.

I remain your most humble friend,
Annie Ferdinand.

Chapter 13: The Search of Ballarat

5th July 1880
Ballarat, Victoria, Australia.

My Dear Charles,

Again I must beg your indulgence for what may appear to be my callous disregard for our friendship in not writing to you sooner, but I pray that I may regain any of your sympathy that I may have have lost when I admit to you that finding James has proved to be much more difficult than I ever imagined it would be.

When I was at home in Europe a common perception of Australia was that it is a vast continent with just a handful of free settlers who are surrounded by thousands of convicts, and your well-meaning words of warning when I stated my intention to undertake this journey has led me to believe that it may also be a common perception in England. This is far from being the truth, however, for it is a truly cosmopolitan society comprising people from almost every country in the world who appear to work together in relative harmony. This situation, while wonderful for the future prospects of the country, has contributed to my lack of success so far. You see, one cannot simply point to a group of people and say those are the French, or to another and say those are the English, as you would expect to be able to do in Europe. For whatever reason a person may have been drawn to these shores, whether it be to seek their fortune or to create a new life for themselves and leave their old one behind, they begin to refer to themselves as 'Australian' almost immediately, no matter what their nationality was before their arrival. I have discovered that there is no English quarter in Ballarat in which I could have expected James to reside.

My search for him began as soon as I had posted my first letter to you. The post office in Ballarat, although not one of the grandest buildings in the city is, nevertheless, an imposing white sandstone structure built, according to the commemorative lintel stone above the entrance, a mere nineteen years ago. The postmaster was exceptionally kind to me when I told him of my mission and he asked me to return on the following day so that his staff could, in the meantime, thoroughly check their records for any reference to a Mr James Pottingley.

On my return the next morning, as promised, I was ushered into a well-appointed office by a prim, mature woman, whose pleasant demeanour warmed me to her immediately. Her smile and the radiance in her eyes as she laid her record book on a polished table indicated to me that she had enjoyed some measure of success and I waited expectantly, my heart pounding, as she opened it at the page she had previously bookmarked. Miss Quinlan, for that was her name, went on to list the dates of a number of transactions between a Mr James Pottingley and a post office box number in Melbourne. The last date recorded, however, was over a month before and the previous dates were at such irregular intervals that it was impossible to establish a pattern to them. Although I was a little disappointed I thanked her and took my leave, undaunted and determined, knowing that at the very least, here was firm evidence that James had not vanished from the face of the earth and that my prayers may be answered soon.

Before I divulge my next strategy to you Charles, and so that your refined sensibilities may not be deceived into believing that I have become ungracious in the reckless pursuit of my quest, I must explain that, with few exceptions, Australians are much less pretentious in their everyday interactions than are Europeans. A pallid smile or a slight doffing of the hat that one can sometimes wrest from a stranger who hurries by on a busy London or Berlin avenue is more often than not replaced by a broad grin and a hearty 'halloo' or a pleasant 'good day to you' in Ballarat. The latter is often shortened to 'g'day' which, despite its apparent brevity, is by no means uttered in a curt or brusque manner, but is delivered rather in a slow and pleasant brogue that aptly expresses the customary unhurried air of Ballarat's citizens.

The Irish, for example, think nothing of breaking into laughter or song, whether alone or in groups, men and women together, at every opportunity. It is so wonderful to witness their unbridled enjoyment of life and I feel that it must be, in part, due to the suffering that has been imposed upon them in their own country in recent history. Class distinction and exclusion from society mean little to them here and I speculate that in the future this will help to form the basis of a unique Australian carefree philosophy.

And so, having defended and, I hope, justified my subsequent behaviour in advance, I shall now proceed with unashamed candour to relate my simple strategy.

I began to walk the streets of Ballarat, asking everyone that I met if they had encountered an Englishman with red hair, green eyes and with a cultured accent. Some had not, but wished me well; many had, but further enquiry convinced me that the subject of our discussion was definitely not James. After several weeks spent in this fashion relentlessly questioning and checking, finding that there was, or had been, an abundance of red-haired gentlemen with a myriad of accents in Ballarat in recent times, I became resigned to having failed to find any trace of my love. I was despondent, Charles. I spent many hours lying alone in my room weeping, the anguish of my failure forming in me a fragility of mind that threatened my very sanity. I knew I could not go on in that way for very much longer. I knew that I had almost reached my breaking point and I examined my reasons for continuing what was rapidly turning out to be a futile search. Indeed, I began to question my motive for continuing to live at all and I do admit shamefully that in my melancholic state of mind, ending my life in that room became a serious prospect of release for me.

A knock on the door interrupted my brooding and I opened it grudgingly, not knowing or caring why anyone should wish to visit me. I was astounded to see that it was Miss Quinlan from the post office. When she saw my dishevelled appearance and my tear-stained face her erstwhile smiling expression immediately became one of tender-hearted compassion, and she set about comforting me in a manner that, in England, would be the reserve of a matronly aunt dealing with an upset child. She sat down, wrapping her arms around me and stroking my hair while rocking gently and softly humming a tune until my sobs subsided, and then when I had regained some composure she told me why she had come. The dear woman had conducted her own unofficial investigation through a friend in the postal service in Melbourne and found that a Mr James Pottingley had made a written request to have his future remittances forwarded to a town called Bathurst in New South Wales. That was as much as she could find out for me, she told me most apologetically, because there seemed to be some kind of secrecy involved in the transactions, and her friend could have found herself in a great deal of trouble if she had probed any further. You and I both know that to be true, of course, and we also know the motive behind the confidentiality of the communications.

I told her she was an angel, and showered her with hugs and kisses, for which she seemed appreciative, and I felt that she fully understood and shared the pain of my aching heart. Intuition convinced me that Miss Quinlan's communion with me was more than that of a kind and sympathetic person. I felt that we were kindred souls, perhaps due to a past episode in her life too that had left her lonely and miserable for a very long time. I resolved, there and then, to be strong and to commit once more to my quest as soon as I am strong enough in body and in mind.

Miss Quinlan has begged me to address her by her Christian name, which is Sarah, and I have accepted her kind invitation to reside with her at her cottage until my recuperation is complete.

I sincerely hope, dear Charles, that I have not given you cause for alarm at what you may perceive as my frailty of mind. It pains me to burden you with my self-indulgent complaints when I know that you tried diligently to convince me of my foolishness and impetuosity in undertaking this task so ill-prepared.

With fresh hope in my heart however, I promise I shall write to you again with the positive news that I am certain you will receive with satisfaction and relief.

    I remain your friend
    Annie Ferdinand.

Chapter 14: Sarah Quinlan

"I cannot thank you enough, my dear Sarah. You have been so kind to me." Annie said as she relaxed on a comfortable divan in the neat living room of the tiny two roomed cottage.

Sarah sat in front of a small ornate mirror near the window. She had undone the pins that kept her hair in a tight bun and let its greying tresses cascade over her shoulders. "Ah, hush now my darlin'. Sure now an' it's glad o' the company I am if truth be known." She picked up a small leather-backed grooming brush and began to comb it through her hair with light strokes. "From the very minute the boys set off on their personal journeys o' adventure I've been sitting here on my own, like the grand old spinster that I am."

Annie was a little surprised, although she realised that there was no reason why she should be. "Are the boys your children then, Sarah?" she said without thinking. She bit her tongue, for she immediately felt that perhaps her blunt question may have been too invasive of Sarah's privacy.

Sarah's face crinkled in a smile and she looked away quickly, but Annie saw the sorrow reflected in her eyes through the mirror. "Ah, faith now, lass," she said, "for it seems that I've led ye' up the garden path! No, not at all my love; the boys were the step-brothers that I nurtured with my own hands ever since they could scarcely put foot to the ground."

"Oh, I feel so wretched," Annie said. "I fear that I have brought a distressing memory back to you, have I not?"

Sarah put down her brush, walked over and sat beside her on the divan. "Not at all *mavourneen*," she said, clasping Annie's hand in hers. "It's grand to be able to hold a conversation about them or anything else, without my own ears being the only ones listening. Sure now the boys are fine an' so am I."

"But you looked so sad just then." Annie persisted.

Sarah sighed. "Aye, it's true Annie; the melancholies do visit me on occasions when I think of my unfortunate da', God rest his soul. He was a fine man who brought me to this country from our own beautiful, but ruined, Ireland. My da's name was Patrick, an' he was still in the prime o' his life when he was left a widower. It was in the aftermath o' the great famine, when it is just a slip of a girl I was, a fresh-faced colleen in only the fifteenth year o' my life. My mam an' my grandmam too, God rest them both, were raised to the glory o' His Presence when the Great Hunger devastated our country. My da' remained in mourning for the most part o' two years, but then he found himself a new companion in Melbourne an' he brought us both, his new bride an' I, here to Ballarat, to this very cottage no less."

"That surely must have been a difficult situation for you to accept, Sarah."

"Ah well, I was grieving for my mam to be sure, Annie, but I was time-worn enough from the hard times we'd been through to understand that my da' was in great need o' forming a new an' happy union in his own life. My stepmam's name was Maude an', glory-be, she must have made my da' a happy man for there was a christening each o' the next two years an' two beautiful healthy boys brought into this life the result o' it all. For the four years after that Patrick and Maude basked in the warmth o' contentment an' I, perceiving my da's blissful existence, was enthralled to be a part o' it, but God forbid, the long lifetime o' peace an' tranquillity that we truly deserved was not to be ours after all. Trouble had been brewing on the goldfields for weeks. The miners resented having to pay the Victorian government thirty shillings each month just to apply for a licence to search for gold. My da', ever the one to stand up for the cause o' justice, - just like his own da' before him, joined the ranks o' the miners in a confrontation with the police. It became known as the Eureka Stockade rebellion an' the poor, unfortunate man was wounded in the affray. I nursed him myself for the better part o' a week while he lingered in agony an' then, finally, he gave up the ghost an' joined his family in the glory o' the saints."

"And where was your stepmother during this time?" Annie asked her, wide eyed.

Sarah shook her head. "Please God the poor woman leads a blameless life for Maude took herself off to Melbourne the minute the trouble started an' we have not glimpsed a hair o' her head since the day she walked out through that door. I will not believe that she purposely abandoned us an' I wish her true happiness until the day she is called before the Almighty to receive *His* judgement. I had already started working at the post office by then so I was able to care for the boys myself an' earn enough to give them both a decent education."

Annie brushed the tears from her eyes. "Sarah, you are such a generous and admirable person. I believe I would not have had the strength and courage to do what you have done."

"Ah well, no! Annie, I'm not at all the generous or courageous individual. The boys are my own flesh an' blood an' it was duty bound I was to help them for that reason alone. But o' course I loved them too an' I still do. They are both in honest work, but it is so far away now that I barely get to see them at all. No! It would only ever have been a charitable act in raising them to manhood if they had not been my own an' I can assure you I almost gave up trying many times over the years."

"And you have done all of this on your own too, no doubt?"

"I have indeed." Sarah said with a sigh. "Oh, glory-be, I have. But it's not been as unpleasant a living as I might have led ye' to suppose, Annie." She quickly brushed her hand through her hair in a defiant gesture that Annie decided must be her own rejection of her innermost thoughts. "Aye, there *were* indeed some promising young bachelors coming in to the post office always giving me the eye to be sure, an' myself no better or worse than any one o' them at giving it right back too. Sure now, there I was, eyeing them an' fluttering my eyelids like I was one o' the commonest trollops on the streets o' Dublin. It became perfectly clear to this vainglorious woman in a short time though, that the attentiveness to her feminine charms evaporated like a shower o' rain in the desert when the young men learned that guardianship o' the boys was a requirement o' any commitment they might think o' making to Sarah Quinlan. An' so here I am now, forty-seven years old to the minute an' with hardly a purpose to my lonely existence at all."

Chapter 15: The Search Continues

8th Sept 1880,
Bathurst, New South Wales.

My Dear Charles,

I have arrived in Bathurst and I am excited at the prospect of renewing my search for James. I must beg your indulgence, however, as I recount to you the events that have overtaken me since I wrote to you last and I hope that in so doing I shall convey to you a more positive attitude of mind than I may have expressed in my previous correspondence.

I remained in Ballarat for a further three weeks in the company and protection of my guardian angel Sarah and it is not by any means an exaggeration and I think perfectly believable that we became as devoted to each other as any two sisters could ever be in the short time that we spent together. I shall impress this notion on you by relating that she often referred to me as Annie Mavourneen. At first this seemed quite strange as I thought, to my consternation that she had somehow forgotten that my name was Ferdinand, but she told me somewhat coyly when I enquired of her, that 'mavourneen' is an Irish term of endearment that is usually reserved for close family members. I began to dread the very thought of saying my goodbyes and leaving her alone once more in her little cottage for, from what she has confided in me, she has already said too many goodbyes in her lifetime, but God has intervened Charles, although not in a mysterious way as is often said, but in a most direct fashion in my darling Sarah's case. She had written to a Catholic priest, she told me. He is a man that she greatly admires, and is a tireless worker in the protection and education of poor and orphaned children, a cause that, for reasons on which I need not elaborate, is close to Sarah's heart.

In her letter she explained her circumstances and expressed a desire to participate in his work in the service of God, in any capacity to which he felt she would be best suited. Several letters have passed between them, followed by a personal interview and the result is that the priest has recommended Sarah to his friend and co-founder of a community of Catholic nuns, whose charter is also to educate poor and orphaned children. This great lady who is at this very time in Sydney to open the order's first school in New South Wales, has invited my beautiful Sarah to join her novitiate. When she received this wonderful news Sarah's life immediately took on a whole new meaning and when I was leaving Ballarat to pursue my own destiny she told me she was at the happiest and most contented point of her whole adult life so far. She assured me she would never be lonely again and was looking forward, in great anticipation, to spending the rest of her days in the service of God.

I was much relieved and delighted for my beautiful sister as I travelled back to Melbourne along the road that had brought me to Ballarat, recognising none of it, because, as I have previously related to you, I believe that I accomplished that journey in a state of bewilderment. This time I journeyed in the relative comfort of the Cobb and Co. coach with its specially strengthened springs, it being much less difficult to depart from Ballarat than it was to gain admittance to it.

The wonderful Mrs O'Hara was once again my strength and my ally even though she was in quite a melancholy state at the time of my appearance. The cause of her anguish, she confessed, was the troubles of a family that she knew well, particularly the mother, with whom she had been very good friends for many years. The woman's name is Mrs Kelly and one of her sons has been killed in a terrible incident with the police. Another son, Edward, whom she affectionately refers to as, 'our Ned', now awaits trial in Melbourne Gaol accused of murder. Mrs Kelly herself has been locked up in the same prison, sentenced to three years hard labour on what Mrs O'Hara believed was dishonest and unsubstantiated evidence presented to the magistrate by a policeman who has a reputation for abusing his position to curry favour with his superiors and further his career at the expense of innocent people

My knowledge of the events leading up to this situation is limited to what I have learned from Mrs O'Hara, but I can only say that the whole population seems divided as to whether these young men are rogues who have committed several murders, or heroes due to their defiance of what many perceive to be victimisation by corrupt police authorities.

Mrs O'Hara has told me that there have been more than thirty thousand signatures to a petition delivered to the Governor of the colony in a bid to save Edward Kelly from the gallows. She doubts whether even that will be enough, however, as the judge has already declared his intention of making an example of the young man. If carried out, I think Edward Kelly's execution may be the subject of spirited debate for many years to come.

A few days after my arrival Mrs O'Hara's melancholia seemed to be banished completely from her mind. I was resting in my room when there was a knock on my door. I opened it and there she stood, her face positively glowing with happiness and I listened enraptured as she related to me the cause of the wonderful change in her mood.

It seems that she, - her first name is Eileen, and our now mutual friend, the good Captain Treloar, have known each other for a very long time and in fact, had a brief romance before he went off to follow the call of the sea. Eventually he realised that his love for her was greater than his love for the ocean, but the voyage had lasted such a long time that, by the time he returned to port she had fallen in love again and was betrothed to another young man.

I should mention that Mrs O'Hara had a wonderful marriage, and there is no question that she loved her husband dearly; hence her gesture of devotion when she presented me with what I now believe, were his clothes when I began my trek to Ballarat. Perhaps she thought he would have approved of their use for a moral cause such as she deemed mine to be. After she and Mr O'Hara settled in Australia, Captain Treloar visited them whenever his ship docked in Melbourne, and he and Mr O'Hara became good friends, but the dear lady has been a widow now for more than ten years.

Jeremy, as she calls Captain Treloar, has now retired, as he told me was his intention when I conversed with him on the ship, and he has returned to Melbourne. The reason for Mrs O'Hara's great joy and excitement is that Jeremy has asked for her hand in marriage and she has accepted his proposal. This then must be the unfinished business to which he alluded that same afternoon aboard the Victoria at Wallaroo. When I left them to continue my travels to Bathurst, it seemed to me that they had wound the clock back forty years or so. Jeremy and Eileen's obvious joy in just being together and their laughter and happiness was infectious and made me tremble in anticipation of my own reunion with James.

My dear Charles, I trust that you will agree that this letter is much more positive than the last. I shall rest now for some days before resuming my quest. Again, I will endeavour to keep you informed of my progress and I hope and pray most fervently that the culmination of my venture is but a breath away.

Your most humble friend,
Annie Ferdinand.

Chapter 16: A Change of Direction

6th December 1880,
Brisbane, Queensland.

My dear Charles,

Much has transpired since my last letter to you which I posted soon after my arrival at Bathurst in New South Wales. I have become convinced that your supposition was correct and that James has indeed developed an interest in prospecting for gold, but it quickly became apparent to me that he would not have remained in Bathurst for very long. It is principally a centre for agriculture and is the terminus of the main western railway line from Sydney, the capital city of the Colony of New South Wales. Interestingly, the rail connection between the major cities of Melbourne and Sydney is still several years away. The closest gold mining area is centred on a town called Hill End, which is about twenty-five miles to the north of Bathurst and so, after resting for a few days, I made my way by coach to that town to resume my search. Thankfully there were no restrictions to my travel plans such as I encountered between Melbourne and Ballarat.

Hill End is much smaller than Ballarat but is, nevertheless, a thriving community of about eight thousand people. Once again I was received very cordially by the postmistress, who went to great lengths to find out if a Mr James Pottingley was, or had been, a customer of her post office. To my great frustration, it seemed that James had never made any transactions there. Had he bypassed Hill End completely after leaving Bathurst, and if so, which way could he have gone? I realised that without answers to those questions my quest was doomed to failure and with no other course open to me, I adopted a similar strategy to that which I had pursued previously, although, as you are aware, unsuccessfully. I hoped that the task, in a much smaller town, would not result in the mental fatigue to which I had almost succumbed in Ballarat.

I began to walk the streets again asking this one and that one if they knew anything of an Englishman with red hair and a cultured accent and, as in Ballarat, the cheerful way in which Hill End's citizens responded to my enquiries delighted me and filled me with hope. At long last, after a week of searching in this manner my efforts were at least partially rewarded. I was weary by then and conducting my search in a most pedestrian manner with little hope of a positive outcome, but I put my questions to a pleasant gentleman who seemed compassionate to my plight and willing to converse at length. He told me he was the mine manager from the Ophir Mine, which was the original gold mine in the area and is named after the biblical city of gold, but my fatigued mind was made instantly alert when he said he remembered hiring a man who fitted the description that I had given him of James. It was odd, he said, that a man with such a fine accent was looking for work as a mine labourer. He, very kindly, offered to look up his records for me and we went at once to his office, a small but comfortable outbuilding near the main entrance to the fenced off mine site. It did not take very long for him to find the entry in the logbook, but you may imagine my surprise to find that the person to whom the manager referred was a Mr James Potts.

This revelation set my mind to racing. I was almost certain that it must be James, as the possibility of such a coincidence concerning two similarly described Englishmen, one a Mr Potts and the other a Mr Pottingley, seemed unthinkable to me, but why, I wondered, would he change his name? Did this have something to do with the trouble that had forced him to flee from England, or had he perhaps learned that I was on a quest to find him, but wished to fade into obscurity and out of my life forever? I decided that I would not even dwell on the latter and that I would venture back to the post office armed with this new surname.

My hopes were quickly dashed, however, when the dear mine manager, in a purely conversational and unintentional manner, pointed out that James had left the employment of the mine after only a few weeks and it was highly improbable that he would have remained in Hill End unless he had taken up a completely different occupation. He explained that this was because the gold at Hill End was contained in deep reefs and heavy machinery was required to excavate and then separate it from the other material in which it was embedded. This was no place for an individual miner and James would have had no other mining company in the area like the Ophir as an option to continue working and living there.

The manager said that quite a few 'new chum' miners like James came through Hill End expecting to find a field where they could stake a claim, but usually left as soon as they realised that they would be working for a company and that it was a ten-hours a day occupation. No matter how much gold was extracted on their shift it did not belong to them, but to the company. Those who stayed could more accurately be described as labourers who worked in a gold mine, rather than actual gold miners, and they were thus known as 'wages' men. I knew that he was likely to be correct, of course, and that James would not have tolerated such a situation as this, but although it was disappointing that I had missed him on this occasion I consoled myself with the knowledge that my stay in Hill End had not been entirely without success.

I had verified that James was indeed, moving from one goldfield to another and had passed through Hill End. I had learned that gold can occur in what is called a reef, combined with other material, from which it has to be separated by mechanical crushing and chemical means. It can also be found in alluvial deposits, where it has been washed down a stream and deposited in the bed of a river. This alluvial gold can be separated from the river gravel by a fairly simple process of washing. Apparently, the gold is heavier than the gravel and sinks to the bottom of the pan as the miner swirls the contents around gradually separating the gold from the detritus. Most importantly, however, I had learned that I was not now searching for a Mr James Pottingley; for whatever reason my new quest was to locate a Mr James Potts.

With no clue as to which direction he had taken I made the decision to travel further north, based solely on the recommendation of the kindly mine manager. He informed me that alluvial gold had been found at a number of sites in the northern part of the continent and prospectors were flocking to the new fields, intent on making their individual fortunes by pegging a claim and panning for gold in the streams. He theorised that, even if I cannot find James himself on one of these alluvial fields I will surely find someone who has known of him and perhaps even knows of his current whereabouts in a much more recent timeframe than anyone in Hill End can offer.

It was in a state of renewed vigour that I boarded the coach, bound once more for Bathurst, and then from there I set out for regions unknown, my confidence boosted by the Ophir mine manager's words of encouragement.

I travelled by coach through the northern half of New South Wales, always heading more or less in a northerly direction, but also acutely aware that James could have decided to return south to the Victorian goldfields, or that he may have given up on his quest for gold and embarked on an entirely new occupation. My confidence again began to fail me whenever I contemplated the possibility that my relentless search for him was already doomed and I gazed out through the coach windows at the neat houses and cottages in each of the many villages and towns that we passed through, reflecting that James could be living and working happily in any one of them blissfully unaware of the misguided and illogical woman who was pursuing him throughout the vast wilderness that was Australia.

The immensity of the task that I faced had once more weakened me, both mentally and physically, with the passing months, so that by the time of my arrival in the Queensland capital of Brisbane I felt that my resolve was as low as it had been even in my darkest hour in Ballarat. I soon came to the conclusion, however, that it was unlikely that another wonderful Sarah Quinlan would happen along to relieve me of my depression and I therefore drew on the last reserves of my inner strength to extricate my mind from its downward spiral. I decided I would recuperate for at least a few weeks in Brisbane hoping that an improvement in my physical strength would result in some relief from the bouts of depression that continued to plague me.

I have discovered that Brisbane is a striking and yet relaxing city, Charles. I was pleasantly surprised and felt immediately comfortable when I learned that the streets are named after the members of our own royal House of Hanover, the streets aligned north-west after the male and the streets aligned north-east, after the female members. There is also, amongst the many daily newspapers that are available, a general weekly news sheet printed in the German language. All of this has, I am certain, contributed to my mental recuperation at least.

The city contains many fine buildings. Government House was completed only ten years ago and Parliament House, an impressive building built in the French Renaissance style, is just two years old. The Brisbane Newspaper Company boasts the largest newspaper building in the world. It is situated on Queen Street and there is a curious tale that, when the basement was being excavated, the stone was found to contain specks of gold. The workers were jubilant and imagined becoming rich, but were considerably chagrined to find that the percentage of gold to the ton of stone was not enough to justify the effort in extracting it. I wonder though, with further advances in methods of extraction in the future, whether the inhabitants of Brisbane will begin to again contemplate the viability of digging for gold in their streets. As you can appreciate I am becoming quite knowledgeable on matters relating to the extraction of gold and I hope, when James and I are reunited, I will be able to discuss the subject with him on equal terms. You see, Charles, this is another example of the liberal Australian culture. There are no restrictions on ladies discussing what would be considered exclusively gentlemen's business in London.

Brisbane is situated on a river of the same name and it is about twenty miles upstream from the estuary in Moreton Bay. The first settlement was initially on the northern bank, but for many years past a large and rapidly growing population has spread across to the southern side, so that the river now bisects the town. It is just as impressive as the Thames and very much cleaner too. As in London also, one fine bridge across it links the northern and southern parts and I have been assured there will be many more constructed in the next few years as the city grows in stature. Ferries also cross the river at many points and these are very well serviced, being met at the terminals on either bank by very efficient horse drawn omnibuses and trams. One must take into consideration and realise with wonder, that Brisbane is a mere quarter of a century old, whereas London predates it by thousands of years.

The town itself, and its near environs, are remarkable for their picturesque heights. Handsome villas occupy the ridges, each one surrounded by tropical gardens bearing myriads of flowers of the most brilliant hues that would be the envy of the gardeners of Crystal Palace. On the western side, there are two or three ranges of lofty hills, which form a splendid foreground for the setting sun.

The manager of the hotel in which I stayed suggested that I take a carriage trip to the top of the highest prominence in the city to gain a better perspective of the landscape of which he was justifiably proud, and he arranged for one of his employees to take me there. That good and knowledgeable man was an Aborigine with a dark brown complexion, long black hair and a broad flat nose, a feature that seems to be typical of their race. He was a fine looking man of superior intellect and of a happy and contented disposition, far removed from the tales of savagery that have been associated with his people, and he told me that his tribe have lived in this area for many thousands of years. He also informed me that the prominence had gained its current title of One Tree Hill when it was cleared of what he called 'scrub' (this is the Australian term for what we might call undergrowth) a few years ago and only one large, shady eucalypt tree was left standing. In the last few months, however, it has been declared a public recreation area, and has since been given the name Mount Coot-tha, which he said, albeit with some contempt, is a corrupted form of the Aboriginal word 'Ku-ta'. It seems that his tribe have collected the honey of the native bee, which does not bear the nasty sting of our European variety, from its slopes and 'Ku-ta' in their language means 'place of honey'. From its summit the mountain presents a magnificent panorama. The distant Great Dividing Range bounds it on the one side, with the sea and sand hills of Moreton Island and the long stretch of the bay on the other. And below the mountain the river adds its beauty to the landscape as it winds through wild vegetation and between cultivated fields, before circling the busy city itself and disappearing into the distant bay.

I was also able to visit the botanical gardens which have been established for only twenty-five years. They cover an area of fifty acres at a bend of the river on its north bank, not very far from Queens Street. Their convenience and beauty draw the busy citizens from their shops and businesses to enjoy a cool half-hour under its shady trees while fanned by the breeze that blows across the river. The collections of plants in the gardens are remarkable; beautiful native flowering shrubs stand side by side with the traveller's tree of Madagascar and the noble date palm from North Africa. Magnificent ferns are protected from the heat of the sun by overhanging clumps of graceful bamboo, and a miniature coffee plantation, whose abundant fruits testify how effortlessly the fragrant bean may be developed in this pleasant climate. The conservatory is also a striking feature, with caladiums and orchids all beautiful in form or tint, while stretched in front of it are ponds, filled with the gigantic lilies that grow abundantly here in hues of white, lilac and pink.

My dear Charles, I am conscious that I have been unrestrained in the praise of my current surroundings, perhaps even overwhelmingly so, but please be assured that it reflects the positive frame of mind in which I now find myself. My recuperation is complete and I feel that I am well enough, both mentally and physically, to resume my journey, and although the trail has gone quite cold I must continue to travel north, because I believe firmly in my heart that this is where James has gone. I will write again from a new destination with, I pray, positive news.

Until then I shall remain
your faithful friend,
Annie Ferdinand.

Chapter 17: The Wild North

16th June 1881,
Port Douglas, Queensland.

My Dear Charles,

It seems impossible that more than six months have passed since I last wrote to you from Brisbane, and again I must ask for your forgiveness and patience as my quest to find James continues.

It was in a small town called Gympie about 100 miles north of Brisbane that my decision to travel further north was vindicated. Using the same method that I had employed previously I found conclusive evidence that James had spent some time there, although he had long since departed by the time I arrived in the town. This confirmation had reignited the spark in me and I was keen to continue on my way, but I was advised that the further north my journey took me, the more hardships I would be likely to encounter, particularly at that time of the year, which is renowned for its tropical storms and flooding rains.

Charles, I remained in Gympie for five weeks and enjoyed the hospitality of some wonderful people who welcomed me into their lives, although it was strange to spend Christmas in such a hot and humid climate knowing that in Berlin and London it would be cold and perhaps even snowing. Towards the end of January I became impatient to resume my search. I had found out nothing further about James in Gympie, but the general accord amongst my new-found friends was that it was almost a certainty that he would have travelled even further north. It became my objective to renew my search in an area known as the Palmer River Goldfields. I had been assured that this was a rich alluvial field being worked by many individual miners with small claims. It has been excitingly labelled a 'river of gold' and I imagined that it would be the type of place that would entice James to try his luck. Getting there has proved to be no easy accomplishment for me, however, and I shall try to describe some of the problems I have encountered so far.

Let me say first of all that the distance I have travelled since leaving Brisbane is similar to the length of the British Isles from the south of England to the north of Scotland, but that is where the comparison ends. There are few towns along the track and the small settlements the coach passed through were nothing more than collections of rough bark huts that have been set up to provide relief stops for the passengers and horses. Fortunately, when I was forced to delay my journey due to a flooded river, it was in a small but comfortable hotel in a town of 700 people, named Rockhampton. Many

British people have made this town their home and this is reflected in the name, as I am sure you have already noted. The town is about twenty-five miles upstream from the mouth of the Fitzroy River where rocks bar the way to further navigation, hence the name 'Rock' combined with 'Hampton', your English name for a village.

There are only two seasons in this part of Australia according to the residents, and they are simply known as the summer 'wet' season, which, as the name suggests is hot and humid, and the winter 'dry' season, which is cool and dry. Now that I have experienced my first wet season I can fully understand why it is so named. I have never seen such volumes of water flowing into the ocean in my life.

By mid-April the waters of the rivers to the north had subsided to a trickle and the sun had dried and hardened the rough roads so that I was able to travel to a small settlement called Bowen by coach, but there was no road to the north from there that was capable of coach travel and I was forced to board a paddle steamer for the next part of my journey.

The Palmer River lies on the western side of the vast range of mountains that I have previously mentioned that has been named the Great Dividing Range, as it divides almost the entire length of the eastern coast of Australia from the remainder of the country. The river is inland from a very small, new settlement on the coast that was established less than five years ago, simply to provide access to the goldfields for the carting of provisions and other necessities. This small settlement was, I have been told, originally opened as the port of Trinity Bay because Captain James Cook passed through the bay on Trinity Sunday 1770, but it has now been renamed in honour of the past governor of Queensland, Sir William Cairns. I hope Sir William will not be too disappointed if he ever decides to visit. It was raining upon my arrival and I was bewildered and horrified to witness the conditions that those hardy citizens are forced to endure. Their small community has been established on a long and narrow sandbank on the seafront, and behind this sandbank there exists an equally long and narrow stretch of mangrove-covered swamp. This alternating series of sandbanks and swamps continues for about eight miles inland until eventually the foothills are reached. It rains often, even in what is supposed to be the dry season and when it does the horses and bullocks, with their loaded drays and wagons churn the muddy roads into a quagmire.

Charles, I feel so much compassion for the unfortunate women in this community who must hold the hems of their long dresses up so high to keep them out of the mud that if it were London it would be considered almost beyond the bounds of decency to see them cross the streets. I hope I do not shock you, my dear friend, by saying that I hope sanity prevails and that the women who must live in this climate attire themselves in garments more suited to their personal comfort than to the social restrictions placed upon them by a society that lives with the advantage of paved streets.

I find myself intrigued by the peculiar, but very practical style of housing that prevails in the tropics, mostly among the more affluent business people, of course. The general population still live under canvas tents or in small slab timber huts with beaten ant-bed floors, but the more substantial houses consist of a central room, or sometimes two, with a very high ceiling and doors on every side opening on to wide verandas that surround the house. I had seen houses of a similar nature in the towns further to the south and these had stirred my curiosity as to the degree of comfort they might permit the occupants to enjoy, so I was fortunate to be invited to stay in one in Cairns by a lovely Prussian couple, Mr and Mrs Sachs. I believe I will not be intruding on their privacy if I convey to you my impressions of their admirable circumstances as I have mentioned that it is similar to many affluent homes in this part of the colony.

The main living room is decorated with various wallpapers and has a decorative strip with a stylised flower design above a picture rail. An upright piano, complete with matching brass candlesticks on either side is the main feature, and the seating consists of cane armchairs and occasional tables arranged against the walls. Framed family photographs are hung from the picture rail and the windows are hung with fabric blinds and valances in a floral print. In the dining room the window blinds are also decorated with valances and with tassels which are replicated on the edges of the tablecloth. The chairs are the finest Bentwood style from Europe with cane inserts, and the solid mahogany table is laid with cut crystal decanters and silver tableware. An archway leads to the kitchen alcove adjacent to the parlour, and the archway is adorned with wallpaper in an oriental theme.

The occupants sleep under mosquito nets made from the finest gauze, in elaborate beds with ornamental counterpanes that would rival that of European aristocracy, which are positioned around the open verandas in order to catch the cool night breezes. These houses have high ceilings and pointed roofs and are perched on wooden posts that allow a breeze from any direction to circulate beneath the house and overall, make for the most comfortable living situation that it is possible to achieve in the tropical climate.

Mr and Mrs Sachs have been successful in business in a community several hundred miles to the south which has the quaint but slightly confusing name of Townsville. Mr Sachs was amused by my perplexity and explained that the inhabitants were not undecided about whether they were living in a town or a village, but had named it after Mr Robert Towns, a businessman who had agreed to provide financial support to the new settlement. He wryly commented that it would have been even stranger if it had been decided to call it Towns town, and he added with, I suspect, a little scorn that Mr Towns had only ever visited the town named in his honour for a period of three days when the settlement was first established and that he had since expired several years ago in Sydney.

My hosts have now extended their business interests to Cairns as quite a few other Townsville business people have done, confident that it will one day become a thriving community and a worthy rival to their former home. I do hope that their expectations are realised and that Cairns does survive as a town well into the future, but I have serious doubts as to its ability to do so, unless the population is made up of the most persevering and enduring stock. There are mosquitoes that cause fevers and tiny biting insects that leave countless marks on exposed flesh and are so small that they are able to pass through the gauze of the mosquito nets. The steamy mangrove swamps are putrid with the odour of decaying vegetation and I shudder to think what else besides, for I was warned not to venture too close to the edge of the sandbanks because large crocodiles lurk in the shallow muddy water and are responsible for the disappearance of many of the community's domestic animals.

I enquired as to why a township had been set up on such an unpleasant piece of ground and was informed that it was because it was the best mooring in the bay. I was sceptical, but learned that a small sister township that carried the name Smithfield had been established near the mouth of the Barron River just to the north of Cairns and that conditions there were somewhat promising and the ground more stable. Unfortunately, it gained a reputation as the wickedest town in Australia and my hosts, a highly religious couple, believe that the residents may have incurred the wrath of God. They said it reminded them of the biblical cities Sodom and Gomorrah, which He destroyed because of the wickedness of their inhabitants; and because Smithfield was washed away and totally destroyed by a flood within several years of its establishment it seemed to them, and to many others, that biblical justice had been done. I cannot help but surmise that the ill-fated timing of the flood has been a blessing to the people who have put their faith in the development of the mud-covered site that Cairns is located on.

I did not wish to burden my Prussian hosts with my travelling arrangements and so I enquired about the location of the road from Cairns to the Palmer River at a carters depot that advertised the carriage of merchandise to the goldfields, whereupon the amused proprietor asked me to kindly accompany him to the front of his store. He pointed towards the massive forest-covered mountain range to the west and said there was a goldfield on the Hodgkinson River beyond the Great Dividing Range and that the Palmer River was further north.

My heart sank, Charles. I could see no way of crossing that huge formidable rampart and I felt that my journey must come to an ignominious end right there on that muddy street. I thanked the storekeeper and my forlorn look must have betrayed my emotions for his amusement immediately turned to concern. When I explained my predicament to him, he told me in a more sympathetic tone that there was indeed a track up the range from Cairns, but it was only suitable for horse and dray. A dray is a two-wheeled cart that is pulled by a single horse and the track had been carved through the mangroves and scrub to the foot of the range and then up by a tortuous route to the plateau at the top. It was much too difficult to be used by regular coaches, he said, and was best left to horsemen and carters of supplies.

Unfortunately for his own business, an adventurer, whose name he said was Christie Palmerston, had found a much easier and more direct route further north. I understood from his tone that the people of Cairns were not too pleased with Mr Palmerston, on whose reports the government relied, to decide which track would become the official road to the goldfields.

There may, of course, have been other reasons for the general feeling of animosity towards this gentleman, since my informant told me of the rumours that abound of his harsh and often violent treatment of the Chinese and the Aborigines. He admitted though, that these rumours conflict with other tales about his deeds of bravery in protecting women and children from attack and rescuing sick and injured prospectors from isolated diggings. Overall, the enigmatic Mr Christie Palmerston sounds very much like an Australian version of your famous English folk hero, Robin Hood.

A new port had been established on the coast that has been given the name, Port Douglas, according to my informant. He also assured me that its citizens, who in many cases are the former residents of Smithfield, have found a better piece of ground to settle on than have those in Cairns. One can only hope that they have learned their lesson and will maintain a level of propriety and decency that will not bring down the wrath of God on them for a second time.

When I told Mr Sachs that it was my intention to travel to the Hodgkinson goldfield by way of the track from Port Douglas, I was pleasantly surprised to learn that he had hired a barge for the purpose of transporting cargo to that community and he, very kindly, allowed me to travel with him. This was fortunate because, as I soon found out, it was the only way to travel from Cairns to Port Douglas. The two are isolated from each other by heavily forested mountains whose steep slopes fall directly into the sea.

Port Douglas is a fine-looking little community and it gives the impression that it has progressed quickly in its three short years of existence. It has about a dozen hotels with more under construction, a courthouse, two banks and a community hospital. Its wide white beach has sand so stable that horse races are conducted on it, and an air of prosperity and confidence in the future was evident amongst the more than 800 inhabitants.

Charles, I am truly frightened by the prospect of what might lie ahead of me as the further I travel, the more arduous my journey is becoming. I do not relish the thought that I might starve to death, lost forever deep in the dense green jungle that is everywhere about me and seems so sinister and foreboding. When these emotions arise to overwhelm me, however, my thoughts turn to your kind, reassuring smile and your brotherly concern and I know that in simply writing to you and sharing my anxieties with you I can feel your presence and your interest in my welfare. That is what gives me the strength to go on with my design.

Once more, let me say that I hope I can furnish you with positive news from my next destination.

I remain,
your faithful friend,
Annie Ferdinand.

Chapter 18: Over the Bump Track

Mr Sachs made sure that Annie was checked in at the best hotel in Port Douglas before he went back to the wharf to oversee the unloading of the barge. After she had settled in she found the post office and posted her letter to Charles and then began the task of trying to arrange transport to the Palmer River diggings. She soon discovered that this assignment was going to be the most difficult of her journey so far. As in Cairns, there were no coaches that catered for paying passengers on the track. It was uncommon, she was told, for a woman to want to go there on her own without having had her transport arranged beforehand or without her husband sitting next to her on a dray holding the reins of a couple of strong horses. It seemed that this was an impediment much greater than the one she had faced before her trek to Ballarat for there was no possibility of walking this time; in fact, unless she could convince someone to take her there she knew she could not go any further.

Once again Mr Sachs came to the rescue. He had contracted a man to take a load of supplies to the goldfields and Annie watched apprehensively from a distance as they discussed whether he might take her along as a passenger. Finally, despite much serious discussion and shaking of his head the teamster threw his arms in the air and walked away and Mr Sachs' smile, as he approached Annie, told her that the transaction had been settled in her favour.

They were to travel in convoy with several other drays carrying prospectors with their wives and children and a dozen horsemen leading packhorses, to deliver supplies to the town of Kingsborough on the Hodgkinson goldfield. She had been told that this was a reefing, rather than an alluvial field, but had also been assured that the reefs were shallow and were being worked, in many cases, by individuals and not companies, so she had made the decision to check that field before travelling on to the Palmer River, if indeed that became necessary.

The teamster was a lean wiry man who looked to be in his thirties, with a weather-beaten brown face, whether burned by the sun or his natural colouring, it was difficult to tell. He sported a thick black beard, and a mop of curly black hair stuck out from beneath one of the wide-brimmed floppy hats that were commonly worn in the tropics. Mr Sachs had brought some of these hats with his trade goods, describing them as 'cabbage tree hats', because they were woven from the dried and stripped leaves of the cabbage tree.

The sleeves of the teamster's red cotton shirt were rolled up to his elbows, revealing a pair of strong muscular arms as brown as his face and covered in a tangle of black hair, and Annie was somewhat startled by the sight of a broad belt about his waist glistening with rifle cartridges. He looked sullen and morose and was unresponsive to her attempts at conversation and she began to worry that the journey might be completed in a dreary silence for he barked orders to his assistant, a little aboriginal boy who looked about ten years old, in a language that was unintelligible to her.

When the load had been secured on the dray she was tersely told to climb aboard and seat herself between the teamster and the boy, and the convoy then moved off to a chorus of whistles and yells of encouragement accompanied by hand clapping and waving. It seemed to be quite a special occasion and Annie marvelled at the enthusiasm of the small crowd and wondered if this was what transpired every time a convoy departed Port Douglas for the goldfields. Her attention was distracted almost immediately, however, as she stared in awe at the majestic peaks that soared above them in a blue haze, merging with the lighter blue of the sky beyond. *How could this route possibly be any easier than the one that ascended from Cairns? Was the remarkable Mr Palmerston who apparently discovered it, really biased against the people of Cairns?* It certainly seemed so. She had also learned that this route had been named 'The Bump track' and this did nothing to alleviate her concerns.

About four miles along the wide and well-maintained road they came upon a small, busy-looking community and Annie began to feel a little more settled. The teamster too, seemed more relaxed now that they were on their way. She began to suspect that her first impression of him may have been misguided and that perhaps he was just someone who preferred not to speak unless it was necessary; someone who, for reasons of his own, cared little for the trappings of civilisation. If that was indeed the case then he had certainly chosen an occupation that was suited to his temperament. As if he'd read her mind the teamster began to speak, although it seemed almost reluctantly. He told her that this thriving little place was called Craiglie, one of the communities where the teamsters and packers who used the Bump Road regularly preferred to live. It boasted two hotels, blacksmith's and farrier's shops, a wheelwright, saddlers and butchers and bakers shops, and the countryside around it was fertile and well stocked with horses, bullocks and cattle, all peacefully grazing.

After about seven miles they crossed a wide river where there was another settlement much like the first and Annie envisaged that if the remainder of the journey was as pleasant, her previous concerns were quite unfounded. This was where they were to spend the first night while the teams were fed and watered and she slept soundly in a modestly furnished but comfortable room, content in the knowledge that she was a little closer to her goal.

By mid-morning of the next day the convoy arrived at the foot of the range and began the ascent up a series of gentle spurs and across wide ridges and the teamster pointed out the advantages of this part of the range as opposed to, what he said, was the much steeper spurs and narrow ridges of the range behind Cairns.

Annie studied him thoughtfully. "I feel I should compliment you on your thorough knowledge of these mountains, sir," she said at length. "Your enthusiasm must surely be the equal of the pioneer of this route."

"That's because I *am* the pioneer," the teamster said. "I surely am. I'm the very pioneer himself." He grinned, revealing a row of even white teeth to Annie for the first time. "I'm begging your pardon, but I assumed the merchant, Mr Sachs, would have told you who I was back in Port Douglas." He raised his hat and replaced it in a sweeping gesture that she felt was almost theatrical. "I'm Cristofero Palmerston Carandini: otherwise known to most people as Christie Palmerston."

Annie laughed. "No! Mr Sachs did not tell me with whom I was to travel and perhaps that is just as well, from what I have been told about *you* Mr Palmerston. If I'd known who you were back there in Port Douglas, perhaps I would have declined the opportunity to accompany you."

Palmerston seemed unperturbed; perhaps even satisfied. "You *have* heard about me then, - obviously from someone other than Mr Sachs?"

"Certainly, I have learned of the great explorer and somewhat, shall we say, - mysterious, Christie Palmerston," she said. "You have supporters who acclaim you to be a great explorer and have named you the prince of pathfinders, while you have detractors who portray you as a ruthless adventurer with some bloodthirsty deeds to your credit. May I be so bold as to ask which of these most accurately describes your character, Mr Palmerston, for your honest answer will either relieve my apprehension or give me further cause for alarm?"

The teamster was silent for a few moments. "Don't rightly know if I *can* give you an honest answer," he said at length. "Maybe I'm a bit of both at different times."

"But you must surely be aware of at least some of the legends that abound about your exploits," she persisted.

"Ah yes, legends or lies; call them what you like," Palmerston shrugged. "Some people make up things about me to make me look bad for their own reasons. I can't help that. You might have heard someone say that I kill the Chinese and steal their gold, but they don't have any proof of that and never will have. The authorities follow every move I make; they don't trust me, but they respect me." He patted the rifle that lay close to his hand. "This Snider is my constant companion, but it's only to look after myself, that's all. The government pays me to find these tracks you know. I got 300 pounds for finding this one we're travelling on and they know they got good value for their money. It wasn't easy, as you'll soon find out, but it's better than the Cairns track and a lot shorter than the original one from Cooktown."

Annie looked surprised. "The *original* track, Mr Palmerston?"

"Yeah, that's right," he said. "It's not too bad in the dry season, but when it's wet the rivers are impassable. There are five major rivers along that route and prospectors heading for the Palmer have been held up for a month or more waiting to get through the flooded crossings, the patient ones anyway. Quite a few of the more desperate, maybe short of food, or just impatient, have drowned themselves and their horses trying to cross when the current is running too swift and the water much too high. After that though, there's *Hells Gate*. That narrow pass is a perfect place for the Aborigines to mount an attack and they've murdered a lot of people there over the last few years. It's aptly named." He abruptly removed his hat and held it aloft in another theatrical gesture. *"Lasciate ogni speranza voi che entrate,"* he said in a solemn tone. He placed the hat on his chest and bowed. "That's Old Italian," he said. "It means, *abandon all hope, ye who enter here."*

Annie laughed. "Ah, yes! The famous final line of the inscription on Hell's Gate, from Dante's Inferno. You are indeed a revelation and you *did* pronounce it as well as any London theatrical performer, Mr Cristofero Carandini. I am so grateful that I have been the recipient of your kindness and that I have not had to abandon all hope thus far in my own particular quest."

Palmerston regarded her curiously and she thought he was on the verge of enquiring about what she meant by her *'own particular quest'* but he remained silent.

"I've heard that the people of Cairns are not too pleased with your success at finding this particular track, sir," she said.

"Yes, I've heard that too," he grinned. "But they might be whistling to a different tune very soon. The minister for Works wants me to examine the ranges around Cairns to find a route for a railway. If I'm successful, as I believe I will be, I'll be their number one citizen; I can assure you of that. All of these small towns are competing with each other for the trade to and from the goldfields. Their very existence depends on it. The one that eventually becomes the most easily accessible will flourish. The others probably won't survive. It's as simple as that – and," he added with a suggestion of arrogance in his tone, "I'm the one who will eventually be the decision maker."

He lapsed into silence again and she began to suspect that many of the stories that abounded about this extraordinary man depended largely on Palmerston's oddly melodramatic personality and perhaps his own peculiar desire for notoriety.

"I wish you every success then, sir, and who, might I ask, is this beautiful little boy, Mr Palmerston?"

"Oh, him? He's my first class assistant. His name is Pompo," he said, rubbing his hand affectionately through the boy's fuzzy black hair. "His tribe raided a homestead that I happened to be visiting a couple of years ago. The settlers defended it, - quite vigorously, and, - well, let's leave it at that. Pompo was left behind and either he adopted me, or I adopted him. Anyway, he's been with me ever since through some of my worst misfortunes, sickness and hunger. He's even saved me from being murdered a couple of times."

Annie fell silent as Palmerston and Pompo chatted in their unknown language, until Palmerston spoke to her again, in English. "Pompo wants to know why such a fine lady as you appear to be is travelling to a rough bush town like Kingsborough, all alone?" he said.

Annie laughed. "Does he now, Mr Palmerston?"

"Yes he does, and you could tell him to mind his own business, but that would be offensive to his culture, Miss Ferdinand. You see they are instinctively inquisitive people, but in a harmless sort of way."

"Well then, I wouldn't like to offend the young gentleman, so you can tell him that I am searching for a very good friend who has been lost to me for more than a year."

Palmerston gave her a probing look and then he and the boy exchanged another flurry of words, after which the youth became quite animated, giggling and pointing at him. He shook his head, gave the boy a playful cuff on the ear and then spoke in English again. "He would like to know if your friend is a gentleman."

"He is indeed."

Palmerston frowned. "And he *lives* in Kingsborough?"

"Is that another question from Pompo, Mr Palmerston?" Annie teased him.

"No! That one's from me." Palmerston continued to frown.

"I don't know where he lives, Mr Palmerston. If he is not in Kingsborough, I shall continue my search further north."

"You must hold this gentleman in very high regard. How do you propose to conduct this search, Miss Ferdinand?"

"Well, first of all I shall find a good boarding house or hotel and then…"

Palmerston laughed, but it was hollow. "…Ah, right then; you'll find a good boarding house or hotel, will you? Let me inform you, Miss Ferdinand, that there are no boarding houses, good or bad, and no hotels that would suit a lady like you in Kingsborough. It's as wild a place as you're ever likely to see in your life. I must apologise for my incivility when we first met, but I supposed you were another 'working girl' looking to make a quid on the goldfields."

"Mr Palmerston!" Annie glared at him. "I am tired of being mistaken for a prostitute in Australia simply because I am travelling on my own. I have only found out what a working girl is since I arrived in this country and I am certainly *not* one of those ladies."

Palmerston heaved an audible sigh of relief. "Well, don't get your knickers in a knot because that's good news to me anyway, Miss Ferdinand," he said. "You wouldn't want to be crossing paths with Palmer Kate. She runs a pretty good business with the miners and she doesn't like anyone arriving on her patch unannounced. Kate is a very good friend of mine. We've spent a lot of pleasant times together, - purely social, of course. I've been worrying over how I was going to tell her I'd brought you to Kingsborough without her being told about it beforehand."

"I shall try to keep out of your *friend's* way, Mr Palmerston." Annie said, her crisp tone and emphasis on the term *'friend'* highlighting her displeasure and conveying to Palmerston quite clearly that she knew exactly how social she suspected he and Palmer Kate to be.

Palmerston looked at her with mild amusement. "Aw, come on now" he said. "What'd you expect me to think? Young women, all dressed up like you are, don't usually go to a pigsty like Kingsborough for the fresh air and healthy lifestyle it offers. It's going to be difficult to keep you out of Kate's way too. She owns the only establishment you might be able to bunk down in for a couple of nights."

Annie stared at him, horrified at the thought of having to enter a whore's house, let alone sleep in one.

Palmerston paused for a moment as if deep in thought, and then he clapped a hand to his knee. "Ah, don't worry about that now; I think I've got it covered," he said. "Since you're not a working girl I know what we can do for you. Do you remember that valley we cut through before we started up the range, and the river we followed upstream for a good part of the way?"

Annie nodded weakly, still shaken by his previous remarks.

"I named them in honour of my good friend, Bill Mowbray. He's the gold mining warden at Kingsborough and his wife, Ellen is one of the nicest women you'll ever meet. She'll be happy to have some decent female company for a change."

Some sections of the road near the top of the range were very steep and they came upon a teamster with a heavily laden wagon, making his way slowly along the track. Palmerston told her that this was the section of the track he'd called *'The Bump'* and neither he, nor anyone else, had been able to find an easier way to get over or around it. The first teamster to arrive at the Bump had to wait until a second one came up behind him. They then had to hook their horse or bullock teams together, pull one wagon up to the landing at the top and then take the teams back down to pull the other wagon up. It worked very well, he said, because everyone knew they could rely on each other. That was the way of the people who lived and worked here and, he told her with pride in his voice, they were known locally as the 'Knights of the Road.'

They conversed quite freely as they progressed up the range and by the time they reached Kingsborough Annie had confided in Palmerston, whom she found to be a sympathetic listener to her plight. He was adamant, however, that she would not find James in Kingsborough and declared it was more likely that he would be located further north. On their arrival in the town, which on the outskirts seemed to be nothing more than a scattered collection of corroding iron clad huts, Palmerston took her immediately to a neat cottage in the main street that he said was the warden's house and Mrs Mowbray, as he had predicted, invited her to stay with them during her time in that outpost, an offer which she gratefully accepted. Palmerston excused himself and turned to go, but Annie placed her hand on his arm. "Thank you for everything, Mr Palmerston," she said. "You have most certainly provided me with the only opportunity I may have to continue my search and I could not have come this far without your assistance."

She was amused, but not surprised by Palmerston's response for he grinned, removed his wide brimmed hat and bowed, holding the hat to his chest. "It is, of course, my pleasure entirely, Miss Ferdinand," he said in a well-rehearsed resonant tone. "And please remember; *do not abandon all hope until the gate has finally closed.*"

"I will remember that, Mr Palmerston; thank you again."

"Then I shall leave you in Mrs Mowbray's safe hands while I attend to my, ah, other business." He winked at Ellen Mowbray and she laughed.

"You're nothing but a showman, Christie Palmerston," she said. "Go on then. I'm sure Kate will be waiting for you."

When he had left, Mrs Mowbray took Annie inside the neat cottage. "Nobody quite knows what to make of Christie." She smiled and shook her head. "He likes to play the tough, mysterious outlaw, as I'm sure you've found out already, but he's got a heart of gold if anyone's in trouble and needs help. I'm sure he gets his theatrical behaviours from his mother. I've heard that her name was Madame Carandini and that she was an opera singer in Melbourne."

Chapter 19: Lessons in Bushcraft

15th August 1881,
Maytown, Queensland.

My Dear Charles,

I suspect that I have now come to the least law-abiding area in all of Australia in my journey thus far, and to present you with my case for reaching that conclusion, let me share with you the details of an incident that occurred several months before my arrival in a dreadful little village called Kingsborough. The sole purpose for the existence of this corrugated iron and canvas town is to provide a service centre for the miners whose alluvial gold claims are located along a forty mile stretch of the Hodgkinson River.

At that time there were somewhere in the region of 400 Chinese miners working in the area. There has been an enduring hostility between the Chinese and the European miners ever since the Chinese were allowed by the government of the colony to have mining licences and it seems that the trouble is due to accusations of claim-jumping from both sides. Evidently, it is a simple matter to differentiate between the shafts put down in the river bed by either side as the Chinese dig round holes while the others are square, but in some instances, there have been allegations of diggers leaving their claims for the evening and returning next morning to find that the shafts have been rounded off and the Chinese claiming ownership of them. At the time I speak of, and for reasons unknown, but probably related to the above, the hostility quickly escalated into open violence. The consequence of this skirmish was that sixty Chinese and ten white miners were killed. The remaining Chinese were forced to flee from the field and have not been allowed to return so far. There have been no arrests made over this incident, nor for any of the many others reported of a similar nature, and it seems that the laws of the country mean nothing to the mining community in Kingsborough.

Many miners, I have been told, have become disillusioned by the Hodgkinson goldfield. It is not as rich, nor as easy to work as the Palmer River diggings from which many of the miners rushed when the Hodgkinson was discovered. Some have already left in frustration and returned to their claims on the Palmer, only to find that the Chinese there have taken over their claims. Consequently, it is a very transient population and a troubled one too, for hostility seems to pervade the very air around the diggings and violence can be triggered by the most trivial of differences.

It became my ardent hope that James had not settled in this uncivilised district, but I knew that I could not leave until I had established with some certainty that he had not. The post office seemed to be unmanned so my initial enquiries as to that possibility were directed to the store adjoining it. I discovered then that the reason the post office was unmanned was that the storekeeper was also the postmaster. This man informed me, in what I thought to be quite a self-important manner, that he was also the town's Justice of the Peace, the honorary secretary of the Hospital Fund, and chair of both the Roads Committee and the Hodgkinson Progress Association.

Naturally, it took me some time to digest this information and I believe I must have stood there, open-mouthed and staring at him, for he seemed to become uncomfortable and to wilt a little under my bewildered gaze. This surprised me somewhat as he looked to be in his forties and he was at least six feet tall, with a huge growth of black beard, black curly hair and a barrel chest that made me wonder what on earth such a healthy and robust looking individual was doing loafing behind the counter of an empty store. He was, in fact, such an imposing figure that I could hardly put words to my request for the information that I desired. Somehow, I managed to pull myself together and relate my unhappy account and by the time I had finished his large dark eyes had softened and he asked me in a rich Irish accent to return the next day after he had made some enquiries. This I did of course, and discovered that he had gone to great effort to secure any information that might have been useful to me from various hotels and shanties during the previous evening. In fact, so much had the poor man persevered in the task that he had woken that morning with a terrible headache, and on my arrival he looked much the worse for wear and a shadow of the impressive man I'd chanced upon the previous day.

Charles, I don't think my words of appreciation for his dedication to my cause, or my cheery smile, made him feel any healthier. He grumbled and groaned in quite a wretched fashion throughout our interview, but between the bouts of self-recrimination and pledges to renounce the drink he called an evil spirit's own foul spirit, he managed to relate that he had been successful in ascertaining that several persons of the description I had given him of James had been in the district some months previously. I was relieved to hear, though, that they too had joined the exodus of miners to the Palmer River. I thanked the man for his trouble and left the store, but not before politely introducing myself. He in turn, told me that his name was also James and he wished me every success in the pursuit of my quest.

Mr Mowbray was quite incredulous, and laughed uncontrollably when I asked him about obtaining transport to the Palmer River and casually mentioned how grateful I was that James, the storekeeper, had been so sympathetic to my cause and advised me to continue my search in that direction. After he had composed himself sufficiently he asked me why, since we were on such good terms, I hadn't convinced the man to take me there himself. I replied that I had assumed that a storekeeper might not be the most appropriate person to advise me on transport opportunities, whereupon Mr Mowbray again burst into laughter. When he had regained his composure once more and noted my confusion, he explained that James, the storekeeper, was in fact no lesser celebrity than the great man who had discovered both the Hodgkinson and the Palmer River goldfields, and who had, by doing so, virtually assured the opening up of the northern frontier of Queensland. He had now gathered several hundred pounds from voluntary subscriptions paid to him by the prospectors of the district to fund another expedition of discovery, and was soon to embark on this new undertaking, an occasion for which all and sundry waited expectantly, hoping to learn of even greater accomplishments than he has already achieved.

The name of this great man is James Venture Mulligan, a household name in the northern goldfields, but one, Mr Mowbray conceded, was almost unknown in the southern regions of Australia. At once I realised why Mr Mulligan had seemed a little deflated at my lack of response to his declaration of the positions which he enjoyed in the community, for I must surely be the only person within several hundred miles who had not heard of his exploits of discovery. I shall thus consider myself privileged to have been able to enlist so readily the assistance of this great explorer whose patronage is so much valued by others in the community, in my quest to find James. This is despite my excitement being somewhat tempered by Mr Mowbray, who is of the opinion that I merely gave him an excuse to visit several more hotels than he usually does when he is not out in the wilderness discovering rivers of gold.

When Mrs Mowbray learned of my need to find transport to a settlement named Maytown, which, like Kingsborough is to the Hodgkinson, serves as the service centre for the Palmer River miners, she asked Mr Mowbray to bring forward his customary monthly journey to that place, and when he agreed she decided that she would make an excursion of it, as she occasionally does, and she and the children would come along for the ride. It is just another example of the sociability of the people of rural Australia and their willingness to assist a stranger in need and is something I have come to accept as part of their nature, but it still leaves me in a state of wonder each time it is my good fortune to be the recipient of it.

The Palmer River was about seventy miles distant and we set out in a two-horse covered wagon. I sat beside Mr Mowbray on a comfortable padded seat, while his wife Ellen and their two children rode inside. This was an excellent arrangement from my point of view, because Mr Mowbray was such an interesting conversationalist and I began to learn a little about what he called 'bushcraft'. When I commented on the sparse vegetation and dry river beds, for example, he told me a tale that I found to be most interesting about a prospector travelling through dry, unexplored territory alone. When he came upon a source of water he would remain there for several days, resting and drinking frequently. When he felt that his body could take no more water he would set out with only a small water bag in the cool of the late afternoon. He would travel by night if there was a moon, and keep going into the early morning until the sun rose above the treetops, then he would rest in the shade during the heat of the day, moving as little as possible to conserve energy. He would proceed in this manner until he arrived at another water source and in this way he could prospect in the most hostile country, where many other men refused to journey for fear of dying of thirst.

Charles, I realise that this tale of how one can survive in the wilderness is probably of little concern to you and it is highly unlikely that either of us will ever find ourselves in such a dire life or death situation, but it does serve to remind me of the tenacity of those intrepid individuals who have opened up this desolate part of Australia for settlement. My dreadful experience in walking from Melbourne to Ballarat had already afforded me an understanding of the harshness of the climate and the fatigue associated with it, but I cannot imagine the privation of travelling through this land alone and with the spectre of extreme hunger and thirst to add to the suffering.

The barrenness of the landscape was transformed just before sunset on the first evening when Mr Mowbray pulled the horses up by a beautiful little running stream that emptied into a large lake a little way downstream from the road. Shady white gum trees surrounded the lake, which he said was called a 'billabong' in Australia, and when he had unharnessed the horses he let them roam free to feed on the rich green grass without hobbling them, knowing that they would be unlikely to wander very far, but also allowing them the opportunity to take flight if surprised by a poisonous snake or some large predator. Mrs Mowbray and I set about gathering wood to make a fire and she pointed out to me the hardwood that burns with a strong heat and very little smoke, and the soft kindling twigs that would get the fire going easily. Once we had gathered enough wood we left Mr Mowbray to the task of starting our campfire, while we women took the children to a secluded spot, to bathe in the cool water. After that we felt quite refreshed and we walked around the edge of the billabong, Mrs Mowbray stopping frequently to sniff the air. I wondered, of course, what she was trying to discover until, with a satisfied grin, she asked if I could smell anything different. I turned in the direction to which she pointed and, sure enough, there was a strange, faint aroma in the air. 'It's a bush tomato plant, Annie,' she told me. We followed the scent to its source and found some shrubs growing in the open, beyond the shade of the gum trees. She became very excited when she saw them, for she recognised them immediately as the species known to her as 'Kangaroo Apple' which, she assured me, was an edible variety. Apparently, there are over twenty different variations of this native fruit, which to the uninitiated look somewhat similar; some are edible, but others are bitter to the taste, and a few are quite poisonous.

It was then Mr Mowbray's turn to bathe and while he was gone Mrs Mowbray soaked the small red and yellow fruit and then buried them in the ashes at the edge of the campfire to roast. She then produced some flour, baking soda and salt from the provisions in the wagon, mixed it all together into dough and placed that in the ashes as well to make a kind of soda bread, which she told me was called 'damper'. We then sat down to, what for me, was an enjoyably different evening meal. The succulent bush tomato between thick slices of damper bread was our main course and then we had damper sweetened with honey, which Mrs Mowbray had gathered earlier from a hive of the native stingless bee hidden in the hollow of a tree. This fine fare was served up with strong black tea, brewed above the flames in a blackened tin can that had once held flour and that Mr Mowbray said was called a 'billy-can'. And as I looked up with gratitude at the clear night sky and drank my tea from the tin mug my thoughts returned to my first meeting with you in London. I remembered your reassurance that you would not offer me tea that was not genuine Indian and of the highest quality. Treasured friend Charles, I know nothing of its origin or its quality, but I can tell you that I enjoyed that tea just as much as if it was the very best London had to offer. To top off a very pleasant evening, Mr Mowbray entertained us, playing some popular tunes on his harmonica while we sang along.

When it became time for us to retire I was invited to spend the night in the wagon with the children, but chose instead to sleep under the stars as it was such a beautiful evening. Mrs Mowbray had gathered the green aromatic leaves of a tree, which she said was called a sandalwood, and she sprinkled some around the edge of the campfire. The scent from the heated leaves, though pleasant to us, she said would drive mosquitoes away. Mr Mowbray rolled out for me, at a discreet distance from where he and Mrs Mowbray were to sleep, a bedroll that he called a 'swag', and I must say, Charles, that I did sleep soundly the whole night long.

In the days that followed I learned a little more of the art of survival in the 'bush' from this happy couple who freely admit to having gained much of their knowledge from the Aborigines that they have befriended over the years. Mr Mowbray pointed to a stand of trees lining a watercourse, for example. He said they were called ti-trees, and that the Aborigines used the leaves for many medicinal purposes, chewing the young leaves to relieve headaches, or rubbing them on the body for the relief of pain and the cleaning of wounds and skin irritations. Another remedy was to cut a piece of bark from a sandalwood tree, pound it between two stones and pour it into boiling water. When it cooled they would drink the solution for the relief of throat infections. Mrs Mowbray then contributed her own interesting information on the subject. She said that the soft and flexible paper-like bark of the ti-tree was stripped off and used in making cradles for their babies, as a bandage for wounds, or as a sleeping mat, and it was also used to wrap food for cooking or for smoking victuals over a fire to preserve them when they were travelling from one camp to another. I was almost disappointed when we arrived at Maytown several days later, having passed the time in such pleasant conversation with this wonderful couple.

Maytown is larger and further advanced in settlement than Kingsborough and has laid claim to being the capital of the Palmer River goldfields, although I have noted that such claims seem to be directly linked to the number of hotels operating in each town. Maytown has six hotels, but I would add that its claim of supremacy is also somewhat enhanced by the fact that it boasts, of all things, a lemonade factory. It also has ten Chinese stores and it would appear that, unlike Kingsborough, Chinese miners are tolerated and Chinese storekeepers are an accepted part of life on the Palmer River. This gives me hope that these people whom I have found to be, with few exceptions, gentle and unassuming by nature, will eventually find their place as respected citizens in the rich tapestry of diversity that I believe the developing Australian culture to be.

Charles, I regret to tell you that I have been unable to discover anything of James in Maytown. A postal service has been established here, but the population is so transient that no mail records are kept and it is a similar situation in the other small communities that have been established along the river. I have been told that the mining claims extend for more than forty miles upstream and the same downstream on the Palmer alone, and that gold has also been found on other rivers in the area too, so I do not know where next to turn. It is quite impossible for me to wander from one camp to another, asking questions. I will not abandon my search, however, for the flame of love still burns within me, but I do need to consider my physical well-being. I know I am becoming malnourished due to the continual travelling in this unforgiving climate and in my weakened state I fear that I have become more susceptible to the fevers that seem to abound in the tropics. I must find a more temperate climate in which to recuperate so that when this journey is completed, James will find me healthy in body as well as in mind.

I have made a decision, Charles. I do not know how this will affect you and I hope, most sincerely, that you will find it in your heart to forgive me because you are my best friend and confidant, but I feel that I cannot continue to burden you with my grievances and the ramblings of my discontented mind. You must get on with your life and forget about this silly woman who intrudes on you with her boring narratives, if you have not already done so. I will never forget you Charles. You were so helpful and inspirational to me when you could so easily have turned me away. I have found that writing to you has helped me to overcome my fears and doubts, but I have decided that it is time for me to stand on my own and I will only write to you again when I have some positive information that I can share with you. Goodbye Charles, God bless you and thank you for everything my dear friend.

I will remain in your debt forever,
Annie Ferdinand.

Chapter 20: An Invitation to Bide Awhile

By September 1881 Annie Ferdinand was in Herberton, a small town nestled behind those mountains that she had stared at with such apprehension from the muddy street in Cairns. She knew that there was virtually no possibility that James would ever have contemplated visiting the town, for it had been established only sixteen months before her arrival and it owed its existence to the discovery of tin on the headwaters of the nearby Herbert River. She had been advised, however, that the bracing climate it enjoyed due to its elevation would assist her to recuperate from the exhaustion that continually plagued her in the tropics, and so she had made the decision that if it was suitable for her needs, she would rest there for as long as it took to recover her strength. She was pleasantly surprised to find on her arrival that the streets were wide and well formed, a number of substantial buildings had been erected and the population had grown in the town's short lifespan to about 400, including 100 children.

Annie's first stop, as had been her past routine, was the post office, to find out if a Mr James Potts was, or had been in the town, and after confirming with the postmaster that the name and description she provided were unfamiliar to him, as she had fully expected, she then enquired about suitable accommodation.

The postmaster informed her that there were three hotels in the town and kindly suggested that she try the Caledonian Hotel at the end of the main street. When he saw the look of doubt in her eyes he hastily assured her that it was a clean and reputable establishment run by an elderly couple and had good private accommodation that was quite separate from the hotel bar. The bar, he added, was frequented mainly by the business fraternity of Herberton, while the other two hotels catered to the considerable thirsts of the hard-working tin miners.

Annie, still hesitant, walked the short distance to the hotel as directed and discovered that it was indeed, an impressive yellow-painted, two-storey wooden structure capped with a red, galvanised iron roof. Wide verandas on both the ground and upper floors wrapped around the building on all four sides and the spaces between each of the support posts were arched with an elegant filigree of white-painted cast iron lace. Satisfied with its appearance of respectability, she walked around to a side entrance where she found a glass-panelled door with the word '*RECEPTION*' engraved on a polished brass plaque that was attached above a large brass knocker moulded in the shape of a heraldic thistle, the floral emblem of Scotland.

She knocked, and several minutes elapsed before the door swung quietly open. A neatly dressed elderly woman, her grey hair tied back in a bun, stood there wiping her wet hands on her apron, obviously having just come from the kitchen. When she saw Annie her eyes widened and her welcoming smile froze momentarily, but in the next instant it returned and she stood aside, holding the door as she gestured politely for Annie to step inside. Annie was a little perplexed and wondered idly what could have triggered the woman's strange reaction, but she pretended not to notice and stepped through the doorway.

"I suppose ye'll be lookin' fer decent lodgings, will ye', lass?" the woman said, as she stepped behind a high desk and opened a ledger. She spoke in a brogue that was unmistakably Scottish, but which she had made an effort to alter enough to be understood.

"Yes, I am" Annie replied. "I'm not sure how long I will stay, but it does seem like a pleasant town and it is certainly much cooler here than it is in Maytown."

"Aye, indeed it is," the old woman agreed, but her smile had faded again and she frowned. "*Maytown*, did I hear ye' say? My, oh my, but that's a rough place fer any lassie tae be livin' in, - an' you travellin' by yerself as well by the look o' it. The people roun'about here are no' a bit like the Maytown bunch. We're all honest hard-workin' folk who widnae dae anybody any harm, an' we're clean livin' people too, ye' know. Anybody that might think they can come tae our wee township lookin' fer bother o' *any kind* is sure to get told tae leave an' no' tae come back. Even the young tin miners are a guid, respectful bunch o' lads."

Annie felt a jolt as she suddenly became aware of the old lady's suspicions. *Oh no, not again. I have been taken for a prostitute once more. This is becoming too much of a common occurrence.* She laughed. "Oh, please let me assure you that I am not one of Maytown's 'working girls'. I merely passed through that town. I am, as you say, a *clean living* person too and I *am* looking for *decent* lodgings." She stopped short of adding that she had gone there looking for a red-headed man as she recalled the distress that it had caused the booking clerk in Ballarat.

The woman sighed with what appeared to Annie to be relief. "Well then, that bein' the case I think ye'd like it here, lass, if ye' dae decide tae bide awhile."

Her voice carried such a tone of entreaty and her old eyes such an earnest look that Annie felt a little uncomfortable; it was almost like the dear old lady was on the verge of pleading with her to stay. But she was now quite certain that the accommodation offered would be appropriate for her wishes. "Yes, then I believe I will stay for a while," she said.

"Well, that's it settled then," the old woman said, the lines around her mouth and eyes crinkling in a happy grin. "I've got a fine wee room for ye' up the stairs. It's at the back, well away from the din o' the bar – an' ye' can have it fer our long-term rate - even if ye' decide ye'll no' bide that long wi' us after all."

Annie was surprised at the woman's generosity towards a complete stranger, and she felt an instant empathy with her. "That is very kind of you, Mrs –"

"Gordon, it is," the woman said. "Mrs Jane Gordon, an' my guid man's out there tendin' tae customers in the bar; his name is Andrew, an' I'm sure he'll be *very* pleased tae meet ye' as well."

Annie wondered briefly about Mrs Gordon's accent on the word 'very', but then she just put it down to her quaint, Scottish way of speaking.

"Okay now," Mrs Gordon said. She bent over the ledger with a stub of a pencil poised above the page. "An' what name shall I put down in my book for ye', lass?" she asked.

"My name is Annie –," she began, but then she stopped mid-sentence as Mrs Gordon's head snapped up unexpectedly, and she noticed that the colour had drained from her face.

"Is something wrong, Mrs Gordon?" she asked, startled.

The old woman shook her head sadly. "No, nothin's wrong, lass; well, ye' see, my wee dochter's name was Annie as well, - an' it's just that, - ye' look awmost the image o' what I expect she'd hae looked like now if she was still wi' us."

Annie saw that look of pain cross her face again, and she became disturbingly aware in that moment that Mrs Gordon was grieving for a daughter who had passed away – a daughter who was also called Annie and who apparently she resembled in some ways. *That certainly accounts for the dear lady's bewildering response to my unexpected arrival.* On impulse, she walked around the side of the desk, put her arm around the older woman's shoulders, and hugged her gently. "Oh, Mrs Gordon, I'm so very sorry," she whispered.

Jane Gordon composed herself and wiped a tear from her eye with the hem of her apron. "It's all right, lass," she sighed. "It's been four years since we lost *our* Annie tae the Ross River fever in Townsville, an' I still think about her, an' I pray fer her every single day o' my life. We had tae get out o' there afore the fever got tae Andrew as well, ye' know. God knows he suffers enough wi' the bronchitis from a welter o' years down the coal mines. It just gave me such a shock when I opened the door an' saw ye' standin' there." She glanced at Annie with a worried frown. "Ye've no' got the fever yerself, have ye', lass? Ye're no' lookin' in the best o' health, ye' know."

Annie shook her head and smiled wearily. "No, I don't have a fever, Mrs Gordon, but I am very tired and I *do* need to rest. It's possible that I may need to rest for quite a long time."

"An' I'll see tae it that ye' dae just that," the old woman said kindly. "Andrew's likely tae get a bit o' a shock when he sees ye', just like I did myself, sae I'd better prepare him fer yer first meeting. I'll get him tae pick up yer bags; I suppose they'll be at the coach office. Is that right?"

Annie nodded gratefully and followed Mrs Gordon as she selected a key from a keyboard on the wall behind the desk and walked slowly up a carpeted flight of stairs to the upper level. She unlocked a door and handed Annie the key. "You get yerself a guid rest now my darlin' an' I'll be right here, if ye' need me."

Annie soon established herself as an accepted member of the close knit Herberton community and she could often be noticed strolling along the main street with Jane Gordon by her side, the two of them laughing and bidding good day to all and sundry as they passed by. At first the ladies would nod and smile and then cast curious, sly glances at the stylish young woman who had appeared out of nowhere to settle in their midst, but any doubts they may have had about the legitimacy of her circumstances were dispelled by the presence of the older lady, who was one of the most respected matrons in the district, and it was agreed that she would never have been seen conversing so happily with a young lady who was not of the most exemplary character. It was even speculated that perhaps they were related in some way, although it was generally agreed that the younger woman's accent was decidedly different to Mrs Gordon's brogue. The men, of course, were not so cautious and their expressions of open admiration as they doffed their hats in deference to her pale beauty earned several of them an elbow in the rib cage along with an icy glare from their slighted escort.

After several months had passed, the cool, bracing mountain air and the motherly attention lavished on her by Jane had returned Annie's general well-being to a semblance of what it had been in London. Andrew and Jane had become more than just her hosts and in fact, they treated her like part of their family. She helped Jane prepare meals in the kitchen while Andrew worked in the front bar and then, after the close of business each day, she joined them for supper and spent the evenings happily discussing the events of the day. The first time she played the piano for them Mrs Gordon burst into tears and even Andrew sighed heavily, but when she stopped, confused, both of them begged her to resume playing and although nothing else was said about it, she guessed that it was something else that she had in common with their poor lost daughter.

Whenever her spirits were low, Jane would hold her in her arms, gently caressing and soothing her and then she would sit her down, wipe away the tears and brush her long hair, a hundred strokes at a time as was the custom, all the time softly singing old Scottish tunes in a dialect that Annie couldn't understand, but loved to hear nevertheless. They talked endlessly; Jane spoke about her life on the coalfields with Andrew, to whom she had been married for more than fifty years. Yet to this day, she confided happily, she could not bear to be apart from him.

Annie would talk about her own past, her growing up in Prussia, her father's persistent struggle to reclaim his estate and their eventual forced relocation to cheaper lodgings in the notorious East End of London so that he could finance his legal struggle. She spoke too about the mother whom she had never got to know, but who still had such a huge influence on her life through the loving memories of her father, and invariably then, the conversation would lead to her dogged quest to find James. Jane, of course, having confessed her enduring love for Andrew could easily relate to the power of her love for James and Annie was comforted by her sympathy and reassurances. It was only occasionally, when James appeared in her dreams in the dead of night, that the despair of his disappearance from her life threatened to engulf her and she would weep silently into her pillow. She understood too well though, from her past experiences, that she must focus on rebuilding her strength for now and she knew that to achieve that goal she would have to keep her mind occupied and immerse herself in the contentment that she had been so fortunate to find once again.

She began to do some voluntary community work to pass the time, and her enthusiasm and cleverness soon attracted the attention of the recently formed School of Arts Committee, a group of civic leaders who were in the process of completing the construction of the School of Arts building. It was to be used for hosting meetings and lectures, but more importantly perhaps, it was to become a temporary schoolroom for the growing number of children of the families who continued to move into the community, and as there were no qualified teachers likely to be sent to the outpost by the Board of Education at that point in time Annie was offered the position of temporary schoolmistress.

She accepted the appointment, threw herself enthusiastically into the role and quickly earned the admiration of the parents and the respect of the children.

The young men of Herberton, whose initial infatuation from a distance had begun to show signs of competitive intensification, grew bolder by the day and each contrived by various means to charm a smile of encouragement from Annie, but Jane was always there to make clear to them in subtle ways, in order to save them any embarrassment and disappointment, that there was little hope of winning the young woman's affection. Eventually, however, she herself persuaded Annie to attend the Saturday evening dances that had become a regular feature in the town since the opening of the School of Arts, and to Annie's surprise, she found that she thoroughly enjoyed the experience and began to look forward to them at the end of each week.

Herberton was growing rapidly and had become the seat of local government for the area by the end of 1881 with the formation of the Tinaroo Divisional Board. As more and more families arrived, Annie's workload increased to the point where she could think of nothing else but the next day's tutoring. It was a situation for which she was grateful and the time passed quickly enough.

She promised herself often that she would write to Charles, but each time she sat down with pen and paper the words wouldn't come to her. What could she say? There was nothing positive that she could tell him and she didn't want him to conclude that she had given up her quest completely. What Charles, whom she still considered to be her dearest friend, might have thought about that was much too important to her. Finally she gave up trying and put it out of her mind, recalling that she had told Charles that she must stand on her own and wouldn't write to him again until she had some positive news, and surely he would understand that nothing had happened to change that situation.

There were many times too when she contemplated resuming her search for James, but the trail was now so cold that she had not the faintest idea in which direction she might find him. She had become so comfortable and contented living here with Jane and Andrew that the prospect of making another impetuous leap into the unknown, at serious risk to her mental and physical health, had become too daunting, especially since the substantial wet season of 1882 made travelling to anywhere, by any means, almost impossible. The members of the school board were also extremely grateful for her efforts and the programme of tuition that she had been helping to set up was far from complete.

Three years after her arrival in Herberton, however, several events combined to unsettle her mind once more. She had corresponded with her papa regularly and in her most recent letter she had assured him that, although she hadn't found James she was quite at peace and satisfied with the quality of her life. His reply was a shock to her, but in hindsight, not totally unexpected.

Annie mein gebliebt tochter,

I hope you have found that my written English is improving each time I write.

As always, I love to hear of your adventures in the great southern land of Australia and I am happy that you have found peace of mind, even though you have not yet been reunited with Herr Pottingley, the man with whom you had hoped to spend the rest of your lifetime.

Annie, mein kind, it is not for me to say, but it has been such a long time that you have suffered in your search for this man. Do you not begin to think that he may not have loved you as you loved him? If he had, do you not understand that he would have moved heaven and earth to return to you as I did to return to your Mama? Is it not the time yet to put that man out of your mind and find another man to love you in his place?

Your letter, in which you told me you were living with a nice family, at peace and happy at last, has been a great relief for me, for I can only now rest in that knowledge and think once more of finding my own peace. I am getting old and infirm in my health, and it will not be very long now until I join Mama, for I feel that she is calling to me, and now that you are happy and settled I must go to her, as I promised her I would.

I have arranged for my assets, such as they are, to be transferred to a trust account in your name. You know that I tried my best to regain my estates, but that my struggle was only partially successful, so I am not able to provide you with the noble life in Prussia that I hoped I would, however I expect that a constant small income will come your way, and I hope your life in Australia will be filled with the happiness that you deserve. In any case Prussia and the other German States are still in turmoil and would not be a good place for you to come to live anymore.

Please, always remember your papa and your mama in your prayers and we two will watch over you together.
Auf Wiedersehen, mein kind.
Your papa,
Wilhelm Ferdinand.

The Herberton School acquired two permanent teachers, and consequently, Annie's workload was diminished considerably, giving her more time on her hands to think about how her life was unfolding. These events were not enough on their own, nevertheless, to induce her to begin what could be another prolonged search, because she realised that the chances of finding James after almost five years were slim, if not impossible.

Many of the goldfields were already in decline and the towns that had grown around them were becoming almost deserted. Much of the Palmer River gold had found its way illegally to China by various means; it was said that when the Chinese took the remains of their deceased comrades back to their homeland to be buried, as their tradition required them to do, the burial urns containing their ashes were often unusually heavy. The Customs clerks generally preferred to turn a blind eye, not relishing the upsetting task of investigating exactly what was inside those jars.

Many of the miners who chose to persevere with their way of life or had families growing in the small towns and could not easily leave, had turned to tin and wolfram as the value of those minerals had increased sharply. It was difficult to predict whether or not James would have followed this course, so the search area had widened considerably. He could be anywhere, perhaps not even in Queensland, or Australia for that matter.

She had almost made the decision to take her papa's advice and try to forget about him and get on with her life; there was a handsome young doctor at the hospital with whom she had danced several times and to whom she was beginning to find herself quite attracted, - when something happened that turned her world upside down yet again.

Chapter 21: Return to the Manor

Charles Pottingley heaved a dejected sigh as the taxicab passed between the familiar entrance pillars of Topsham Manor. He had not bothered to look up at the arch bearing the welcoming inscription in Latin for he knew it so well, but the significance of its translation was not lost on him on this occasion: *'Enter in peace and depart in friendship.'* He seriously doubted now that any associate who had ever visited his father beyond this arch had entered in peace, and it was just as certain that few would have departed in friendship, unless they had complied with the demands of Lord Pottingley without so much as a whimper of dissent. He shook his head to clear his mind of the brooding anger that continued to embitter him; after all, the wording of the message that bore his father's request for a meeting was not quite the same as the brusque summons that he had often received in the past and did not create the anxiety in his mind that such a meeting would then have presented. The massive oak entrance door swung open as the driver pulled the horse up opposite the broad staircase and the familiar figure of Parsons emerged.

Charles paid the tax, alighted from the cabriolet, and turned to look up at the ivy-covered walls that had sheltered him from the day he was born until just three years ago. It had been a most difficult decision for him to leave, of course. There were so many wonderful childhood memories in every nook and cranny of the old house. His eyes misted over as he thought of the misery his dear mother must have endured for most of her married life and the wretchedness that he had been completely unaware of until that day in the parlour when she had poured her heart out to him, but it had been more than five years now since she had released herself of the burden of living.

The imposing facade of hard and uncompromising principle that Lord Pottingley had always presented to his family, and indeed to the world, had collapsed in an instant when Charles confronted him with the fact that he was the cause of the tragedy of his mother's death. It was the turning point in their relationship for Charles had never dared confront his father before in his whole life and Lord Pottingley, unused to being challenged by anyone, least of all his only remaining family member, was forced to listen in wretched guilt as Charles berated him with the reality of his protracted ill-treatment of his beloved mother. Lord Pottingley resigned from Parliament, exiled himself from society, and spent his time in isolation at the manor, brooding over his loss of both a devoted wife and an unloved son.

The footman's voice broke into his thoughts. "It was good of you to come so promptly sir," he said, his eyes downcast.

"Oh yes, Mr Parsons, I received the note only yesterday," Charles said. He studied the footman's grave face as he handed him his overcoat and hat. "There seemed to be some urgency in my father's *request* for my attendance. Is he not well?"

"To be honest, sir, I feel that Lord Pottingley's health has declined quite significantly, although he would never discuss this with the likes of me or the other servants, of course. His physician calls in regularly, certainly much more now than he did a year ago, and although he is commonly a pleasant enough gentleman, he often looks grim-faced when he takes his leave. I think Lord Pottingley will be relieved that you have been so kind as to take the time to see him, Mr Pottingley. He will not consent to having any visitors apart from the doctor. He is in the library now, sir, where he spends most of his waking hours. Shall I announce you?"

Charles shook his head. "Thank you, Mr Parsons, but that won't be necessary." He winced, remembering that for him to walk in on his father unannounced would have been quite unacceptable up until five years ago. He strode down the long hallway and stood for a moment to compose himself outside the door to the library, that special place where he had spent many an hour in happier times conversing with his mother. At last he raised his hand and knocked twice and a muffled voice from within bade him enter.

Lord Pottingley was seated at the oak reading desk with a scatter of papers strewn over its polished surface. The heavy drapes that had hardly ever been closed except on the coldest winter nights, were now drawn over the windows, admitting little light even though it was a bright, sunny afternoon and Charles guessed, from the haze of tobacco smoke hanging in the air that the windows behind them too were closed. His first thought was that it may as well have been a stranger who had just walked in, such was the expressionless stare on his father's pale face, but then a flicker of recognition passed over the gaunt features and Lord Pottingley stood up slowly and with obvious difficulty. He held on to the desk for support with one hand while the other was clutched to his side. "Ah, it's you, Charles; I thought it was Parsons coming to fuss over me again," he said, his voice thin and hoarse. "I wasn't sure you'd come."

"I wasn't sure I *should* come, Father. I thought it might open up old wounds that haven't yet quite healed, – and, forgive me, but perhaps it has."

"I know Charles. Believe me, I know how much you loved your mother and I understand how much you must still miss her." His already stooped shoulders sagged even further. "And I do appreciate that your mother opened her heart to you in her final cry for help. You had every right to ascribe the blame for her state of mind to me. I am guilty as charged. I was blind, so immersed in my own prominence and in the things that I alone coveted in my life that I never considered what she wanted, which was nothing more than for all of us to be together as a happy family. In my self-indulgence, I abandoned the only woman I have ever loved and neglected *both* of my sons." His voice wavered and grew heated. "It's much too late for me to redeem myself, but *please*, never consider following my example, Charles. When you do find the love of your life, if you have not already done so, for God's sake tell her you love her and show her that you do, because she may be taken from you too soon and your heart will not heal easily."

Charles was bewildered as he listened to his father's impassioned words of remorse, and his mother's closing indictment became chillingly clear in his mind. *'Charles, you and your father will regret this, each in your own way, for the rest of your lives.'* It was true, he thought; just as his father was being tormented by grief and regret right there in front of him, his mother's words would inevitably plague him with that simple message for the rest of his life.

Lord Pottingley's frail body began to shake, his face contorting with pain. "Charles, my physician has instructed me to ensure that my affairs are in order," he said with an effort. "I may not have to suffer under the strain of my guilt for very much longer." His lips twisted in a laconic smile. "Certain it is that it will not be for as long as I made your poor mother suffer."

Charles didn't answer, but he gripped his father's arm to steady him and then helped him to be seated.

"That is why I have asked you to come here today, Charles. I know that I can never atone for my wrongdoings of the past, but I hope that you will assist me in taking some measures in that regard. You and James will share equally in my estate, and I want you to make him aware of that and let him know of my regret at what I have done to him. I must entrust you to make my peace with him."

Charles shook his head. "If only I could locate him in order to do so, Father. James seems to have gone to some considerable effort to conceal his true identity, and from what I have heard he has even changed his name."

"That much is true, Charles, and I am not aware of his reason, if he has one, for adopting a *nom de plume,* but he has been claiming his remittance from a post office in a small town in the northern part of Australia for the last four years now, so it should not be *too* difficult to find him. The town is called, let me think now, I have it here somewhere." He shuffled some papers around on the desk. "Yes, here it is. It's a gold mining town called *Charters Towers*."

Charles felt a cold shiver run down his spine. There it was, as simple as that. *A gold mining town called Charters Towers in the northern part of Australia.* But it had been three years since he had received that final heart-rending letter from Annie, the letter that had made him realise how unfulfilled his life was without the two women he loved, and the catalyst that led to the confrontation with his father and subsequent departure from the emptiness of Topsham Manor. Had she found James? Her last communication was from the northern goldfields area of Australia. He knew that much, but he had no idea of how big an area that could be or of how many people inhabited the region. James could be but a stone's throw from where she was living, or he may be many miles away. Annie had said that she would write to him if she had any positive news so it would seem that she had not been successful. He realised, with a jolt, that his father had continued to speak, but he had no notion what he had said and he could only nod in agreement, for the lump in his throat precluded any further discussion on his part.

Charles made the necessary arrangements to vacate his apartment and move back to Topsham Manor at his father's heartfelt request. It was a tough decision, but Lord Pottingley had pleaded with him and the look of relief on Mr Parson's face when he announced to the staff of his intention to return resolved any remaining misgivings that he had entertained on the wisdom of it. In any case the physician had informed him personally of his opinion that Lord Pottingley had very little time left and the upkeep and order of the manor would fall to him sooner rather than later. He mulled over in his mind whether he should attempt to contact Annie and let her know that James was probably living in the town called Charters Towers, and he wished with all his heart that he could travel to Australia himself to locate her and personally deliver the news, but that was out of the question at this particular time, considering the state of his father's health. If she had already found James, of course, then he would be able to establish contact with him to express their father's remorse and to welcome both he and Annie back to London.

I remember so well the morning Annie left to travel to Australia and I had to scold myself, for I hoped, in that moment of madness, that she would not find James and would come back to London to be with me. I have, since that day, fought to remove such an unpalatable sentiment from my mind with only moderate success, but I accept, now that James's location has probably been ascertained, that my forbidden dream can never be realised. The honourable course of action is to do everything I can to unite them in happiness.

He was still appalled that such a disgraceful thought had ever crossed his mind for he constantly reminded himself that it was just another indication of his similarity to his selfish father. He determined that his only recourse for now was to take a gamble and send a telegraph message to the last place from which Annie had written to him. It seemed to him an unlikely place for her to settle, but perhaps someone would know where she had gone and forward the message on. He didn't need to go through her letters to find it; he'd read them so many times before.

It was called Maytown.

Chapter 22: End of the Search

"Mr Mowbray, how nice it is to see you again. I trust that Mrs Mowbray and the children are well?"

The gold mining warden stood awkwardly in the private sitting room of the Caledonian Hotel holding his hat in his hands. He grinned. "Yeah, we're all fine and well, Annie, thanks for asking. We've moved from Kingsborough to live in Maytown now. It's for the sake of the little ones, you know, a bit more civilised there. You look great too. Mrs Gordon here must be feeding you up on her famous Scotch stews."

Annie flashed a devoted smile in the old woman's direction and Jane's lined face lit up with pleasure.

"Get away wi' ye' now, Bill Mowbray, yer aye full o' the charms fer the lassies, an' you wi' a wee wife an' two bairns at hame waitin' fer ye," she said. She averted her eyes, pretending to be embarrassed, but then laughed cheerfully. "Can I get ye' a cuppa tea, Bill, or a wee dram of somethin' a bit stouter, maybe?"

"I'd love to stay, Mrs Gordon. Thanks for the offer. I've got a couple of appointments that I need to attend to first, but I will come back later to partake of your great hospitality." He turned to Annie. "I thought I'd drop in here first to deliver this message. It came through on the electric telegraph line to the new Maytown Post Office the other day. The postmaster didn't know who you were, so he asked me if I'd ever heard of you; me being a long-time resident of the district, I suppose. He was shocked when I told him I *had* and even more so that I remembered you'd passed through about three years ago and I thought I knew where you were. He'd only made a casual enquiry and hadn't really expected anyone to remember, but I told him you were a friend who was special to me and my wife, and I offered to deliver it to you. It's come all the way from London, Annie, and I thought it might be important."

Annie had listened to him with alarm bells ringing in her mind. *From London? Is it about James?* Her eyes were wide with anxiety as Bill Mowbray placed the piece of paper in her trembling hand. She studied it for a moment and then put her hand to her lips to stifle a cry.

Jane threw an arm about her shoulders. "Are ye' all right, lass?" she said, alarmed. "It's no' bad news is it, my darlin'?"

Annie shook her head. "It's from Charles," she said, her eyes suddenly brimming with tears.

"Ye mean yer man's brother that ye've aye talked about writin' tae?"

Annie nodded. "Dearest Charles, he was so kind to me and I have been negligent in not writing to him in a very long time. I feel so ashamed." She suddenly felt weak and leaned on the piano for support, clutching the telegram in her shaking hand. "He has discovered recently that James has been settled for some years in that large town to the south called Charters Towers." She frowned and looked enquiringly at Bill Mowbray. "I thought it was a reefing goldfield like Hill End in New South Wales, so I had already dismissed it as a place where he might reside for any length of time."

"Yes, it is a reefing field like Hill End with a few big companies operating, and there are more wages men there now than prospectors, but there are still a lot of individuals working their own shafts too," the gold mining warden said. "The Towers is about eighty miles inland from Townsville."

Later that evening after dinner Annie listened eagerly as Andrew told her what he knew about the town. "Some o' the larrikins among the locals like tae call it 'Charlies Trousers'. It was supposed tae be called Charters Tors at furst. Ye' see, Mr Charters was the gold commissioner an' a *'tor'* is one o' those rocky roun' hills in Wales or in the south-west o' England. Some chap who came from ower that way thought the hills roun' the Towers looked a wee bit like his tors back hame. He must've had a guid imagination all right, but naebody else had the faintest clue what he was on about sae it got tae be called Charters Towers instead. "There's that much gold under it they've got their own mining exchange. It's the second biggest city in Queensland now, after Brisbane o' course. About twenty-five thousand at the latest count I've heard. It's nae wunder a lot o' the people who live there call the town, *'the world'*, they're that proud o' it."

"In that case, Mr Gordon," Annie laughed excitedly, "I must go and see *the world*. I shall then be able to write back to dear Charles with the good news that I am sure he will be waiting to receive."

Jane and Andrew were naturally distraught at the prospect of Annie's departure and made her promise that if she were to be unsuccessful in her endeavours she would return to Herberton. They both understood well enough, though, that it was something she had to do. She would never be able to settle down now, knowing that James may be only a few days' coach ride away, so it was with sadness that they waved goodbye to her as the coach rumbled through the main street.

The new coach road that linked Herberton and Charters Towers directly had recently been opened and the route avoided the worst of the Great Dividing Range to the east, so the journey to Charters Towers was relatively comfortable. Annie had formulated a plan in her mind. She would make Charters Towers her base while she systematically searched the surrounding goldfields that Bill Mowbray had told her about, including Ravenswood and Mount Leyshon, both of which he'd said were still yielding large quantities of gold. Her strategy proved to be unnecessary, however, for within a day of arriving in the Towers she'd met with complete success.

"Yes madam," the busy clerk at the Charters Towers central post office told her, "there is a Mr James Potts in town and yes, he is a red-headed Englishman. Are you *related*, perhaps?" The clerk's tone was cautiously tentative and Annie was puzzled by his attitude.

"No, sir, I am not related to Mr Potts, but I do need to speak with him on a private matter," she told him.

The clerk frowned, "Pardon my curiosity madam," he said gravely, "but you are quite obviously a lady of some ranking and I feel it is my duty to warn you that many of these miners are somewhat rough, to say the least. That is not to say this would be true of the gentleman you wish to speak to, of course, but I may benefit you with the advice that the post office can arrange delivery of messages promptly and discreetly if you so desire, and the charge for this service is minimal if you wish to avail yourself of it."

"Yes," she said with a wry smile; "I am aware of that and I thank you for your concern, sir, but I *really do* need to speak with the gentleman personally." She could hardly contain her excitement. James was so close. The clerk shrugged his shoulders, wrote the address and some directions on how to get there on a slip of paper, and handed it to her with a look of forbearance on his face.

She smiled gratefully, thanked him again and walked out of the post office with the piece of paper that she anticipated would herald the end of her heartache clutched tightly in her hand. She felt elated and light-headed as she walked briskly back to her lodgings to bathe and change into her prettiest afternoon dress. Then, her preparations completed, she walked the few blocks to the address that the clerk had provided.

She was apprehensive and yet exhilarated as she turned into the street. It had been five years since she had seen James, yet she felt that her love for him had not diminished at all. Her heart was beating rapidly in her breast as she found the cottage, a dilapidated little building with yellowed paint peeling from its rough timber walls and a high sloping iron roof that looked like it was rusted beyond repair. The appearance of neglect that it presented to the street was completed by a wrought iron gate that creaked and groaned on its hinges as she pushed it open. A short gravel pathway bisected a small unkempt garden and she walked along it, the prickly weeds on either side irksome as they caught on the hem of her dress. *James had certainly come a long way from the opulence of Topsham Manor,* she thought, with a distinct feeling of uneasiness beginning to grip her.

A mere six paces beyond the gate three worn, wooden steps led up to the front door, which was closed, but the horizontal wooden laths that functioned as windows on either side were open. She could hear raised voices from within the cottage and hesitated at the bottom of the steps.

"…Don't you dare come near me…" A woman's voice was shrill and full of alarm. "…you're drunk, and you've been out whoring again, haven't you?"

There was the ominous sound of breaking glass, and the woman screamed. "I've had enough this time. I'm leaving you and I won't be coming back. I mean it James…"

A child cried out and Annie, dismayed by the commotion, stepped backwards. Suddenly the door was thrown open and a woman rushed out and scrambled down the steps, holding a baby in her arms and dragging another older, crying child by the hand. When she saw Annie she stopped, confused. Tears were trickling down her face.

"Who are you?" she sobbed. "What do *you* want?"

Shocked by her unexpected appearance, Annie answered breathlessly. "I've – I've come to speak to James Pottingley."

The woman stared at her through her tears for a moment and then shook her head in disgust. "Another of his *working girls*, aren't you? He hasn't even told you his real name. It's not Pottingley; it's James *Potts*. Have you no shame? Are you so brazen that you will even come knocking on our door in broad daylight? Did he not tell you that he has a wife and two children, or *did* he tell you and you just don't care about that?" She strode to the open gate where she stopped and turned again to face Annie. "You're welcome to him," she said, the pitch of her voice changing to one of weary acceptance. She turned and glanced towards the doorway. "God knows I've done everything I can to keep that scoundrel happy for more than four years now, but it's no use trying anymore."

She looked again at Annie with a puzzled frown. "You don't seem to be anything like his usual *conquests*, as he likes to call them," she said. "You sure enough look like a proper lady." She nodded towards the open door. "But if you are, what in the world would someone like you see in that useless brute, James Potts? Believe me *lady*, if that's what you really are, he'll do the same to you as he's done to me, and probably others before me too. He'll put on the charm and tell you he loves you, but once he gets what he wants from you he'll turn into a monster. I don't think that man has ever loved anyone in his life, or if he has, something wicked has happened to him since then. I often wonder if he truly hates all women for some reason and enjoys hurting us, but I won't be coming back to find out. You just be careful of him, lady." She threw a sullen glance at the doorway once more, turned her back and walked away along the street with her little red-haired son crying by her side.

Annie stood there dumbfounded, staring at the woman's back as she hurried away. From inside the cottage there was a crash and the splintering sound of furniture falling over, and she spun around as a man emerged, rolling drunk and holding on to the doorway for support. She recognised the red hair immediately, and his face; it was burnt by the sun, but there was no mistaking it was James.

"Wha-ssh you want, woman?" he slurred, "squinting in the late afternoon sun.

She stood motionless, her mind in turmoil. Could this really be the man she had been searching for, the man to whom she had given her love and had longed for during all of the sufferings that she'd endured to find him? *He must look into my eyes, Papa, and tell me he does not love me, just as he once told me he did.*

"James," she cried in horror, "James Pottingley. It's me, Annie."

He put a finger to his lips and looked furtively up and down the street. "Potts," he mumbled. "I'sh, James Potts." He frowned in confusion. "How'd you know my name was, - oh, never mind." He reached out towards her and she backed away as his rough hand brushed her upper arm.

"Thash' right, now I remember you," he said with a smirk. "You jus' couldn't stay away, could you sweetheart? You're the one from the Mossman Hotel." He looked her up and down with a lecherous grin. "You're wearing those fancy clothes jush' for me, aren't you? Needn't have bothered, you know, I'll have you out of them in no time at all. Well then don't just stand there, come on in." He looked up the street and giggled. "Jenny's gone again. She said it was for good this time, but she'll be back; she always comes back. You know why, darlin'?" He burped loudly. "She's got nobody else to look after her. Tha'sh right, she's got nobody else but me. Ah, don't worry about her though; she'll spend the night at her friend's place so we'll have plenty of time to get to know each other again. Picked her up in Ballarat, you know. Did I tell you that before? Should've left her there, but the stupid whore managed to get herself pregnant." He grinned and winked at her, but his green eyes were glazed. "Sorry; shouldn't have said *whore*, should I? Didn't mean to offend you. Should have said *working girl* instead." He giggled again, but then shook his head and ran his fingers through his hair in frustration as Annie had seen him do so many times before. "Said she'd kill herself if I left her. I should have told her to go ahead. The only woman a man needs is the one he can buy, – right sweetie? We don't need any of that emotional nonsense between us, do we? And I *can* pay, you know. She thinks she gets all my money for groceries and stuff like that; always asking for money to feed the kids. Well, she was the one that *wanted* them, wasn't she?" He laughed derisively. "I've got money coming in regularly that she doesn't even know about."

Annie stood in shocked silence as he rambled on drunkenly, her eyes blurred with the tears that had already started to trickle down her face.

"Come on in then," he urged her again. "Wha'd you say your name was?"

"James, how could you do this to me?" she sobbed. "It's Annie Ferdinand, James. You told me you loved me."

He stared at her, trying to focus and then, abruptly, his eyes widened and his expression changed to one of horrified recognition. "Annie? - Annie Ferdinand?"

"Yes James. Do you remember me now? You *never* loved me, did you? It was all emotional nonsense to you. Your poor, wretched wife was right. You've never loved anyone but yourself in your whole life."

"Annie! No! I mean, - please, you don't understand. You see, it was my mother…" His voice faltered.

Annie shook her head. "Do not blame your mother for your present circumstances, James. She loved you so much that she could not endure to remain alive after *your father* sent you away. Your heartbroken mother died because she loved you, James. It is your father alone whom you must hold accountable."

He stared at her blankly for a moment in stunned silence, and then he gasped. "I didn't know, Annie, honestly; I thought…" He reached out to clasp her in his arms.

Annie took a step backwards. "*Honestly,* you say? Oh no, James, do not speak to me of *honesty,*" she said. "You told me so many lies and I *trusted* you."

He shook his head, but his attitude suddenly changed and he smirked at her. "Yes, Annie, it is true. I never loved you. I used you, as I have used many women who have had the misfortune to be involved in my life, but it doesn't matter now, does it? You've obviously been searching for me or you wouldn't be here now, so let's make the most of the time while we can." He lurched down from the top step, but Annie had backed away again out of his reach and he was caught off balance. He swayed to his left and tried to steady himself, groping for the doorjamb. He missed it and cursed loudly, and then with his arms flailing wildly, his body twisted awkwardly and he fell backwards amongst the weeds in the garden bed where he lay stunned and gasping for breath.

Annie Ferdinand stared in disgust for what seemed a very long time at the motionless figure of the man who had betrayed her and her whole body began to tremble as the love and hope she had cherished for him throughout the past five years ebbed away. Gradually the trembling began to subside and was replaced by a feeling of numbness, as if a cold hand had closed around her heart. Her body stiffened, her eyes glazed over and with her mind void of any emotion she turned her back on her shattered dreams and walked away along the road without even once looking back.

It was much later, when she was alone in her room that the full realisation dawned on her. The searching and the yearning had been futile from the very beginning. Everything she had been through - from the journey to this country in the unwavering belief in his commitment to her; walking the streets asking questions of strangers; the episodes of depression into which she had fallen after her continued failure to find him; the letters to Charles so full of hope and anticipation, - all of it had been in vain. The man she had cherished so much and to whom she had devoted her very existence had never loved her at all, but had merely used her for his evil-minded pleasure. He was a womaniser who had, without a doubt, pursued her with a singular purpose on that very first day she had met him on a London street. *Why else would someone of his social standing be prowling the streets of the East End?* He had even admitted to having purposefully followed her, a grim warning in hindsight that his intentions were perverse from the beginning and yet she had recklessly preferred to ignore her papa's dire warning about the danger of conversing with such men. She had deluded herself into believing that she could trust her own intuitions. She had confided in him, told him there could only ever be one man to whom she could give herself in love, but he had chosen to ignore her feelings to satisfy his lust. *We don't need any of that emotional nonsense between us, do we?* She buried her face in her pillow and sobs wracked her body as her mind reeled with the enormity of the revulsion she now felt for him.

Later still, that revulsion became merged with a feeling of self-loathing. *'Why was it not obvious to me that he was a wolf waiting for the opportunity to pounce on a defenceless lamb? Was I really so defenceless, or did I venture into the field a willing participant? Was I so desperate to satisfy my own base needs that I deliberately ignored the signals that would have been apparent to any lady of sincere righteousness?'*

The self-loathing fuelled her doubts. Had she actually *allowed* herself to be defiled? Her body was her sanctuary; wasn't that what her papa had always taught her? Her mama had been her model of virtue, but she had failed to live up to her mama's ideals. *'I was too vain to believe that I could have been wrong, Mama. I have failed you and Papa because I was so vain.'*

It was her conceit, her preference for stylish clothes and fine hats that had been her downfall and the cause of her misery, she was now certain of that. Vanity had caused her to fall from the grace of chastity into the abyss of promiscuity and she knew in her heart that her papa and her mama would be watching over her with humiliation at the dishonour she had inflicted on the Ferdinand family name. The despair of that perception was so overwhelming that it subdued all other feelings of loathing and torment in her mind, and she welcomed it, letting the hopelessness wash over her and sweep her along in an inescapable current that threatened to tumble her into an immense black void. She was at the vestibule of Dante's entrance to Hell's Gate and she was ready and willing to pass through it.

'Abandon all hope, ye who enter here'.

But not yet; no, not yet; she rallied her thoughts briefly. Mr. Palmerston was right when he said *'Do not abandon all hope until the gate has finally closed'.* The gate had *not* closed. And there *was* something she knew she must do before she could allow her mind to slip away into the refuge of unconsciousness. She must destroy all traces of her conceit and arrogance and thus remove any connection with the decadence of her past that could ever remind her of her failure and her shame. She must ensure that no man would ever be able to tempt her into the pursuit of lascivious pleasures or look upon her with lustful eyes ever again.

'The Gate of Hell has not closed yet; there is still time to save my soul'

With a mighty effort she raised herself up and opened the door of her wardrobe; she took out her finest dresses and, one by one, began to rip them apart.

Chapter 23: In Pursuit of a Dream

Several months had elapsed since Charles had moved back into Topsham Manor. There had been no reply to his telegraph message to Annie and whether or not by mere coincidence, James had stopped claiming his remittance at about the same time as the message was sent. Was there a connection? Surely Annie would have written to him if she had been reunited with James. No; it was logical to assume that his message had never reached her. Moreover, what of James himself? He may not even be in Charters Towers now. The fact that he had not claimed his remittance may well be an indication that he was on the move and had not yet informed the post office of his whereabouts, or it may be that he had struck it rich on the goldfields, was financially secure, and had no further need for dependence on what he probably considered an unwelcome link to the family who had disowned him. He could be anywhere.

Despite the best efforts of the most illustrious physicians that London had to offer, Lord Pottingley's health continued to deteriorate, but when his long-anticipated demise eventuated he did not go peacefully in his sleep as perhaps the bewildered physicians, unaware of the exact cause of his infirmity, would have expected. It happened instead in a passionate outburst of grief and self-reproach which culminated in an apoplectic seizure.

After his State funeral, as befitting his status as a Lord of the Empire, and a respectable period of mourning, Charles began to think about the settling of his father's extensive affairs, but before Lord Pottingley's last will and testament could be executed it was necessary to establish exactly what had happened to James. With nothing to deter him now and with the double mystery on his mind, he made the decision to travel to Australia and investigate for himself.

In much the same way as Annie had, Charles found the small, run-down cottage in Charters Towers. He pushed open the creaking wrought iron gate and walked the few steps along the overgrown gravel path. It was ominously quiet as he knocked on the paint flaked front door. There was no answer. He knocked again and a child cried out from somewhere inside. The wooden slats of the window opening were pushed apart slightly.

"Can you give me some more time please?" It was a woman's voice, plaintive, appealing. "I might be able to pay the rent next week."

Charles was startled. "I'm terribly sorry madam," he said, "but I have not come here to solicit rent money from you. I merely desire to gain some information, if you please."

"What kind of information? Who are you and what is it you want?" The slats were prised open a little more and he saw a pair of eyes peering out at him. "My God, you look so much like him, except he had red hair."

"If you mean James, then I have obviously found the correct, ah - house." He glanced at the peeling paint and the rusted iron, leaf clogged gutters above the window opening. "Yes, I am his brother Charles."

"He said his family lived in England."

"We do, or rather I should say, - I do, but I have come to give him some news about that very subject. Is he home, perhaps?" He heard a muffled sobbing, followed by a click as the door was unlocked and then opened.

"You'd better come in Mr Potts." The woman stood aside and Charles ignored the misuse of his name, assuming that she must only have known his brother as James Potts. He removed his hat and stepped inside the tiny front room, which was sparsely furnished with nothing more than a rickety table and a mismatched pair of wooden chairs. A child sat on the floor playing with a toy and another younger one lay asleep on a rug. Both had red hair.

Charles studied the woman's face. She was pretty, but there were dark rings around her eyes and her hair was dishevelled.

"Please have a seat, sir," she said in a voice that was weary and drained of energy. "God knows it's about all I've got left to offer you."

"Thank you. Please call me Charles, Mrs…?"

"Potts!" she said, wiping her eyes with a small cotton towel. "I'm Jenny Potts, Charles." She nodded towards the children. "These are your nephews."

Charles' head reeled. *James was married, but not to Annie, and he had been married for quite some time by the look of the children.* "You're my brother's *wife?*" he gasped.

She shook her head, but even her look of dejection didn't prepare him for what was to come. "No, not his wife, - not any more. I'm his widow now. James is dead, Charles."

Charles sat down heavily and slumped forward in his chair for several minutes, both hands covering his face. When he'd recovered a little from the shock he stood up and took her hands in his. "I'm so sorry, Jenny. I should have realised something terrible had happened when he stopped claiming his remittance. I thought he had moved to another location or…"

"…His remittance?" She stared at him with a blank look. "I know *nothing* about any remittance."

"He never told you he was receiving money regularly from his father in England?"

Her thin shoulders sagged. "No, - not at all." She shook her head and pushed a stray greying strand of hair from her face. "Your brother was a man of many secrets, I know now, but he wasn't always like that. When we first met he seemed to have so much energy and vigour. That was something that attracted me to him. He was keen to learn all about the gold mining and he worked a few shafts that had been abandoned, but they didn't produce much for the effort he had to put into them. His hands were getting so badly callused that sometimes he could barely swing a pick or hold a shovel. I had to bathe them in brine to keep them from getting infected."

Charles's face was grim. "Manual labour was not something he had been used to in England, Jenny. Perhaps that is the most unfortunate part of James' life story. He had everything given to him by our father except what he needed above all, - love and acceptance." He pursed his lips and sighed. *James had not undertaken any kind of work in England.*

"We shared the disappointments, but we had some good times too, Charles." Jenny managed a weak smile. "When he found a little gold he behaved like a different person altogether. He got so exuberant, planning for our future together. He was sure he would eventually find the biggest nugget in the whole country, and I was a part of it, caught up in his enthusiasm too, yearning for the success that would make us rich. We moved on from one field to the next, chasing the dream, but by the time we arrived here in the Towers he was a spent force. We struggled to make ends meet and sometimes he'd go out and find a bit of work to keep us going." She hesitated before adding, "At least that's what I thought he did until now."

"And you have only ever known him as James *Potts?*"

She nodded. "That's what he said his name was when we got married. I don't think he had any intention of marrying me, but he was an impulsive sort of man and we just did it one day when he was in a really happy mood. Is Potts not his real name then?"

Charles frowned. "No; it's Pottingley." *So that is probably why James has changed his name to Potts. He would not have wanted Jenny to know that he was receiving a regular remittance under the name of Pottingley, although he eventually would have had to inform Father's acquaintance in Melbourne of the change to avoid confusion at the post office. Annie's fear that it may have been because he was trying to disappear from her life was wrong; it was much more basic than that.*

James was simply protecting the little secret of his remittance. He dismissed the thought from his mind as Jenny continued.

"As I said, I think James had many secrets he didn't share with me. He rarely spoke about his father or you either, Charles, and on the few occasions he did, it was with no affection and only while he was in a drunken temper. I knew he had been sent to Australia against his will and I believe his drinking problem stemmed from some injustice he felt about that, but he would never talk about it to me when he was sober."

"Did he speak well of our mother?"

"James hardly ever spoke well of any woman, Charles and he would never discuss his feelings towards his mother, but I have long suspected that *she*..." She glanced apologetically at Charles. "...your mother, I mean, - was the cause of his callous attitude towards other women. I think he felt disappointed by her in some way and he was never able to get over it."

Charles shook his head. "If you are correct in your suspicion, Jenny, then my brother was sadly mistaken. Mother was told little about the sorry affair that necessitated his immediate departure until he was already beyond her comfort and support and *I* must shoulder the blame for that on my own now. Dear Mother, - she loved James so much that she could not bear to live with the knowledge that he had been sent away without so much as a word of farewell; - but he would not have known about that. If he *had* known, perhaps things would have been very different, not just for James, but for all of us." As he spoke, Charles was also thinking about just how different it may have been. *'Mother would have done everything in her power to persuade my father to take a softer approach with James and even if she had not succeeded in that endeavour she would have at least ensured that Annie was reunited with him soon after her arrival in Ballarat. It could have ended happily ever after for all players including you and I, Jenny, but it was not to be or we would not be sitting here today discussing my brother's premature demise.'*

He quickly pulled himself together in an effort to regain his usual outwardly civil demeanour, although deep inside, his mother's words still tugged at his heart. *'Charles, both you and your father will regret this final betrayal of me; each of you in your own way, for the rest of your lives.'* Lord Pottingley had already paid the price; perhaps now it was his turn. "Please tell me what happened to him, Jenny, if it's not too difficult to talk about?"

She nodded and daubed her eyes with the towel. "It was about four months ago," she said. "He'd been drinking heavily as he often did, and he came home smelling of cheap perfume and falling around, knocking things over. I told him I was leaving him for good, but he just laughed because he knew I *always* came back. One of his conquests, as he called the women he associated with, even came to visit him as I was leaving. He had probably planned to get me out of the house so he could be with her, because she looked so shocked to see me still there. She *was* quite different though, *that* one. Looked like a real lady, well-dressed and not a bit like the others I'd seen loafing around at the front of the tavern door."

'Annie?'

"I stayed with a friend that night, and it rained quite a lot; a real tropical downpour it was, and when I returned home I found him lying in the garden. He'd been there all night and he was all wet and shivering. I helped him inside and got him dried off, but he never said a word after that. It was like he'd had a great shock of some kind. Even after the shivering stopped he just lay there running his hand through his hair like he always did and shaking his head as if he couldn't believe something. He died three days later. The doctor said it was pneumonia."

Charles's eyes narrowed and his voice quivered in hope. "Are you sure the woman who visited him that day was one of his, ah - conquests, Jenny?"

"No, I'm not sure at all. In fact, I never saw her before that day and I haven't seen her since, but it's a big town so she may still be around here. She couldn't have known him *very* well though."

Charles's heart had begun to pound in his chest, but then immediately he felt a stab of disappointment. "Why do you say that?"

"Well, she even got his name wrong..." She stopped mid-sentence and stared at Charles wide eyed.

"What is it Jenny?" he said.

"I've just realised something, Charles. I thought I'd heard that name before. I'm sure the woman said she wanted to speak to James *Pottingley*. Does that mean *she* knew him before I did?"

Charles tried to remain calm, but he felt an odd sense of dread. "If she was the person whom I believe her to be, then she certainly did know James before you did and finding him in the circumstances and in the condition you have described would have devastated her to such an extent that I fear for her state of mind. The person to whom I refer is a dear friend of mine whose name is *Annie Ferdinand,* and she may have been searching for James for a very long time, - perhaps as much as five years, - and unaware that for most of that time he was already married to you."

Jenny Potts had composed herself and her sad expression changed to one of what Charles could only think of as acceptance; perhaps acceptance that James's deception had extended far beyond his sordid one-night affairs. It was obvious that she had still held out a small vestige of hope that he *had* really loved her despite his infidelity, but now that too was gone. "I do feel sympathetic towards Miss Ferdinand for the distress she has endured, Charles," she said, "but please don't be offended when I suggest that she may have been the more fortunate of the two of us. I may also have inadvertently saved her from the full awfulness of witnessing your brother's degeneration because I believe she left not long after I spoke to her without ever entering into the house."

"I see." Charles said thoughtfully. "And what is it that has prompted you to come to such a conclusion?"

"Well, this may sound rather silly to you, but I could always tell if James had been with a woman *inside* the cottage when I wasn't there, even though he would deny it and try to hide it from me by cleaning everything. That small expression of guilt in itself always gave me hope for our future happiness together, but there were no signs of your friend Annie ever having been inside. I mean, there was no lingering scent or anything like that to indicate she'd been here. A woman can tell, you know, Charles. And she definitely had an expensive fragrance when I passed her at the bottom of the front steps. No, forgive me Charles, but James was so drunk that afternoon that he probably fell into the garden and couldn't get up, - and I'd wager that your friend just walked away and left him to it. She probably doesn't even know he's dead."

Jenny Potts was shocked to learn that she was now a very wealthy woman, due to the inheritance she could expect as James's widow. Charles arranged for her to collect the remittance money from the post office and paid her a generous advance that would suffice to keep her in relative comfort until his father's will had been finalised.

He was quite certain that the well-dressed woman who had visited James at the cottage that day was Annie, *but where was she now?*

Chapter 24: The Journey to Nowhere

"Mrs O'Hara. How nice it is to see you out in your garden."

The woman was on her knees digging out some weeds with a small trowel and she peered up from beneath a wide-brimmed sun bonnet. "Oh! God in Heaven above, you startled me." She looked around hastily. "And where have you come from, my love? I didn't hear any carriage arriving."

"Why, from Ballarat of course, Mrs O'Hara. Don't you remember? I went there to look for, - something: didn't I? I promised you I would come back and here I am."

The woman got to her feet with an effort and wiped her hands on her apron. "Yes, of course you did. From *Ballarat,* did you say?" She regarded her unexpected visitor curiously; a woman much younger than her who would not have looked out of place amongst the fashionable set in Townsville or Brisbane, - except for one thing: the clothes that she wore may have been stylish once, but now they hung off her in tatters and she was leaning on an old baby carriage that she had been pushing along the road.

"I'm Mrs Ryan," she said, "and you're a long way from Ballarat, my dear, if you mean the one in Victoria. Which direction did you come from?"

The young woman pointed along the road. "There," she said. "From Ballarat; I walked all the way there from Melbourne and now I've walked all the way back just to see you and Captain Treloar again"

"You'd better come inside, love." Mrs Ryan said. "You're a bit confused I think. A bit too much sun, maybe. What's your name then?"

"Why it's Annie, of course," the woman said in a plaintive tone. "Surely you remember me Mrs O'Hara?"

Mrs. Ryan frowned and shook her head. "I don't think we've…" A slight movement from inside the baby carriage caught her eye and she glanced at it anxiously. "Whatever have you got in that old cart now Annie? It's not a baby I hope?"

"No, no, of course it's not a baby. It's my puppy. I found him in Ballarat. That's why I went there, isn't that so, Mrs O'Hara? He's a little Alcacian dog, like the one my papa got for me from Alcace when I was a little girl. I have named him Captain, - after Captain Treloar of course. I hope the good captain will be pleased." She uncovered the puppy and held it out for the woman to see. The little dog whimpered and wagged its tail.

"Ah, yes," she said, "a little German shepherd dog. Well then, you'd better bring him inside out of the sun." She took Annie's arm and led her inside the cottage.

Mrs Ryan pulled a pair of chairs out from the small wooden table in her kitchen and sat down opposite Annie. "Charters Towers is about thirty miles in the direction you said you've come from and Townsville is about fifty miles the other. Ravenswood is away on that other road. This is Ravenswood Junction. You're in North Queensland, my lass, - and a long way from Ballarat."

Annie stared at her blankly and hugged the puppy. "But I went to Ballarat to get my little Alcacian; did I not, Mrs O'Hara?

Mrs Ryan nodded tentatively. "I'll make us a nice cup of tea, lass," she said, "and then we'll try to sort this out." She put the kettle on the wood-fired stove and then sat down again opposite her surprise guest. "Annie, whatever has happened to you?"

"Why, nothing really, Mrs O'Hara. I walked all the way to Ballarat as we agreed was the best course when Cobb and Co refused to take me and you gave me the wheelbarrow, the shovel, and the clothes that I needed to disguise myself as a destitute miner. We had such a wonderful time doing that, did we not?" She paused and a frown wrinkled her brow. "I think I met some lovely people in Ballarat, but I am really not sure now." She smiled. "But it matters not, because now I am back here with you, as we arranged. I will not want any of my good clothes, however, as I have…" Her smile faded and her voice faltered as she searched for the right words. "…I have *decided* that I will not have need of them anymore."

Mrs Ryan had never had to deal with anything like this before. Her husband had died many years ago and she had spent her years as a widow tending to her vegetable garden and doing the occasional work at the community hall in Ravenswood Junction. "Annie, my love," she said. "I don't know where you've come from or where you're wandering to, but I know this much, - you need looking after. You're going to stay here until I find out what this is all about."

Annie looked at her intently for a moment. "Oh, Mrs O'Hara, you look so much younger than when I left. Captain Treloar must be looking after you so well. How is the good captain and please, please, tell me about your wedding? I would love to have been there." She paused and her voice faltered as uncertainty clouded her features, "but I had to go to Ballarat to find – *something, didn't I?*"

Chapter 25: The Reality of Defeat

Charles Pottingley reluctantly acknowledged that there were no ladies who matched the description of Annie Ferdinand in any of the boarding houses and residential hotels in Charters Towers. He had conducted a thorough search of the town himself and had paid several other people to conduct enquiries on his behalf, but it had become obvious that a sizeable part of the town's population was transient and anyone who had not been sighted for several months was relegated to that classification and swiftly forgotten.

Jenny Potts had never seen the unknown woman who visited James on that eventful day, either before or after it, and she speculated that it was most likely she had left the town immediately. The enquiries Charles conducted appeared to confirm her suspicions, although, admittedly, his search had been focussed on finding that singular woman whose presence was fixed forever on his mind; the Annie that he'd known and loved in the past.

'No, no, Annie. I could never do what you are asking of me. I could never forget you now.'

Annie's appearance could have changed significantly over the past five years and Jenny's terse description of the unwelcome *visitor* to her home during the upheaval of her leaving James was understandably sketchy, but on the other hand, a common whore, well-dressed or not, would not have arrived suddenly out of nowhere and then disappeared again just as quickly. The demise of one of her customers would have had little effect on such a person, - certainly not enough for her to leave town immediately after, unless she felt she'd contributed in some way to his death and wanted to avoid the legal repercussions that could have followed.

'Of course if we couldn't find James it would be a different story…'

Charles remembered the words of the Police Inspector at Scotland Yard and grimaced, for it occurred to him how ironic it would be if James had indeed met his end by the hand of someone who had now absconded from justice.

But no, there was also the fact that the woman knew his name was Pottingley, and although he conceded that she could have been someone who knew James in Melbourne or Ballarat, or perhaps even someone in Charters Towers to whom he had revealed his name while in a state of intoxication, he needed no further confirmation. Everything that had transpired so far suggested that, in all probability, it was Annie who had visited the cottage that day, and he was also certain that she would have been broken-hearted to find that James was a drunkard, married and had children, after searching for him for so long in the belief that he still loved her. She would not have wanted to cross paths with James ever again, but if Jenny's reasoning was correct and she had departed immediately without entering the cottage, she would not have known that there was no possibility of that happening, with James' death three days later.

Would she have retraced her steps to one of the frontier towns that she had passed through and mentioned in her letters to him? There would be no point in that now that she had found him, unless she had already made a new life for herself and had simply called on him to let him know that she no longer loved him. After all, she must have been living in one of those towns in the northern part of Queensland if she had received the message he had sent to Maytown. On the other hand, perhaps she had *not* received it and it was mere coincidence that she had found out where James was living at around the same time that he had been told his whereabouts by his remorseful, dying father. Had she returned south, to Victoria or New South Wales, where she would find solace with the good friends he knew she had made in those places? Or had she even returned home to grieve with her father in Prussia?

The possibilities seemed endless. He knew that it was just as unlikely that he would find Annie by scouring the length and breadth of Australia, with no clue as to which route she had taken, as it had been for her to find James. And if he *was* fortunate enough to locate her, would he be rewarded with the happiness that he yearned for, or would he find that she wanted nothing more from him than mere friendship, - if even that, considering that he would be a constant reminder of the man who had betrayed her?

It had gone much too far beyond friendship for him, of course, but just as he had felt so helpless each time he had read one of her letters in the cold comfort of his club, he felt equally powerless now as he stood on the dusty street of a small town in Australia where he was certain she had walked only weeks before. He turned away, finally forced to concede defeat. He could do nothing further here and could only live in hope that she would one day make contact with him. He would wait for that day, he told himself, even if it took a lifetime of waiting.

Chapter 26: A Seasoned Traveller

She placed another hardwood log on the campfire and it crackled into life as she prodded at it with a stick, turning the embers over so that it flared up before returning to a dull orange glow. The dogs had fed on a large snake they'd caught; she suspected it was the non-venomous type known as a python. The dogs seemed to know instinctively when they should back off. They were now curled up just out of range of the heat from the fire. She cut up what remained of the snake, wrapped it in tree bark and pushed it under the warm cinders at the very edge of the fire; that way it would only singe enough to preserve it for the dogs to eat the next afternoon.

'And now it is my turn.'

She foraged in the bottom of the old baby cart that held all of her worldly possessions for the tin that contained the tea leaves. She took it from the waterproof oilskin pouch in which it was wrapped to protect it from the weather, scooped a little tea into a smoke-blackened billycan that she had filled with water from the creek and placed it on the edge of the fire. And while that was simmering, she prepared the damper bread and the bush plums that she'd gathered earlier that afternoon. Dear Mrs Mowbray had taught her how to recognise some of the edible native fruits and since then she had experimented with different varieties, very carefully of course, because some were quite poisonous. She'd had a few scares in the early years and on some nights she'd had to go hungry after ruining her evening meal by adding berries that looked appetising, but were bitter to the taste. Hunger is a swift educator, however, and she'd quickly learned which of them to avoid.

When she'd finished her simple but satisfying evening meal she removed the pins holding her hair in a tight bun and let the long tresses fall around her shoulders. After bathing in the cool water of the running creek, she carefully combed it as she did every evening, holding an old cracked hand mirror and counting the strokes of her brush until she had reached exactly one hundred. Her hair was beginning to turn grey as the years crept by, but that was nothing more than an observation for she had learned long ago that vanity brought misfortune to the woman who permitted it to consume her. Such misfortune had something to do with her reason for being here and for the way she chose to dress, but more than that she found impossible to remember. She simply knew that she was content with the way things were and there was no reason to change.

She went back to the stream and washed the clothes she'd worn that day, clothes she'd made from old sugar and wheat bags, - nothing that might attract unwanted attention, - like the man on the dray who'd spoken to her today, - but comfortable enough nevertheless.

She bent over and patted Captain on the head and the big dog sat up and wagged his tail. It was always the last thing she did each evening when they were travelling and he would sit there fully alert until she had retired to the rolled out swag. He would then slowly circle the camp several times, stopping occasionally to listen and to sniff the air and when he was satisfied there was no danger lurking nearby he would lie down a short distance away, on the opposite side of her to where the other dogs lay.

She'd picked up Captain as a pup from the outskirts of a town.

'Was it the town called Ballarat in the Colony of Victoria? That's where Mrs. O'Hara and her Captain Treloar live. She'd named her puppy after the dear captain, of course. Oh, how nice it will be to see them again...'

It was so difficult to remember those details. *'Yes, so long ago.'* She'd been walking along the road pushing the baby cart and noticed the little body lying under the shade of a tree. At first she had believed that he was beyond help, but when she went over to check on him he had raised his head weakly and whimpered. She'd given him some water and cleaned the dried mucus that had sealed his eyelids together and then she'd held him in her arms until she'd thought he'd recovered enough to stand on his own.

"You must go home now little puppy," she'd told him gently. But there were no houses anywhere in sight and she'd stood there looking around and wondering what to do while he sat and looked up at her with big dark pleading eyes. Eventually, she'd reluctantly decided that her only option was to simply walk away and hope that he would find his way back to wherever he'd come from, but that was not to be; he'd trotted along happily behind her at a distance and each time she stopped to tell him to go back he'd sat down on the road and wagged his tail, holding one little paw up to her until she'd relented and picked him up. He'd been so gentle when he licked her hand that day. Now, after all the years they had spent together, her faithful companion was getting a bit grey around the muzzle, but she noted, with gladness in her heart, that he was still a strong and healthy dog despite his age.

Tomorrow she would be at the Gordon's Caledonian Hotel and good old Mrs Gordon, always happy to see her, would sit her down and sing delightful Scottish melodies in the evening while she cut the stray ends of her hair and combed it. Mr Gordon would fix that squeaky wheel on the cart and repair the tear in the canvas top without even being asked. He always seemed so happy and was always ready to do those little things without even being asked, and she had long ago formed the suspicion that he kept a little hoard of parts just for her cart.

Why *had* she left the Gordon's to walk along this road to nowhere anyway? What drove her to leave the security and the love that was always given to her so willingly at the Caledonian Hotel and that she could not bear to be away from for long?

'That's it settled then lass. I've got a fine wee room for ye up the stairs, well away from the din of the bar and ye can have it for our long-term rate even if ye decide ye'll no' bide that long wi' us after all.'

And what about the other people too that she loved and who clearly loved her in return? There was dear Sarah, who treated her like a sister and always begged her to stay longer, and of course, the wonderful Mrs O'Hara, who waved goodbye to her with such placid acceptance whenever she felt compelled to leave, the only sign of her melancholy, the cotton handkerchief that she clutched in her hand and used to daub at the tears trickling down her lined face. Why, indeed, *did* she always develop that longing to set off on a pointless journey, - on some kind of mission that even she could not comprehend, far removed from the people that she felt the most comfortable with? It was too frustrating to think about for very long. She only knew that she *had* to do it.

Finally, she rolled her swag out on the soft grass of the riverbank and was soon drifting off to sleep to a chorus of croaking bullfrogs, whirring crickets and all of the other nocturnal sounds of the bush. A long time ago she had been terrified by those sounds, but not now; she would sleep soundly as she always did, knowing that Captain and the other dogs would guard her against inquisitive snakes and would wake her at first light. Mr Mowbray had called it *piccaninny dawn*. He'd told her long ago that a piccaninny was an Aboriginal child and that piccaninny dawn signified the birth of a new day. It was so easy to remember things like that, she thought with a wry smile. Why were there so many other things she couldn't remember?

By the time the first golden rays of the piccaninny dawn had crept above the eastern horizon, the baby cart was laden with her 'swag' and the leather water pouches filled and stowed. She doused the remains of the campfire and carefully covered it over with damp sand to prevent it from smouldering and perhaps flaring again. The dogs had already drunk from the creek until they were sated, knowing that they would only be able to share what water she carried in the cart until they came to the next waterhole. There the little party of travellers would rest in the shade of the paperbark trees on the edge of the billabong during the heat of the day and would continue their journey in the coolness of the late afternoon. That was just another piece of bushcraft she had learned from the Mowbray's that the hardened prospectors always employed to conserve their energy. The dogs were always keen to be off in the cool of the early morning, but she sensed that today they were a little more eager than usual. They knew where they were going; they had travelled the same road so many times before.

Chapter 27: The Gilbert River Hotel

George, the owner of the Gilbert River Hotel, had been idly wiping a stained grey cloth over the polished surface of the timber slab that served as the main bar. He finished with a flourish just as the door was pushed open and a man walked in. George's beady little eyes lit up. This was his first customer for the day, and it was already late afternoon. He'd had no customers at all yesterday, except for Frank of course, but then it would be stretching the truth to call *him* a customer since he lived on the premises and earned his keep doing odd jobs.

The man closed the door behind him and removed his wide-brimmed hat before he approached the bar, as was the custom. "Tied the old horse up in the shade at your water trough. Is that all right with you mate?"

George grinned, and his heavy jowls quivered. "Yeah, that's what it's there for. Sorry, I didn't hear you pull up. Are you driving or riding?"

"I've got a single horse dray outside, mate. I just came from Georgetown with a few emergency supplies for the good people of Croydon."

"Emergency?" George's bushy grey eyebrows were raised. "What kind of emergency? They had a good supply of grog the last time I was there."

The man laughed. "Yeah, I'm sure they did, but they've run out of tea and sugar and stuff like that."

George grunted. "Oh yeah, right," but his scornful look suggested that he didn't think a shortage of tea and sugar constituted an emergency situation. "Croydon's still a day's ride away," he muttered. "Are you planning on staying here tonight or pushing on a bit further?"

"I was planning on staying if you've got a bunk for me and a yard for the horse," the man replied. "It's getting a bit late anyway and the old pony reckons he's had enough for the day. He refused to budge another foot when he spotted your trough and thought I was passing right by it."

"Okey-dokey," George said, the relief showing in his face, "Smart horse that one o' yours. There's no place to bunk down between here an' Croydon anyway, unless you'd think about camping out rough. Half-Pint will give him a good feed then stable him for the night, an' I'll get my Mary to make up a bed for you in the main bunkhouse. She's Scottish an' she cooks up a tasty beef stew so I'll wager you won't go hungry tonight."

The man looked relieved. "Sounds great, thanks a lot."

George heaved his heavy frame off the bar stool. He waddled to the end of the bar, pushed open the swing doors that led to the kitchen and eased his ample frame through them, disappearing for a minute at most before reappearing. He eased himself on to the stool again and it creaked ominously under his weight, but he didn't seem to notice. "Right then, it's all fixed good as gold mate; your bed will be ready an' Mary's happy she's got somebody else to cook for besides me an' him there." He jabbed a thumb in the direction of the only other occupant of the bar, a weather-beaten little man with skin the colour and texture of parchment. He was perched on a bar stool, subtly blending in to his surroundings in the darkened corner, elbows on the bar and scrawny shoulders slumped forward.

He grinned toothlessly in greeting. "Don't eat too much of Mary's stew or you'll finish up a big lump o' blubber like *him*." He shook his head so that the few grey hairs that remained fell over his forehead. "An' it's no wonder he's lost all his customers. He's got no manners; - can't even introduce us properly." His grin disappeared and he glared at George. "Got no manners, have you, Tiny?"

George scowled, but he thrust out a plump hand towards his customer.

"Sorry, mate, I'm George, otherwise known as Tiny, - for obvious reasons," he said, "…an' he's Frank. I own the place, but he thinks *he* owns it too. I'd bar him from coming in here for a day for being sarcastic towards me, but then I'd have to bar him every single day of his life an' I'd end up feeling sorry for him. Anyway, my Mary won't let me bar him because she's so fond o' him; calls him her wee Half-Pint, would you believe?"

Frank's grin reappeared. "See what I have to put up with from the big man? Mary's the only reason I stay here," he said.

The man shook hands with George and then Frank. "I'm Tom," he said, "but most people call me Bluey, also for obvious reasons."

George looked at the man's hair and chuckled knowingly. "Yeah, you an' every other bloke with a ginger mop in the country. Right then, Bluey; would you like a drink o' something a bit stronger than *tea*?" he asked hopefully, albeit with a touch of contempt in his voice.

Tom's eyes drifted to the near empty shelves behind him. "Yeah, sure would, but have I got any choice, Tiny?" he said. "It looks like you're waiting for a grog run yourself."

"Yeah, been waiting for a long time now," George agreed. "Got rum an' beer, but the beer's a bit sour; been standing too long. Rum's all right though; goes down well if you don't swill it too quick."

Tom looked at George's shot glass on the bar. "If it's what you're swigging yourself, then it can't do me any harm either I suppose," he said evenly.

George reached under the counter, wheezing as he produced a bottle of rum and a shot glass. He poured the rum and re-corked the bottle.

Tom picked up his glass. "Not many left on the Gilbert now is there? It looks almost deserted. When I came through here last time it was a busy little place."

"That must have been a long time ago." Frank said. "It'd have to be four years at least. Yeah, you're right though. People don't stop here anymore. Not since they pushed the railway through to Croydon."

Tom nodded. "And a year after they pushed it through, the government decided to cut the service back to one day a week. That's why I'm driving over there now. I got a telegraph message telling me they'd forgotten to bring the tea an' sugar an' it's going to be pure hell for the men until it arrives." He shook his head. "The things I have to do to make a quid – and maybe save a few marriages along the way!"

George was philosophical. "Oh well, it wasn't just the railway that killed the Gilbert River diggings off. We were well on the way to becoming a ghost town before that. It's been about ten years since they built the road from Herberton through to Charters Towers. They bypassed us then and that was when we started losing some of our trade. There were five hotels here, but then the mine closed. That was the end of trading for the other four and pretty well the death knell for Gilberton as a town. We're just about finished too." He gestured towards a charcoal sketch in a frame that hung on the wall at the far end of the bar. "We had a six-stamp battery here that crushed ore fourteen hours a day. That's it over there. They dismantled it and transported it to one of the working mines in Ravenswood I think, or maybe it was Charters Towers; I can't remember. The mine wasn't ever a grand one anyway, but it kept us in steady work and it kept the town going. It's happening all around the north now. The small towns can't survive once the miners have gone."

Frank nodded, "It was taken to Charters Towers. That's where it went and it's still working there." He glanced at Tom. "I used to work there myself a few years ago, Bluey. I think I'll go back there again sometime and find some work."

George feigned disgust and shook his head so that his heavy jowls wobbled from side to side. "A few years you say? You came here in eighty-seven. Let's see now, it's been more than eight years since you left the Towers. You'll never go back there Half-Pint. You're getting too old for that kind of work, mate."

Frank looked hurt. "I could still work a full shift, Tiny, don't you worry," he said. "And, anyway, the work is nowhere near as hard as it used to be when I was a wages man there. The pick and shovel days were over when they started following the gold bearing seams deeper. It's mainly mechanical now you know"

"Well, I wish you would go back to the Towers and get some work." George snapped. "Then you might just be able to pay me back your bar tab. Cripes, considering how much you owe me, if that ever happened, I'd close this place up and retire to the coast a wealthy man, for sure."

Frank glared at him. "Hang on now, lard-man. If it wasn't for me working my keep here, this place would've fallen apart years ago. The fact is I'm doing you a big favour you know. Who'd chop the wood for Mary's stove if I left? – I reckon you couldn't even pick up the axe, ya' big lazy slug. Anyway, let me see my bar tab, and I'll tell you what *you* owe me in wages."

George glanced towards the door to the kitchen. "Keep yer shirt on Half-Pint. Mary might hear us, and you know *I'm* the one who always gets the blame when we get loud." He looked a bit uncomfortable. "You know I haven't kept any bar tab, ya' scrawny little weasel."

Tom looked from one to the other and laughed uncertainly. "Hold on, lads. I'm sorry. I didn't mean to start a brawl. You two are actually good friends, right?"

They both looked at him in surprise. "Yeah, of course we are. What'd you think?" George's deep-set little eyes twinkled with mirth. "Don't worry about us, Bluey. It's just our way of dealing with the boredom, isn't it, Half-Pint?"

"Yeah, that's right." Frank said. "If you hadn't come in when you did we'd be arguing about something else entirely. It's usually the most excitement we get in a day."

All three men lapsed into silence for a few minutes and then Tom said casually. "I had a little bit of excitement myself this morning on my way here. I know it's going to be hard to believe, but there was a woman walking along the road pushing a cart, - not a wheelbarrow, but a baby type cart; - right out in the middle of nowhere, she was. She had three big dogs walking alongside her. I thought it was a man at first; she had an old cabbage tree hat on and a pair of miner's boots." He shook his head as if he was bewildered by what he had seen. "It was only when I got close enough to get a good look that I realised it was a woman. She had her hair tied up in a bun, - you know, like the older ladies still do."

"I hope my Mary hasn't heard you say that if you want a big plate of stew tonight," George said, throwing another glance towards the kitchen. "She can be a bit sensitive to being called an older lady, you know…"

Frank whacked the bar with his open hand. "Ah, that's great news. Annie's on her way here again,"

Tom was startled and then looked puzzled. "*Annie?* You know her?"

George nodded. "She would've been wearing clothes that look like they've been made out of grain sacks, right?"

"Yeah, right enough, that's her," Tom agreed. "She was shuffling along pushing that old cart, bent over it as if she was really intent on getting to somewhere, - like she was on some kind of a mission to get to wherever she was headed. I haven't seen anything like that since I left the Victorian goldfields about fifteen years ago. It was common enough back then to see prospectors shuffling along from one goldfield to another, shoving a cart or wheelbarrow with all their belongings piled on it. They usually had a kind of vacant look in their eyes so it was no use trying to start a conversation with them. It was all about the gold. Nothing else in the world mattered to them when they had that gold-fever. *They* were always men, though, and the weather was cool enough for them to be able to walk a fair distance. But I've never seen a woman walking along a road in Queensland looking like that – and the weather's a bit different here to what it's like in Victoria. Her name is Annie, you said?"

Frank's lined face had lit up in a beaming smile and his scrawny shoulders no longer slouched over the bar. His voice had almost an adolescent hoarseness to it when he answered. "Sure is, Bluey, it's our Annie all right. We just know her as *Annie Bags*." He held up his glass in a silent toast and then abruptly turned away, burying his face in the relative privacy of the dark corner. He cleared his throat and added. "She's a *real* lady, but she never dresses in fine clothes. She always wears rags."

George regarded the back of his friend's head with an expression of grave forbearance and then turned to Tom. "Nobody knows where she came from, or what happened to her, or who gave her the name Annie Bags," he said. "My Mary thinks there's at least some truth to the rumour that she was a *real* lady a long time ago, - maybe even European royalty. Mary says that Annie certainly always acts like a lady an' she has a bit of a posh accent, although I have to admit that

I've never heard her say very much at all. You didn't talk to her, did you Bluey?"

"Well, yes I did," Tom said, "but mind you, the conversation was pretty short and one-sided. I just said hello and asked if I could give her a lift. I had plenty of room on the dray. She just kept staring straight ahead, - never looked at me once. Just shook her head and looked a bit confused - frightened, I suppose. The horse was getting agitated because her dogs were growling, so I left her to it and went on my way. It left me feeling a bit odd." He looked from one to the other. "Have you ever accidently frightened a wallaby that's been grazing on a nice patch of grass and minding its own business and then felt really upset with yourself that you'd intruded on its peace?"

George nodded in agreement, although it was doubtful that he had ever actually disturbed any grazing animals in his lifetime.

"That's the only way I can explain the feeling I had. I kind of wished I'd been able to slip on by and let her get on with what she was doing without noticing I was there."

"You're probably lucky you didn't press the point too far an' left when you did," George said. He glanced at Tom's hair again, "particularly with you being a ginger mop. She doesn't seem to be too inclined towards men in general, but men with red hair are definitely the nastiest creatures on the planet. It seems she can't tolerate you blokes for some reason, Bluey. I don't know if that's true, mind you, but that's what I've heard. Maybe you're lucky she *didn't* look directly at you, or she might have set those dogs on you."

Tom still looked troubled, but he shook his head. "No, I don't think she was in that kind of frame of mind. It wasn't anything malicious I saw on her face. Like I said before, it was just a vacant, haunted kind of expression I saw when I first caught up with her, like she was in another world or something, but then she became confused and frightened when I stopped and spoke to her so I guess she wasn't expecting me to do anything like that." He looked from one to the other. "Where do you think she'd be going to now?"

"She's going everywhere an' getting nowhere," George said. "I don't think *she* even knows where she's heading for. How far away from here was she when you passed by?"

Tom thought for a moment. "Just on the other side of Eight Mile Creek, I reckon," he said eventually.

George nodded. "There's a billabong downstream of the crossing at the Eight Mile, an' there'd still be plenty of water in it. She doesn't come that way when she knows it'll be dry, but that billabong rarely dries out. She'll sleep out tonight an' get here by late tomorrow afternoon probably. Mary will have her room ready for whenever she turns up anyway."

Tom's eyes widened. "She stays *here*?" he said.

"Sure does," George nodded. "But don't worry. She won't bother you if you stop here on your way back." He jerked his thumb over his shoulder towards the back of the hotel. "We've got some rooms right out the back, away from everything. We haven't used them much. They were supposed to be miner's quarters when the Gilbert looked like being a very big field, but needless to say that didn't happen. We'd let her stay there for nothing, but she always insists on paying her rent. She'll stay for a few weeks, maybe a month or more depending on the weather an' how she feels an' then she'll be on her way again when something in her brain tells her it's time to go. She always leaves her room spotless an' spends a lot of time washing her rags an' combing her hair. Sometimes Mary combs it for her. Annie loves it when she does that an' sings some of her Scottish songs, an' she really settles down an' relaxes. It's like Mary is her second mother or something. I can never understand what Mary's warbling on about myself an' I don't think Annie does either, but she likes to sit an' listen anyway. You wouldn't even know she was here a lot of the time. She talks to Mary a fair bit though, but Mary says it's hard to understand what Annie's all about."

"Ah, - so she gets on all right with other women, then?" Tom said.

"Yeah, well, - some of them anyway." George agreed. "But it's like I said, she seems to be fine with women who tend to mother her a bit. I suppose she feels safe with them. The strange thing is though, she insists on calling my Mary, Mrs Gordon."

Tom gave him a perplexed stare. "Why's that so strange? She probably doesn't feel she knows your wife well enough to be on first-name terms with her."

George frowned and shook his head so that his jowls quivered in unison. "No Bluey. That's not what's strange about it. Our surname isn't Gordon; it's Johnson. Mary used to try to get it through to her a long time ago, but she just accepts it now. This Mrs Gordon must have been someone Mary reminds her of; someone she trusted or was related to in some way. Like I said, she won't talk to me at all – gets a bit of a frightened look on her face if I get too close to her, especially if her dogs are not nearby. I don't take any offence to it because she's the same with most men."

Frank cleared his throat again and they both looked at him. "Annie talks to me," he said, staring into his glass with a self-conscious smirk on his face.

"Yeah! Sure she does, Half-Pint." George agreed. "But only when she thinks you're Mr Gordon, - whoever he is, - or *was*."

"Well then I don't *care* about that." Frank retorted, his voice strained with indignation." Mr Gordon must have been good to her and I'm quite *happy* she thinks I'm him."

George regarded Tom with a meaningful smile. "Half-Pint here fixes her cart whenever it needs a bit of attention, - an' sometimes when it doesn't too."

Frank still looked uncomfortable and he glanced at Tom, his face flushed. "Of course I do, Tom. It's what any *real* man would do for a real lady like Annie. Tiny hasn't got any notion of how to treat a woman properly and attend to her little necessities in life; that's one of the reasons she won't talk to him."

"George laughed and pretended to show his displeasure at the slight on his manliness. "Yeah, your right; - I don't, but then you go around scrounging bits an' pieces from all over the place an' hoard them in the tackle shed just in case Annie comes along an' needs her cart fixed..."

Frank scowled. "...I like fixing things, ya' big lump."

"Yeah, an' you like being close to Annie too," George said, contented that he'd hit a raw nerve. "In fact I reckon you're really..."

"...Yeah, right, get on with the story." Frank said. "You're just lucky Mary felt sorry for *you*, Tiny or you'd be single too."

George appeared to be satisfied that his long-held suspicion of Frank's affection for Annie had been confirmed and he continued unabashed while Frank still scowled at him from his corner. "We know of a few other places Annie stays at an' there are probably more that we don't know of, but they're mostly out of the way, just like we are. Sometimes she stays with Miss Aldridge, the postmistress at Croydon, in a spare room at the back of the post office. Annie calls her Sarah, or Miss Quinlan, depending on the circumstances an' her mood at the time. - Oh, an' sometimes she gets called *'mavourneen'* as well."

"Mavourneen?" Tom said. "That's Irish, isn't it? I'm sure my mother used to say that a lot when we were little."

"Then you must have had a happy childhood." George said. "My Mary is from the south-western coast of Scotland where they reckon they can just about see the Irish coast on a clear day – if they ever get one. The Gaelic they speak there is much the same as in Ireland an' she told Miss Aldridge it means, 'my beloved' or something similar."

"That would've put a smile on Miss Aldridge's face, I'd wager." Tom grinned.

"Sure did." George told him. "Mary said she was so happy she was crying. Miss Aldridge looks after Annie like she's her younger sister. She's never been married herself and lives on her own, so she loves to have Annie there for the company she gives her. Where she picked up the word 'mavourneen' though is anybody's guess. She's got some kind of an accent for sure, but it's definitely not an Irish one."

Frank nodded and re-joined the conversation, having forgotten his hurt feelings for the moment. "Miss Aldridge saves some of the old hessian bags that are too old to use for the mail deliveries anymore so that Annie can make her sack dresses," he said. "She's offered to buy some decent dresses for her, but Annie won't have anything to do with that idea. We've all come to the conclusion that she wears the rag dresses so that men will think of her as an ugly old woman and just ignore her."

George agreed. "Yeah, that's for sure an' it works well for her in most cases. I'd say she could afford nice clothes if she wanted them, an' even if she couldn't, as Half-Pint said, Miss Aldridge would buy them for her an' so would my Mary an' probably a lot of other people too, but she doesn't want them."

"Miss Aldridge knows more about her than anyone else, as far as we know." Frank chimed in. "But she doesn't say any more than she has to. Being the postmistress she says it's part and parcel of her job to keep things like that confidential information, - which we agree it is. The only thing she's told us is that Annie gets an allowance sent to her every couple of months from somewhere, - Germany, I think she said. She keeps it in a safe deposit box until Annie turns up to collect it. It's odd though, because after a while staying with Miss Aldridge and seeming to be perfectly happy, she gets it into her head that she *must* go and she wanders off to some other place, maybe here, or somewhere else further south like Ravenswood Junction. She's been seen walking between Townsville and Charters Towers and on the Ravenswood Road and even out west as far as the Cape River diggings."

"We spoke to Miss Aldridge about her odd wanderings last time we were in Croydon, - as we always do, because it's so puzzling to us all." George said. "She agrees with us that Annie isn't deliberately holding anything back from any of us or hiding the truth about whatever or whoever she's searching for, - or trying to get away from, whatever the case may be. Her brain seems to have shut something out that she really *can't* or doesn't *want* to remember."

Tom's face showed his dismay. "I take my hat off to Miss Aldridge and to you and Frank and your good wife Mary for doing what you've done to look after her, but has anyone ever tried to get her to a hospital or something? I mean, women shouldn't be wandering around in the outback on their own, dressed in rags. It can't be safe for her out there - and what about her being out in the sun? It must be as hot as Hades on some of the tracks around here."

"Sure is hot," George said. "An' she looks a bit tanned from her years out in the sun, but she protects herself pretty well under that big floppy cabbage tree hat that she wears an' she rubs some kind of paste on her skin – made out of some native fruit, I reckon. Mary says if you get close enough to have a good look at her you can see that she's got nice, fine skin even now. She's pretty safe out there too, generally. It's an unwritten law in the outback that you respect other people's ways of running their lives; leave someone be when they want to be left alone an' help them when they let you know they need it, because you never know when *you* might be the one that needs support. I'll agree that it's pretty unusual for a woman to be travelling on her own the way she does, but she knows where all the waterholes an' billabongs are. She carries food an' water for herself an' her dogs in that old cart, - an' as you found out for yourself, those dogs would tackle anything an' guard her with their lives if they thought she was in any danger."

Frank laughed suddenly, and the other two men turned to look at him inquisitively. "Tiny," he said chuckling, "You'd remember that young fella' Davies, wouldn't you?"

The publican grinned. "Yeah, sure." he said, "I remember him all right. He was a puny little lad from the city, trying to convince everybody that he was a great bushman. He couldn't even ride a horse very well. The horses knew it too because a couple of the quiet ones, who'd never tossed anybody in their lives, threw him off just because they knew they could get away with it so easily. It must have affected his skull in the end, or maybe he was *always* a sixpence short of a quid, as they say."

"He was as thick as two planks of wood." Frank agreed. "He'd heard that Annie was on her way and he thought he'd go out and have a bit of fun with her, - get her on her own out there, if you know what I mean. For some crazy reason he believed he could come back to Gilberton and brag about what he'd done to her and everybody would laugh along with him and slap him on the back because he'd been such a big shot. Complete idiot, he was. Those dogs of Annie's nearly took him apart. Serves him bloody right, mind you. He came limping back into town, wailing blue murder and calling for the doctor to patch him up and for the magistrate to lock Annie and her dogs up. The doctor had to do his duty, of course, but the magistrate was more interested in making sure he hadn't harmed Annie in any way. Nobody else had any sympathy for him either and a couple of the lads were intent on stringing him up in the nearest gum tree. They were bush-hardened men themselves, and they had all heard the legends of Annie and her wandering ways. Quite a few of them had doubted that she even existed until then, and most found it difficult to believe that a woman could survive in the outback on her own, but the one thing they were all in agreement with was her right to go about her life the way she chose to without any meddling from mongrels like him. The doctor advised him to get out of town in a hurry otherwise, he reckoned, the fool was beyond his help and would soon be more in need of an undertaker than a doctor. In the end he scurried back to wherever he came from with his tail between his legs before the boys could get at him."

"I heard that the bugger still walked with a limp for years after that," George chipped in. "An' he's told whoever wants to listen to him, that he got it breaking in a huge brumby stallion. Annie wandered in here a few days later, an' Mary fixed up her room out the back as usual. It was just as if nothing had happened to put her off her itinerant ways; - probably in her mind nothing *had* happened anyway."

Tom laughed with the others, but his face still showed some concern. "It must have been something quite tragic that made her brain snap like that," he said.

Frank stared up at the empty shelves, or perhaps beyond them at nothing in particular, but the other two knew that it was to shield his moistening eyes from them, for he cleared his throat more loudly this time and there was no mistaking the emotion in his voice "Some mongrel *has* done the wrong thing by our Annie, that's for sure," he muttered, almost to himself. "And I hope whoever he is, or was, rots in hell for it. As far as I'm concerned though, the harm was done long ago and right now Annie's like any other little wild thing out there in the bush. It's like you said before, Bluey. She gave you the feeling that you'd like to have been able to slip on by without her noticing you were there." His voice rose and he sighed audibly. "I agree. Annie's living her life the way she wants to live it and nobody else needs to hinder her or meddle in what she's doing. She always looks healthy enough to me so her chosen way of life is not doing her any harm. Leave her be I say, and eventually she might find what she's been looking for all these years."

George uncorked the bottle and filled all their glasses. "This one's on the house, gentlemen," he said.

Tom looked intently at the pair of odd characters he'd been drinking with. He'd noticed a perceptible change in their relationship evolve even as he sat there. No matter how well they felt they knew each other, he realised that George had learned something about Frank that day that would probably remain with him for a very long time. Frank wasn't just the old ex-miner who lived in the corner of his bar. He was a man with strong feelings about something he believed in and Annie and her simple lifestyle was close to his heart. His belief was confirmed when George spoke again.

"I know you've always fretted about Annie's well-being, Half-Pint," he said quietly and sincerely. "But I've never heard you put it into words as well as you have now. Let's drink to her health as we regularly do." There was no humour in his voice as he held his glass aloft and the other two men followed suit in a similarly earnest manner,

"Here's good luck to the lady who dresses in rags.

We all hope you find what you're looking for, Annie Bags."

Chapter 28: The End of the Road

"Good dog Andrew," she said, reaching down and patting the old dog on the head. "We shall be at Mrs O'Hara's cottage tomorrow." She coughed again and the dog whimpered, knowing instinctively that there was something wrong with her. He trotted a short distance to where a fallen log lay in the shade of a large tree and barked once. She managed a weary smile. "Yes, Andrew, I believe I will rest for a while." She pushed the old cart off the formed road and through the long grass to where he stood wagging his tail.

The cough was quite persistent now. It had started as a niggling little irritation in her throat and had gradually worsened, sapping her vigour during the past few weeks as she walked the road to Ballarat. In times gone by she would have easily been there by now, relaxing with dear Mrs O'Hara and sharing yarns about her recent, *perhaps not so recent now,* marriage to Captain Treloar. That was what the captain called them, *'yarns'*; so many strange words in this English language that she misguidedly thought she had mastered long ago in Prussia. Good old Captain Treloar; it had been quite some time since she had heard his yarns; perhaps he was still away on a voyage. *Adrift on the high seas.* That was the explanation Mrs O'Hara had given her the last time she had enquired about his health, and she always remembered to ask about the captain because she could see the wonderful effect that it had on her.

Her face positively glowed with happiness, and I listened enraptured as she related to me the cause of the wonderful change in her mood.

She sat down on the log and sighed as the strain was taken off her tired legs. The previous evening she'd cut a piece of bark from a sandalwood tree, pounded it between two stones and poured it into boiling water. When it cooled she drank the solution. It had always worked in the past, giving her relief from any irritation in her throat, but not this time. This was different, - and to make matters worse, she'd noticed flecks of blood in her saliva.

Andrew lay at her feet, his old grey muzzle almost touching her boot. What a wonderful dog he'd turned out to be. She remembered the night when a wild boar had invaded their camp. Her faithful Captain, and Andrew, who was not very old at the time, stood their ground between her and the angry pig. They dodged its huge tusks and attacked its exposed hindquarters, finally managing to chase it away while she stood spellbound and paralysed with fear. When it was over old Captain, although exhausted and with several puncture wounds of his own, went over to where Andrew lay panting for breath and began to lick his cuts clean. It was as if he was saying; *good job young man. You'll make a worthy successor when I'm gone, so I'm going to make sure you survive.* She'd never dreamed she'd have another dog like Captain. She still grieved for him, though she knew he was at peace out there somewhere. It had been quite a few years now, but she remembered so well that fateful night when he'd left. He'd circled the camp as he always did, checking for signs of danger, but with steps much slower than she'd ever seen him take before. When he returned, he'd nudged Andrew, and the young dog had followed obediently. The two of them had circled the camp together and, with that done, Andrew took up Captain's position on the opposite side of the campfire. Old Captain limped over to where she lay and licked her hand. It was his way of saying goodbye. He walked slowly away, stopping to nudge each of the other dogs in turn with his nose before looking back at her one last time, then, with his tail drooping, he disappeared into the night. In the morning she'd called him, thinking that he'd just been a bit sick, and Andrew had gone to the edge of the clearing and howled, but Captain was gone. From that time on Andrew had made the rounds of the camp.

She was about to stand up and resume her journey when one of the young dogs barked and stood sniffing the air. He was looking back along the road with his ears pricked. She knew instantly what it was.

Their advertisements assure the traveller that their coaches are as comfortably appointed as any you will see on a London street and also, curiously, that the wheel springs have been specially strengthened to cope with the rough tracks that pass for roads in Australia.

The Cobb and Co. coach rounded a bend in the road and rushed towards her in a cloud of dust, but when the driver saw her, still seated on the log, head down and her faithful dogs gathered around her, he quickly reined in the horse team and the carriage came to a stop. The windows were pushed open and several passengers' heads appeared despite the swirling dust, trying to get a glimpse of whatever it was that had caused the unscheduled stop, while from inside the compartment a chorus of irritated voices yelled objections to their inconsiderate curiosity. She turned her head away.

'No, please go away. I shall walk as I have always done. The municipal authority in Ballarat has ordered you to only allow passage to single females who have demonstrated a legitimate reason for travelling to their city and I can give you no legitimate reason for my journey. I cannot remember why I am going there.'

Chapter 29: Ravenswood Junction

As the name suggests, the community of Ravenswood Junction had been established in 1884 when the spur line to Ravenswood was completed on the Great Northern Railway between Townsville and Charters Towers at Mingela siding. The tiny police station had initially been opened as an outpost of the Charters Towers Police Headquarters, but now after more than twenty years as a one-officer station the renewed mining activity at Ravenswood had made it necessary for the commissioner to appoint a constable to assist Sergeant Kennedy, the resident officer in charge. The young man had been in the position less than a month, but he was already proving to be a handy acquisition to the station, according to Kennedy's reports.

Kennedy looked up from his paperwork as the constable pushed open the door to the duty room and poked his head inside. "We've picked her up now, Sergeant," he said. "It was just like you said. I would have had a devil of a time getting her to cooperate if I hadn't taken the widow Ryan with me. Even so, she still refused to sit on the front seat of the dray and rode in the back with her dogs and the old cart with all her belongings in it. I reckon those dogs would have eaten me alive if I'd gone anywhere close to her without her consent, but one word from her and they were like pups. Strange thing though, she was very happy to see the widow Ryan, but she calls her Mrs O'Hara."

He stepped inside the office, flipped his hat on to the hook behind the door and ran his fingers through his short black hair, a habit he'd developed when something perplexed him. "Mrs Ryan told me the gist of the story, - well, as much as *she* knows anyway, when we were on our way out there. The poor woman's been calling the old lady Mrs O'Hara since she first turned up on her doorstep with a pup wrapped up in her cart, - seems like it started about twenty years ago – and she said she'd walked all the way from Ballarat. *Ballarat in Victoria; would you believe that?* Mrs Ryan reckons she came from the direction of Charters Towers. She called the pup Captain after some bloke she expected Mrs Ryan to know quite well and she still asks about him every time she visits. She's been coming here ever since – always walking, - with her dogs in tow. What do you think of that?"

Sergeant Kennedy underlined a particular paragraph on the page and then gave the constable his full attention. "Yeah, I've heard a bit about her over the years and I don't rightly know what to make of it myself, Dan. It might be someone in her past that the widow Ryan reminds her of, maybe someone she knew before she went crazy." He pointed his pencil stub at the handkerchief still knotted around the constable's neck. "I see you went prepared, like I told you to."

"Too right," Dan replied, undoing the knot as he spoke. "She was sitting by the side of the road coughing up a little bit of blood, just like the coach driver's report said. His other passengers weren't too keen on her getting on the coach, but it didn't matter anyway because she wasn't going to leave her dogs out there on their own. It looks like she might be developing a fever too. We took her straight to Mrs Ryan's place because she has her own room there when she's not walking the roads. The old lady reckons she's always been pretty healthy until now. She's happy to look after her until we can get her to Townsville Hospital. I've arranged for her dogs to be fed and put in the compound at the back of the hotel and I've got her cart with all her belongings in the lock-up."

"Yeah! Good work Dan." The sergeant nodded. "You're pretty sure it's contagious I suppose?" he added, hoping that the answer would be negative. He was disappointed.

"I'm almost certain of it," the constable said. "I reckon she's got tuberculosis for sure. I just read recently that somebody has discovered what the germ is that causes it, but there's no cure for it yet."

Kennedy shook his head in wonder. "Now where'd you read something like that? You're destined for better things than picking up drunken miners, Dan."

The constable grinned, "I did think about going into medicine once, but I couldn't stand the sight of blood."

The sergeant stared at him in silence for a moment, and then his mouth twisted in a grin too as he realised his constable was teasing him, as he often did. "So you decided to become a policeman instead? Maybe you're not as smart as I just gave you credit for, sonny boy."

The constable's face was suddenly serious. That poor old woman is going to die if she doesn't get treatment soon, Sergeant," he said, "And if it is tuberculosis, she needs to be in an isolation ward before she infects everyone around the district. I've already advised Mrs Ryan to wear a mask whenever she's near her."

Kennedy nodded. "There's a place attached to the Townsville General Hospital called Reception House, where they have an isolation ward to accommodate people with all sorts of contagious diseases, and there's a train going through to Townsville tomorrow," he said. "See that she gets on it. - Oh, and have a message sent through to Charters Towers that they need to hook up the leper van to the back of the train."

Dan raised his eyebrows. "The *leper van?* She definitely hasn't got leprosy, Sergeant"

"Yeah, I know that, Dan, but that's just what they've nicknamed the railway carriage that's used when a patient has to be transferred from any of the outlying towns to the Townsville Hospital. It doesn't matter what they've got, leprosy, fever, tuberculosis, or any other disease they think might be contagious, the leper van gets hooked up on the back of the train to take them there, isolated from the other passengers. There's a couple of beds and some seats in it. They even take lunatics to the asylum at the Townsville Gaol complex in it, but the lunatics are always tied down to the bed for their own safety, as well as everyone else's, of course." He drummed his pencil stub on the desk with a worried frown. "Let's face it, Dan, we don't want to be accused of starting another epidemic. There are plenty of fevers going around in the Ross River district already.

"Righto," the constable said, "I'll do that, - and I'll get the post office clerk to wire through to Townsville Hospital, so they can be ready to pick her up from the railway station in the horse-ambulance."

"Thanks, Dan." Kennedy said. The constable had turned to leave when he stopped him. "Just one more thing," he said. "Would you regard me as being old, Dan?"

The constable had a puzzled look on his face. "No, not at all Sergeant, why do you ask?"

Kennedy grinned. "It's fortunate for your career prospects you knew what answer I was expecting. *I'm* fifty-five lad, but you called *her* an old woman. The truth is Annie Bags is probably about the same age as me, from what I've been told."

The constable thought about that for several seconds. "You know Sergeant," he said finally. "When I saw her sitting by the side of the road in her old bag dress and looking so sick, I thought to myself. You poor old lady, you must have been a beautiful woman once. She's very pale and thin, but you can see that she still has fine features beneath it all. Why would a woman like that go out on the road, wandering from one place to another instead of settling down in a cottage somewhere and living out her life peacefully?"

Kennedy shook his head. "Don't know, lad. The widow Ryan told me she's not destitute and always insists on paying her way, so that's not her problem. The police sergeant in one of the small towns out west had her arrested for vagrancy a few years ago. He was new to the district I think. She was taken to the coast and put before the magistrate, but he threw her case out and ordered her to be released when he found she had several hundred pounds in her bank account. The unfortunate part of that particular story was that the police had already had a lot of her animals put down."

"She had *other* animals besides the dogs?" Dan said, shaking his head in wonder.

"As far as I know, she had quite a few cats following her and even some rats," Kennedy said.

"*Rats?*" the constable shuddered. "Rats and cats don't follow people Sergeant," he said, "- unless you're the Pied Piper of Hamelin."

"Wha…Oh yeah, well that's probably just another rumour, Dan." Kennedy shrugged. "There are plenty of them around about her. It's always bothered me to think of her wandering out there on her own of course, but I thought it was best to leave things as they were. She didn't seem to be in any danger and she certainly wasn't doing anyone any harm. The police can sometimes be too obstructive, I believe, and meddle in peoples' affairs we don't need to concern ourselves with."

Dan retrieved his hat. "Yeah, I agree with that, Sergeant. No need to stick our noses in where they're not needed. Maybe she's had something terrible happen to her, though, - a long time ago, Sergeant, like she's been attacked or someone has tried to kill her even."

"Sure, I think you're right that something terrible *has* happened to her a long time ago, Dan," Kennedy agreed. "But I don't think it would have been bodily harm. That would be apt to make her shut herself away in my opinion, not wander along the roads putting herself at even more risk of that sort of thing happening to her again. No, I think she's been mentally ruined by some brainless twerp who's gone off and left her or something; maybe run off with another woman. It's odd, though, that she's not short of a quid. She must have somebody sending her money. I'm thinking it could be a family member, but then if she has family why haven't they taken her in and looked after her? Mrs Ryan wouldn't have much to give her and it doesn't grow on trees either, does it?" He threw down his pencil and cleared his throat. "I'm going to try to find out if she has any relatives. I don't know if I'll have any success though. I've only ever heard of her being called Annie Bags and that's surely a name that's been given to her by others. While you're gone I'll go through her personal belongings, I hate doing that, but it might give me a clue as to who she is and how we can help her."

Dan shook his head and shot Kennedy a worried glance. "If it *is* tuberculosis she might be already beyond help, Sergeant."

"You'd better go and organise that transport, Dan." Kennedy said. "I need to finish this report before I check her belongings."

"Sure, Sergeant," the young constable said with a grave look on his face. "It wouldn't be a good thing for my morale to see my tough boss break down and cry now, would it?" He closed the door quickly, before Kennedy could find something to throw at him.

Chapter 30: The Isolation Ward

Annie was admitted to the recently completed New Townsville General Hospital, the old one having been destroyed during a cyclone just two years before in 1903.

The usual routine tests were conducted on her although it was obvious to the doctors from the beginning that the young constable's tentative diagnosis was correct and she was suffering from tuberculosis, or *consumption* as it was commonly known. As there was no known cure for the disease she was immediately transferred to the isolation ward in Reception House, a palliative care facility for the terminally ill, where every attempt would be made to make her comfortable as the sickness progressed towards the inevitable conclusion.

There were two other patients in the isolation ward, their beds spaced as far apart as possible from each other and from Annie's, to give what little peace and quiet might be achieved from the separation. She could tell though, that both were elderly and emaciated and by the regular cries and groans, that their bodies were racked with pain. Neither one of them would have to suffer much longer. Did either of them have any family, she wondered idly, and what might become of them when they succumbed to the disease? Would they be buried in pauper's graves with no proper service to send them to their own paradise, wherever that may be? Surely they deserve *some* reward for the suffering they are enduring in this world. *'How long will it be until I too have declined to the same moribund state? I know I have been brought here to await the release from pain that death will bring me — it is simply a matter of time, but what will happen to my loyal Andrew and my other dogs? Who will look after them? And will I be buried in consecrated ground? I must be buried in holy ground if I am to be reunited with Mama and Papa in Paradise. My dear Sarah would ensure that I receive a proper burial, but she will not know of my passing. I must tell someone; Sarah will be a holy sister soon. Perhaps I can get a message to her through the visitor who regularly comes to pray over us.'*

She had only ever seen one visitor to the ward, a nun who appeared quietly at mealtimes each day, spoon-fed the two elderly patients and prayed by the bedside of each of them in turn. She then made sure they and Annie were comfortable and then glided silently out again. From her stooped back and shuffling walk it seemed to Annie that *she* must have been elderly too, but it was difficult to tell because only part of her face was visible beneath the starched white cap that came down over her forehead and the white wimple that passed down either side of her face and underneath her chin. A brown-coloured cowl covered her head over the cap and a voluminous brown habit with a monogram of blue braid on the front hung to the floor. She spoke softly with a slight accent and occasionally Annie could hear her humming a lilting tune that seemed oddly familiar as she went about the ward.

Apart from the nun, a doctor and a nurse made a brief cursory check each day, the former commenting on the ongoing deterioration of each patient in turn while the latter made appropriate notes on the medical charts attached to the iron rail at the bottom of their beds. Following these examinations several young orderlies would arrive to perform all the usual housekeeping chores, changing sheets, washing floors, bathing and administering to the needs of the elderly patients. *They* laughed and talked amongst themselves behind their surgical masks as they worked, but when the catering staff entered they never spoke, coming in with similar surgical masks over the lower part of their faces and unloading the trays containing the food on to a table by the door, thankful no doubt, that the old nun was always there to dispense it. They would then depart quickly, casting hesitant glances over their shoulders at the doomed patients; such was the fear of contracting the disease that was known colloquially as *the white plague.*

Time passed. Was it days or weeks? She couldn't tell how long she had been languishing in this state, drifting in and out of troubled sleep. The fevers came and went and the coughing fits became more regular and intense and it was then, when her body told her that the pain had reached an almost unbearable level that her tired brain began to welcome the thought of death.

A kindly doctor, on one of his visits, had told her that people with respiratory diseases like consumption often lapsed into a euphoric state as the disease progressed; something akin to the feeling of elation that people rescued from near drowning had reported having. This response of the brain to a restricted supply of oxygen was known medically by the Latin term *spec phthisic*, which she knew translated as 'hope of the consumptive', and it reputedly had even been known to produce bursts of creativity in artists and poets. The doctor advised her to hold on to those moments and treasure the times when her clarity of mind and sense of profound happiness detached her from the drab surroundings and the pain she was forced to endure.

It seemed like good advice and when the feeling of euphoria eventually began to manifest itself, she relaxed and allowed her mind to be carried along on a wave of enchantment, floating across the inviting threshold of this other mysterious realm into a brightly lit dream world where happy scenes from her life long ago were being re-enacted. It was like watching her whole life flit by as she watched in detached fascination and she welcomed the images and the memories they brought back, a few of which she remembered she'd carried with her on her long journey to nowhere, but there were others that had not occupied her confused mind for many years.

She found herself once more in the Caledonian Hotel in Herberton over twenty years before. It was after supper and Mrs Gordon was holding her close as she talked excitedly about the next school project she was preparing for the children. Oh, such joyful, contented evenings she had spent with Mr and Mrs Gordon. And then there was the Saturday evening dance in the School of Arts building. What a happy time that had been for all; the young men had seemed intent on whirling her and the other young ladies around on the dance floor until everyone was enjoyably exhausted, - and there, prominent amongst the crowd, that good-looking young doctor had caught her attention as he smiled charmingly at her again. She'd been so close to encouraging him to pay court to her, - but then she remembered a solemn promise she'd made to God and to her papa when she was a child. She'd promised that she would only ever give her love to one man, just like her mama had, for she wanted so much to be like her mama. *'Yes, and I found that man. He told me he would love me forever, and I believed that he would. I gave him my heart, - did I not? But what has happened to him, and why is he not with me now? Ah, now I remember, - he had to go away.'* That was it, but there was something else, something important that she couldn't quite recall. *'No matter; it will come later. Treasure the moment and let the fond memories come back at will, just like the doctor advised.'*

Then, in the flutter of an eyelid, she was transported even further back in time to Ballarat, her tears of joy mingling with those of her dear friend Sarah Quinlan as Sarah recited the letter she had received, notifying her of her acceptance into the convent. Dear Sarah had liberated her when her spirits had been at the lowest. But why had her spirits been low? Indeed, why had she gone to Ballarat to begin with? What was it she had sought there? Did it have something to do with the man to whom she had given her heart? There were so many questions still unanswered.

There too was Mrs O'Hara, seated in the garden of her lodging house in Melbourne, laughing in boundless joy along with the dapper Captain Treloar as they prepared for their coming wedding. They made such a perfect couple. Captain Treloar had been in command of the 'Victoria', the ship that had brought her to Australia. Why, indeed, had she ventured to Australia at all? She had been living in London temporarily with her papa and had met someone; a man had befriended her. He'd been so compassionate towards her. His name was Charles. Yes, Charles had been so kind to her, but... as kind as he was, he was *not* the man to whom she had entrusted her whole life. That man was... *He'd been forced to go away and leave me. Why?*

Her friends had been so caring. They had all inspired her at different times and in different ways, *but I never found the complete happiness that my friends all wished for me to have. No, and the reason for my failure is close by.* She became frightened suddenly, for she sensed that in her dream world there was a dark side, in which sinister, dim shadows lurked, shadows that disturbed and distressed her for some reason. She had almost succeeded in shutting them out, but they were still there, insistent, hovering just below her consciousness, and now they were becoming a little more clearly defined.

Perhaps the doctor was wrong. Perhaps she shouldn't have allowed her mind to venture to this other world after all, because the tender memories of her friends were being replaced by some that she didn't care to evoke, and she felt powerless to do anything about it. But it was too late to try to gather her strength to fight against the memories being thrust at her. A shadowy figure began to materialise out of a haze. *'Am I seeing this through a veil of tears?'* It was a man. He was dressed roughly, - like a miner, and he had red hair. *'I do not care for men with red hair, but I cannot remember why. Did I not love a man with red hair a long time ago? Yes; he was the one who was forced to leave me. It had something to do with his family. I think that is why I came to Australia. But it couldn't possibly be this man. No, - not him.'*

The man's speech was slurred, and she couldn't comprehend what he was saying or why he was speaking to her in such a manner, but he seemed familiar, nonetheless. She was still mulling over this unwelcome intrusion into her dream when, abruptly, the shadowy figure's expression changed to one of horrified recognition and he reached out as if to take her in his arms, but she recoiled from his touch and shook her head firmly. *'No! Go away, you horrid creature. Get away from me. You are not welcome in my dream. I only want to think of pleasant things before I die, and I believe you will not bring enjoyable memories back to me.'*

But the apparition persisted and he held his hands out to her, palms upward in a familiar gesture of appeal; his expression had changed to one of regret, and as she looked up at him his face and his red hair seemed to be surrounded by an aura created by the mist in the yellow circle of gaslight behind and above him. The green eyes that once, a long time ago, had shone with a heavenly radiance and had been so soft and kind, now held a steely glint of coldness in them that she hadn't noticed before.

'*What does that mean – before? Have I truly known such a man as this in the past? Did I not love him once?*' She shook her head again resolutely. '*No! I want you to go away. Whoever you are, you are from my past life and I do not wish to visit that part of my life ever again. I shall die in peace.*' The apparition cast his eyes downwards and ran his fingers through his tousled mop of red hair, and she shivered as she remembered that it was one of the little characteristics about him that had appealed to her. But where and when had she seen him run his hand through his hair like that? '*Was it at the theatre in London?*'

The man's mouth began to move and she heard an intonation, but the sound was hollow and faint. '*Oh Annie, it's me – James Pottingley. Don't you remember me? I love you, Annie. I truly love you, and I promise you that you will never be alone again, my beautiful Annie.*'

Annie stared at the apparition in confusion. '*James Pottingley?*' A million thoughts crowded her mind and sent it racing. This was the red-haired man that she had loved and pursued because he had professed his love for her, and she had believed in him. It was he whom she had trusted and he who had betrayed her. '*Yes! Now I do remember you, James Pottingley. I remember your words of love, and I know now that they meant nothing to you. I gave you my heart and my body and I followed you across the oceans of the world with hope always in my heart, but you never did love me, James. You shamed me. But my papa taught me to be strong, - much stronger than my mama ever was. He told me I must be strong on the inside as well as the outside, - and I was strong, James! I did not succumb like my mama did. I was strong enough to shun you from my mind and I have completed the penance for my sin of vanity. I do remember you, James Pottingley, but it is with revulsion. I do not love you anymore.*'

The shadowy ghost of James Pottingley smirked at her. '*Yes, Annie, - it is true. I never loved you. I used you, as I have used many women who have had the misfortune to be a part of my life, but all of that is irrelevant now, is it not? You have endured a long and difficult penance, and if you come with me I shall ensure that you suffer even more, but you will come with me, Annie. I was able to take your heart and your body so easily and now I want to take your soul as well. Come with me, Annie. You know you cannot continue to live your life without me. No woman ever could. Are you going to wander those dusty roads forever trying to forget me?*'

He cocked his head to one side, listening, as if something beyond the mist had attracted his attention, and behind him Annie saw an ancient iron gate. It was opening slowly, - invitingly, on silent hinges. Above the gate an inscription was engraved into the bridging arch, but of the nine lines that it contained only the final one caught her attention.

'Lasciate ogni speranza voi che entrate.'

She laughed. *'Read the inscription, James Pottingley. It is from Dante's Inferno. The last line means 'abandon all hope, ye who enter here'. You took my heart and my body, but you cannot take my soul. Yes, I have survived, James, and you are mistaken. I shall endure without you and you cannot ever induce me to enter the realm of the underworld through this gate to hell.'*

The presence's evil green eyes were locked on hers with what she perceived to be a curious mixture of regret and spite, but with her words it became agitated. *'What do you mean, Annie? There is no gate to hell. Your twenty years of penance were all for nothing. Come to me. Jenny will be away until tomorrow and we can enjoy our time together. Come on in, Annie.'* He beckoned to her and took a step backwards. All of a sudden the movement of the gate distracted him and he stared at it in disbelief. That disbelief then turned to despair and a look of fear passed across his face when he looked down and realised that he had already stepped through the vestibule and the gate was quickly and silently closing in front of him. And even before it had completed its path his features had already begun to twist and distort and melt away. Hell's gate closed with a final metallic click and the mist around it shifted and cleared, - or had she blinked the tears away? She could now see beyond the shadows where the spectre had been lurking and there, in all its grandeur, she recognised the imposing facade of Topsham Manor.

A man's voice softly called her name, "Annie!"

She knew that voice; it was kind and caring. Strangely, it seemed to be coming from a long way off too, just as the dream ghost had, but it was not quite the same. No, this was from *outside* her dream, and it was the voice of a man whom she trusted, a man who, she believed, had been with her in spirit throughout her heartbreaking years of searching. "Is it you, Charles?" She struggled to cry out faintly.

"Annie!" the voice repeated; it sounded closer and more urgent.

"Charles?" She opened her eyes wide, but she was at once confused and disappointed. It wasn't Charles Pottingley who bent over her; it was just another grey-haired doctor with a surgical mask covering the lower part of his face, bending over her with a look of concern in his eyes. *'What does this doctor want of me? Doesn't he know I am beyond help now, and that I am going to die?'*

"They made me wear this mask." The man glanced towards the door and then pulled the mask down under his chin. "Annie, it's me, Charles."

Annie was overwhelmed. "My dear Charles," she cried. She raised one hand weakly and touched his cheek. "Is it really you, or is this just another beautiful dream? If it is a dream then it is so real that I can touch you." Her eyes strayed to his hair. "Your hair is grey now, Charles. How could I possibly imagine *that* in my dream?"

"It is not a dream, Annie. I am here with you now at long last." Charles clasped her hand in both of his and kissed it gently. "How can I begin to tell you how much I have yearned for this moment? You have rarely been out of my thoughts in the last twenty-five years." He shook his head forlornly. "I remember your words to me before you left England to search for my brother. You said that nothing was likely to happen to you, but if anything did then I must forget about you and get on with my life. I told you then that it would be impossible to forget you, Annie, and so it proved to be. I have never married. I did not take my seat in the House but devoted myself entirely to my business. Apart from that I have lived a somewhat reclusive life. When I found out about your present situation, it was almost more than I could bear, because I had upheld my belief that one day we would meet again, and I realised that perhaps this time I had lost you forever."

"And I too have lived a solitary existence, Charles. I did find James, but unhappily, it was not the kind of reunion that I had anticipated."

"Yes, I am aware of that." Charles said miserably. "And if I had known of the condition of his life at that time I would never have sent the message that I must assume reunited you with him and caused such a catastrophic outcome. The knowledge that I was responsible for whatever had happened to you as a result of that meeting has caused me much melancholy in the past and finding you in this way has re-ignited the pain."

"You could not have helped me at that time, Charles. I was beyond any assistance from anyone. I alone had to deal with the demons that tormented me." She paused, reflecting on the bad dream that Charles's timely intervention had just released her from. "Dear Charles, I have to tell you that I do not think James is, - with us anymore."

Charles nodded. "Yes, I am aware of that too, Annie. But let us talk of such things another time when you are well enough."

She gazed at him tenderly. "Another time may not eventuate, my treasured friend. This hospice is for the terminally ill, as I am sure you already know."

"I will not accept that prognosis, Annie. Now that I have found you again, I will not let you go so easily this time. I will find the best doctors money can buy. I will leave no stone unturned in my determination to alleviate your suffering and to nurse you back to good health."

"How then, *did* you find me, Charles?" Annie felt tears welling in her eyes.

"A policeman, Sergeant Kennedy, from a town called Ravenswood Junction, contacted me. You had my name and the address of the Kensington Club in London amongst your possessions. I could scarcely believe it when the message was delivered to me, but I organised my affairs in record time because, you see, I have been ready for such a possibility for many, many years, hoping beyond hope that this moment might come. I don't expect you to ever love me. That would be too much to ask of you, considering what you have gone through at the hands of my cruel brother, but you have nothing to fear now, for I will care for you as long as I live, unless it is your specific wish that the last remaining member of the Pottingley family go away and forever leave you in peace."

Annie gripped his hand with the little strength she could muster. "I would not wish that of you, my dear Charles. We agreed long ago that you and James were diverse characters in many ways. I am able to appreciate that now. I can confidently add that James Potts means nothing to me now."

'Lasciate ogni speranza voi che entrate.'

'Abandon all hope, ye who enter here.' You took my heart and my body, but you cannot take my soul.

Charles acknowledged her deliberate use of the surname James had adopted with a slight smile of satisfaction. If it assisted the healing process to reject any connection between himself and his brother then he would accept that gratefully.

Annie slept peacefully that night.

Chapter 31: Doctor Jones' Prognosis

Charles requested an interview with Doctor Jones, the hospital superintendent, and was pleasantly surprised to be invited to meet him in his office the very next day.

"Thank you for agreeing to this meeting, Doctor Jones," he said as he was ushered into the chamber by an administrator. "I realise that you must be very busy. The hospital seems to be a hive of activity."

"Welcome to Townsville, Lord Pottingley," the doctor said as they shook hands. "It's not often that we get a visit from an English gentleman."

Charles laughed. "From what I have learned, sir, nobody seems to care very much about English gentlemen or the titles such people carry with them here in Australia, - a refreshingly different state of affairs to the deferential treatment accorded to those of rank in London. I would certainly feel much more comfortable being addressed formally as plain old Mr., or in your case, informally as Charles."

"As you wish, Charles, and you must call me David. Yes, regrettably our new hospital is always busy; it is already too small because Townsville is growing so rapidly, as is the population of Queensland in general. It certainly doesn't seem like it has been more than four years since Federation."

Charles's face was blank for a moment and the doctor grinned, more than a little mischievously. "I'm terribly sorry for seeming presumptuous, Charles," he said. "I had supposed that a gentleman of your importance would be aware that the colonies of Australia became a Commonwealth of Federated States on the first day of January 1901"

"Oh yes, I *was* aware of it, of course, David. I had read about it in the Times of London." Charles nodded. "I was simply thinking, as you were, that it seems a more recent event. Has it made any difference to you in terms of good government?"

The doctor shook his head. "Not so much here in North Queensland. There was great jubilation to begin with and later that year we celebrated a very brief visit from the first Governor General of Australia, Lord Hopetoun, who happened to be passing through, but we now have two separate governments to deal with instead of one, and the new federal government sits in Melbourne, so it is even further away than the Queensland government in Brisbane." He indicated a wicker office chair. "Please be seated, sir, if you will." He walked around the plain wooden desk and seated himself in an identical one behind it. "The reason I was so prompt with my invitation is that I have an acute interest in this particular case, as you shall learn in due course. I would not, under normal circumstances, discuss the personal details of a patient under my care with anyone who is not a direct relative, but I recognise that this is an exceptional circumstance and I have been advised that Miss Ferdinand has nominated you as her primary carer."

Charles could not resist a smile. "That is indeed music to my ears, David," he said. "To care for Annie is my only purpose in life now."

The doctor nodded. "Well then, Charles let us discuss the disease that has brought Miss Ferdinand to this hospital. Have you ever heard of Doctor Robert Koch?"

"Yes I have, an eminent physician by all accounts and the most recent winner of the Nobel Prize for Medicine."

"He is, and I am sure you are aware then, that he has done some magnificent research in the identification of the bacillus that causes tuberculosis at his clinic in Prussia, and he truly deserves the honour bestowed on him. We are, nevertheless, still a long way from finding a cure for this terrible disease."

Charles shook his head ruefully. "There must be something that can be done for Annie. I cannot accept the judgement that it is a forlorn and hopeless condition with no possibility of reprieve and simply stand by helplessly as she slowly fades away."

"I can fully appreciate your vexation and I would have suggested taking her to a sanatorium, Charles. There are many of these recuperative facilities in various parts of the world where fresh mountain air and good nutrition has been demonstrated to have a beneficial effect on consumptives. I'm sorry to say though, that no such facilities have been established in Australia as yet and Miss Ferdinand is much too fragile to undergo the stress of a long overseas journey. I doubt that she would see the end of such a voyage, quite frankly."

Charles clutched at the notion instantly and his eyes lit up in anticipation. "In that case, David, and with your consent of course, I will take her to the closest mountain retreat that I can find. Fortunately, my means are considerable and I will spare no expense in ensuring that Annie receives the very best of care."

Doctor Jones' voice was full of sympathy. "You must love her very much, sir, but I must warn you again. This is a very contagious disease that Miss Ferdinand has contracted. It is responsible for about one in every five deaths in Europe at the present time. There is a very high risk to *your* own health and the bacillus does not discriminate between the rich and the poor. Hermann Brehmers Sanatorium in Germany, which has been operating for over forty years and is considered to be the best in the world, still only boasts a fifty per cent chance that a consumptive will survive for more than five years."

Charles was resolute and his voice was charged with emotion. "I have spent twenty-five years regretting the day that I let Annie walk out of my life, David," he said. "Please be assured that my own health is of minimal concern to me. Whatever time that Annie and I have left together is all that matters to me now."

"Then take her and care for her, Charles," the doctor said gravely. "There is a small town high in the mountains of the Atherton Tablelands about two hundred miles north of here. It has a small, but well-appointed hospital if it indeed became necessary for her to be admitted to it. The town is named Herberton, and I know it well because I worked there as a young doctor. I am certain that Miss Ferdinand will also be well acquainted with the town once her memory improves."

Charles was bemused. "How can you determine that with such confidence, sir?"

"I stated earlier that I had a personal interest in this case," the doctor replied. "It is only recently that I have become aware of her true identity. You see, Miss Ferdinand was admitted to the Townsville Hospital under the only name that people everywhere have known her by for many, many years, - *Annie Bags*."

Charles frowned and placed his hand over his mouth to stifle a groan. "When I received the message from Sergeant Kennedy that a woman who went by the assumed name, Annie Bags, had my name amongst her possessions, I knew immediately that it was my long-lost Annie Ferdinand and I agonised about what she must have endured to have had such a name bestowed on her. I have also heard a few of the accounts that apparently abound of the itinerant Annie Bags since my arrival."

"Quite so, sir, as have all of us," the doctor said. "As Annie Bags she has become something of a 'bush' legend over the years, and the folk who live and work out there on the stations and small settlements have been relentless in their defence of what they regarded as her right to live her life whatever way she chose to. I imagine they have admired and respected her as a kind of a symbol of their own independence from the shackles of big city life and wanted her to enjoy that liberty without any interference from officialdom. I personally envied her on occasions when things were becoming chaotic here at the hospital and I fancied a much simpler lifestyle such as she had. In fact, I only began to have a feeling of disquiet about her identity when I had a conversation with Mrs. Ryan from Ravenswood Junction after Miss Ferdinand was admitted. That kindly widow told me that Annie Bags had stayed with her on many occasions over the previous twenty years, but had always called her Mrs. O'Hara and talked about places that she expected Mrs. Ryan to remember, but the widow had only heard about. That in itself was of no particular significance to me, of course, as I had never heard of Mrs. O'Hara and it merely set the alarm bells ringing about my patient's mental state of health, but then Mrs. Ryan went on to say that Annie also often spoke about returning to visit her very good friends, Mr. and Mrs. Gordon at the Caledonian Hotel in Herberton. Now that revelation stunned me, for I realised immediately, to my horror, that the itinerant Annie Bags was, in fact, the wonderful Annie Ferdinand who had boarded at the Gordon's Caledonian Hotel while she worked at the school in Herberton all those years ago.

I was well aware that Miss Ferdinand had become very close to Mrs. Gordon at least and, I suspect, Mr. Gordon as well. It also confirmed my suspicion that her mental condition was as fragile as her physical condition because Mr. And Mrs. Gordon had both passed away a very long time ago. Mr. Gordon succumbed to a lung disease. He had been a coal miner and he died at our hospital in Herberton within a few months of Miss Ferdinand leaving us. Mrs. Gordon, who had been in relatively good health, I might add, followed him to the grave very soon after. I remember their passing very well because it left such a lasting impression on me, as a young man, to witness the devotion of this lady to her departed husband. We could only presume at the time that she simply did not want to live any longer without him as we failed to find a valid medical reason for her rapid decline."

The doctor looked melancholy and he paused in obvious reflection. "The passing of Mr. and Mrs. Gordon so shortly after Miss Ferdinand had left Herberton had a profound effect on many of us. You see, I can assure you that you are not the only one who loved her, Charles. She had captured the hearts of possibly every young unmarried man in Herberton at the time and probably some of the older ones as well. I certainly fell head over heels in love with her, but she never seemed to notice the adulation she received from all of us, although she did seem to enjoy the Saturday evening dances in the School of Arts building. I managed to spend some wonderful time on the dance floor with her, although we all realised quickly enough that none of us had any hope whatsoever of capturing her attention because she was clearly committed to someone else. I was one among many who were distraught when she left town, but we were aware that Mr. and Mrs. Gordon had invited her to return to live with them if anything went wrong and, because she didn't, we just assumed that her dreams had come to fruition."

The doctor got up from behind his desk and walked over to the large window. He stood there looking out at the sailing boats anchored in Cleveland Bay, and beyond to Magnetic Island and his voice was tinged with sadness as he continued. "If only someone had learned the truth about what had occurred after she left us, her life could have been so much different. Whatever tragedy it was that induced her to embark on her solitary journey must surely have involved a man after she left Herberton, because of her subsequent abhorrence of men in general. I can assure you that she showed no such tendency when she was living with the Gordons." He turned to face Charles and regarded him with a puzzled look. "She obviously did not succeed in finding *you* though, Charles. Had you perhaps, returned to England without her knowledge? You see, the one thing that poses a dilemma for me about this whole sad affair is that she carried your name and address with her throughout all those years. Why did she not try to contact you in London when she had the means at her disposal to do so at any time?"

Charles stared at him in bewilderment for a moment as the doctor's words sank in and then he shook his head vigorously, "No! No! I'm terribly sorry, David. I have unwittingly misled you. Let me assure you it was not *I* whom she sought. If it *had* been me, sir, we would have been the happiest couple in London for all of our lives." He clenched his fists and closed his eyes briefly. "I can readily understand how you have been deceived. You see, it was not I, but my brother James whom she loved so much that she followed him when he was forced to flee from London to Australia. We, - his family that is, believed at the time that he would be wrongly implicated in a serious crime, and we arranged for his hurried departure. I had not even met Annie until after this had taken place, but I then felt responsible, or should I say irresponsible as it turned out, for endorsing her decision to come to this country in a bid to find him. My dear Doctor Jones, you are correct in your theory that a man was responsible for the tragedy that befell Annie after she left your Herberton community for when she found my brother, to put it in Annie's own words, *it was not the kind of reunion that she had anticipated.*"

The doctor frowned and paced the floor in front of the window for a few minutes as he digested this information and then he smiled and nodded. "Ah! That certainly sheds a new light on what has hitherto plagued my mind since I learned of your existence, sir. We do not have a psychiatric unit at the Townsville Hospital, although I am hopeful that we will have one at some time in the future. It is therefore left to individual doctors to conduct the most basic of psychiatric assessments of the patients under our care. We do our best of course, but we are certainly not infallible and you should not take what I might say now as anything more than an opinion."

Charles glanced at the doctor with a worried look, "Are you going to tell me that you believe Annie is *insane*, David?"

The doctor was emphatic in his reply. "Certainly not, Charles, but until your revelation about your brother's involvement in this tragic affair the facts that I had before me were confusing, to say the least." He walked back to his desk, sat down and clasped his hands in front of him, elbows resting on the desktop. "I must once again test your knowledge of medical persona. Have you heard of Doctor Sigmund Freud?"

Charles paused, gathering his thoughts, and then he nodded, "Yes! I do believe I have read something of that particular *doctor*," he said. "Is he not a charlatan who stands accused of dabbling in mysticism and mesmerising his patients so that he can delve into their innermost thoughts?"

The doctor smiled wryly. "The person who is perceived to be a charlatan is often-times the pioneer, sir. From the astrologer came the modern science of astronomy. The respected chemist of today was, long ago, accused of alchemy and witchcraft and more recently the mesmerist has become the experimental psychologist. Doctor Freud is certainly the neurologist of whom I speak and yes, you are correct in the observation that he *was* accused of dabbling in mysticism by some reports. And, yes again, he did undertake some experiments using Franz Mesmer's methods of monitoring the human brain's impulses on his own disturbed patients, - but he has abandoned that form of treatment because it proved to be ineffective for many of them. He has now been instrumental in developing a treatment that has been labelled - *psychoanalysis.*"

Charles looked surprised. "You speak as if you acknowledge that this gentleman's unorthodox conduct has some academic merit, David," he said.

The doctor nodded. "There has been much debate on the issue of the legitimacy of psychoanalysis, especially amongst the medical fraternity, but since Doctor Freud's latest theories were published several years ago there has been a growing acceptance of them and recognition of their value in the treatment of patients who display symptoms of neurosis."

Charles frowned again. "Neurosis, you say, but you agreed that Annie is *not* insane, David."

"Yes I did and I still do," the doctor said in a tolerant and patient way. "Neurosis is a term used to describe the condition of excessive anxiety or indecision in a patient and that person may also be socially maladjusted, but it is certainly not insanity."

Charles looked relieved to a small extent. "I had not read of the advancement in this field of medicine, but if as I suspect, you believe that Annie has become neurotic is there a possibility that this new psychoanalysis would be available to assist her to recuperate?"

"Well no, sir, of course it would not be possible for Miss Ferdinand to consult with Doctor Freud. His neurological practice is located in Austria and as I have said, it would be impossible for her to travel so far. In any case, I don't believe that such a consultation is justified considering her positive reaction upon *your* arrival. In fact, Doctor Freud has commented that, *if we can identify the origin of a patient's neurosis, it goes away.* Perhaps you were the catalyst that enabled her to identify and come to terms with the origin of her most recent and probably her most extensive episode of neurosis and, as Doctor Freud postulated, *it has simply gone away.*"

"…Her most recent episode?" Charles stared at the doctor in dismay.

"I shall explain that observation in a moment, Charles, if you will allow me to continue with my hypothesis. I have mentioned Doctor Freud's treatment simply as a means of enabling us to understand, feasibly, why Miss Ferdinand would have left behind the security of her friends and loved ones and embarked on her long, lonely journey on the fringe of reality. It may benefit us to try to understand her apparent transference of the identities of persons she had known and presumably highly esteemed before she was traumatised, - into those of individuals she has encountered since then, and it also may explain her abhorrence of men in general." He paused and studied Charles intently. "If you object to exploring these possible scenarios, sir, then I would be happy to leave it at that."

Charles was impressed. "No, not at all David," he said. "It would be a relief to me to understand anything at all about why this tragedy has occurred, and I have found your knowledge and perception to be faultless so far. You have obviously given this a great deal of thought before my arrival on the scene."

"Yes, I have, but as I said previously, there was so much confusion in my mind about who the culprit was who had disaffected her, that the pieces of the puzzle did not fit as snugly as they do now with your revelation about your brother. I thank you for your confidence, Charles, and I ask for your patience as we explore the possibilities." The doctor leaned back and clasped his hands on his lap. "The term that Doctor Freud has ascribed to what I believe Miss Ferdinand's condition to be is *psychological repression,* which is a particular form of neurosis."

Charles frowned, but said nothing.

"We have no control over this repression. It's an action of the brain to remove certain feelings or memories from our consciousness and hide them, so to speak, in our unconscious. We *all* use repression in our everyday lives. I suppose you could say it's a kind of defence mechanism that the brain uses to protect us from anxiety. It throws up a mental shield against situations with which we may not be able to otherwise cope."

He paused for a moment, and Charles nodded slowly. "I think I understand you so far, David. Please go on, if you will."

"I'll try to simplify it as much as possible, sir, but I must emphasise again that this is just an opinion of mine based on what I have read on the subject and perhaps in the future it will be proved to be quite inaccurate."

"I do understand, but in the meantime, David, I am happy to rely on your knowledge and expertise."

"Thank you Charles. You see, emotionally healthy adults use repression to prosper in their everyday relationships by separating conflicting emotions and thoughts and removing those that do not fit in with what is considered to be socially acceptable behaviour."

Charles frowned and shook his head.

"Let me give you an example," the doctor said. "I may not care to work with a particular colleague because I feel that my skills and knowledge are inferior to his, but my mind will suppress the emotion of jealous dislike that I feel towards him because my admiration for his skill is the stronger emotion and I know that I can learn from him. Do you understand that concept sir?"

Charles nodded. "I suppose that is why we can exist side by side with a wide assortment of individuals with different beliefs to our own. In the course of my business affairs I have many times been forced to cooperate with people for whom I held little regard. I have often heard it expressed, *'I don't have to like him – I just have to work with him'.* Is that what you mean?"

"Yes; a good analogy, sir, and that is what most of us who are emotionally healthy would do. We would simply suppress those emotions of dislike and get on with the job at hand. It is clear, though, that Miss Ferdinand was not emotionally healthy when her trauma occurred and she was not able to make, what we may call, rational decisions to minimise the effect of it on her psyche. Indeed, her injured brain decided that the only option was to completely suppress the character of your brother along with all the pain and suffering that he had caused her, from her conscious memory."

Charles felt a lump rise in his throat and swallowed hard. "I suspected all those years ago when I read her letters that Annie was emotionally unstable, David, but I refused to believe it and in my defence I must say that I was entirely powerless to do anything about it. I had no forwarding address with which I could contact her and implore her to return to me. I had let her go and no matter how many tears of regret I shed for her as I read her words over and over, I knew that I had to accept my failure to protect and comfort her in her time of greatest need."

"I do sympathise with you sir," the doctor assured him, "but you may receive a little comfort when I state that, in my opinion, Miss Ferdinand's psyche was already damaged by then. She had convinced herself that your brother loved her, that he had never intentionally been guilty of any wrongdoing and that everything would be made right when they were reunited. She had made, or accepted, convenient excuses for his deplorable and cowardly exit from her life without so much as a letter of explanation. Yes, I believe she may have, well before your brother met her, already exhibited signs of advanced psychological repression. That is what I alluded to when I mentioned her *most recent episode of neuroses*. Where this may have originated is difficult to pinpoint; - something in her family history, perhaps? Was there a time in her life as a child when she was forced to repress memories of something that greatly affected her; the failure to understand the separation or death of someone close to her? We will probably never know, but I am left in no doubt whatsoever that you are correct in your assertion that when Miss Ferdinand finally located your brother after she left Herberton, the reunion had a profound and devastating effect on her already fragile mind. Her neurotic defence mechanism would then have begun the process of pulling all of the painful thoughts into her unconsciousness and preventing them from re-entering her consciousness.

If anyone had cared to notice she would have exhibited inexplicable naivety, memory loss and a lack of awareness of her own situation and condition. She would have made a drastic modification to her personal identity or character to avoid any further emotional distress and she would have dissociated herself temporarily from her previous life, isolating herself from anything that was likely to result in the resurfacing of those painful memories. That I suggest, is why she did not return to her friends, but instead took to aimlessly wandering the roads without actually knowing why she was doing it.

Men universally would have been repugnant to her, particularly men who resembled your brother, because her conscious mind would have decided that a man who looked like he did could readily unlock those painful memories from her unconsciousness. She would have avoided contacting them or even looking at them. She would also have ensured that her appearance attracted no man to her either, hence the drastic action of dressing in rags when it is obvious that she could have bought and worn fine clothes if she so wished. Her total isolation could not last indefinitely, however, because her consciousness would have been forced to find a balance between isolating her from the painful memories of her past and the need for self-preservation. As we know now, it allowed her the small consolation of befriending certain women who invariably reminded her of someone else she had loved and trusted and who was now lost to her, and she succeeded in transferring identities from one to the other. This was a clever compromise by her consciousness and I would wager that, if any of those previous recipients of her affection had assisted her in any way in the pursuit of your brother, those memories too would have been sifted out and consigned to her unconscious and she would only remember the otherwise joyful experiences associated with those people."

Charles had listened in fascination to everything the doctor had said, and he slumped in his chair as he realised that it made so much sense and the enormity of it began to overwhelm him. "Why couldn't someone have understood this and done something about it twenty-five years ago David?"

The doctor shrugged his shoulders. "You must understand, Charles that twenty-five years ago we were still grappling with the mysteries of mesmerism and hypnotism and discussing dubious subjects like animal magnetism. Until Sigmund Freud came along and set us on the path to enlightenment, Miss Ferdinand would have been diagnosed as simply having *hysteria*, a word that literally means 'uterus' in Greek because it was considered to be a purely female affliction, a belief that persists among some people to this day. It was thought to be caused by a problem associated with a woman's uterus. Hence, the removal of that organ is referred to as a hysterectomy. We have certainly come a long way in understanding the complexities of the human mind in the last twenty-five years and we can only wonder with awe at the advances we may expect in the next century."

"I am truly amazed by the clarity with which you have explained your conclusions, David," Charles said," but I have one final question that gnaws at me and I beg you to answer it frankly, with no regard for my feelings." He paused, gathering himself for the worst news. "Is there any possibility that Annie can fully recover from this neurosis?"

"I *will* be frank with you sir," the doctor said. "I can tell you with some certainty that Miss Ferdinand has a much better chance of escaping from her mental prison than she does from her physical prison now that you are here to care for her. As a matter of fact, you may very well be the only person in this part of the world who can help Miss Ferdinand to return to some semblance of normality and I wish you the very best of good fortune in your endeavours."

Charles was grateful. "Thank you so much, doctor. I am indebted to you for your reassurances and your attention to our needs."

Doctor Jones was dismissive. "I just wish we had a cure for the terrible disease that may yet be her undoing. But I have one final question for you too, sir, if I may be so bold." He hesitated and Charles waited expectantly. "What of your brother James?" he said. "Is he ever likely to return to cast the dark shadow of misery over her once more?"

"That can *never* happen, doctor." Charles said, and there was no suggestion of sentiment in his voice. "You see, I came to Australia once before, about twenty years ago, seeking both Annie and my brother. My motive for finding each was diverse, but the upshot was that I found neither. I did discover that James had died, probably from pneumonia leaving a wife and two children and from what I learned from his poor widow his death probably occurred immediately after I believe Annie finally located him. Significantly, David, I can say with some certainty that she would have been one of the last people, - if not the very last, - to see my brother alive."

They each rose from their chairs and walked to the door, and the doctor held it open for Charles. "Ah, such irony, sir," he said as they shook hands. "If Miss Ferdinand had arrived but a few days later and your brother had already expired, she would certainly have grieved, but probably would have accepted her loss and returned to London, perhaps, as you suggested earlier, to spend the rest of her life with *you.*"

Chapter 32: A Divine Reunion

Charles revealed to Annie the essentials of the discussion he'd had with Doctor Jones. He told her of the doctor's suggestion that the clear mountain air of the Atherton Tablelands may have a beneficial effect on her health and he was delighted with her enthusiastic response when he proposed that they take up residence in Herberton.

"Dear Charles, of course I remember Herberton," she said. "And yes, I remember Mr. and Mrs. Gordon very well. They were like my second family and I lived with them in the Caledonian Hotel. There are so many wonderful memories that are returning to me of my experiences in that charming little town. It will be like going home again."

Charles arranged for a complete new wardrobe of fine clothes to be delivered to the hospital and had her transferred to a private room overlooking the bay as he went about the business of organising their relocation. And when the time finally came to leave Townsville, they went together to say goodbye to Doctor Jones.

"It's good to see you looking so well, Miss Ferdinand," the doctor said. "I'm so sorry about the way your life has been touched by suffering for all of those years. If only I had…"

"…Doctor Jones," Annie scolded him gently." Charles has told me of his admiration for your extraordinary skill and rationality, but I have serious doubts that either you or anyone else could have been of any assistance to me in my personal struggle, so please don't feel sad on my behalf. Most of the memories that are coming back to me are of delightful friends and places and it may be quite improper of me to say this," she glanced at Charles in embarrassment," but *you* sir, were a major figure in that wonderful part of my dream when I recalled the Saturday night dances in Herberton, and how we danced so well together."

The doctor's face shone with pleasure. "Yes, we did dance well together, Miss Ferdinand. We were the envy of the town as I recall. But I don't think either of us would be faring so well now with the current dance craze. It's called *'ragtime'* and it appears that the participants are intent on contorting their bodies into a wide range of impossible postures. I often wonder what the young people will think of next."

Annie laughed. "I have not heard of that, doctor; I have quite a lot to catch up on I should think."

"Please don't try it, Miss Ferdinand. It can only contribute to the workload that we doctors are already faced with." He turned to Charles and grinned. "Don't be at all anxious about our apparent familiarity, Mr

Pottingley," he said. "I was fortunate in meeting and courting another wonderful lady a couple of years after Miss Ferdinand left Herberton. We have four children, and are still very much in love after twenty years of marriage."

Charles had some business that required his attention and Annie walked the short distance down the hill to the Strand that fronted Cleveland Bay and looked out on the imposing mountain backdrop of Magnetic Island. She held a small silk handkerchief in her hand so that if she had cause to speak to someone on the way she could protect them from possible contagion. She unlatched an ornate gate and entered a well-maintained garden with a stone paved pathway that led to a wide porch enclosing the front door of Saint Patrick's convent; a large ornate wooden building located next to the school of the same name. She knocked on the door and was admitted to a comfortable parlour by a young novitiate who regarded her curiously as she spoke through the handkerchief that she held to her lips. But after hearing her request the young woman excused herself and returned a few minutes later with a mature nun, who introduced herself with a friendly smile as Agnes, the Mother Superior of the convent.

Annie frowned, feeling a little uncertain as she noted the black habit that the nun wore. It looked nothing like the one worn by the elderly nun that she sought. "I'm not sure now that I have come to the correct convent," she said. "I was directed to come here, you see, but I was looking for the holy sister who visits the consumptive sufferers at Reception House. She wore a brown habit with a blue monogram."

"Ah yes," Mother Agnes said. "You *have* come to the correct convent. It is after all, the only one in town, and it is Sister Mary Gerardus that you are seeking. It can be very confusing I know, but we who are dressed in black are of the Order of The Sisters of Mercy and she is a Josephite."

"Oh, I see." Annie said, but still with a frown of uncertainty.

The nun smiled patiently. "The Sisters of Saint Joseph of the Sacred Heart began their teaching ministry here thirty-two years ago. They also established this convent, but the Sisters of Mercy took over the ministry six years later when the Josephites were recalled to New South Wales. Over the years a few of the 'Brown Joeys' have returned to Townsville to teach along with us." She laughed, and her eyes twinkled with mischief. "I think they like to keep a watchful eye on us to ensure that we are doing the right thing. Sister Mary Gerardus has been here for about four years, but she has long ago retired from teaching. Her eyes have deteriorated too much now for her to be able to teach the children, so she has chosen to spend her remaining time with us, praying for, and visiting the sick in Reception House. By her own volition she has isolated herself essentially from the rest of her sisters in God because of the risk of contagion. She is a wonderful example to our novitiates, - and indeed to all of us."

"Ah, then that is certainly the lady to whom I wish to speak. Where may I find her, if you please?" Annie said. "I would like to thank her for her care and her prayers during my own treatment in Reception House."

Mother Agnes looked at the clock on the wall and nodded. "She would have made her way back down the hill from Sacred Heart Church at her own slow pace by now. She still insists on trudging up there every morning for Mass, even though she's about seventy years old and becoming quite frail. She always sits well away from the other parishioners because of her contact with the consumptive patients." She sighed and pursed her lips. "It used to be so convenient for us when we had Saint Joseph's Church just around the corner, but the old wooden church collapsed when a flood washed away the foundations three years ago. We are all hoping that a new church will be built there soon. You would have passed through our beautiful garden bordering the Strand when you arrived, Miss Ferdinand. Take the pathway to the left when you go out the front door and you will find her there in the shade of the banyan tree."

Annie found Sister Mary Gerardus sitting quietly praying on a wooden bench in the convent garden. Her eyes were closed, but she opened them and looked up with an impassive gaze as she approached. "Please do not come too close to me if you have regard for your own welfare, my visitor. I am the comforter of the consumptives at Reception House."

"Dear Sister." Annie said. "That is why I am here. You see, I *am* one of the consumptives. I hope I am not intruding on your prayers. I just felt that I had to come and say goodbye and thank you for your care at Reception House as I am being taken to a retreat in the mountains to assist with my recuperation."

"Annie my love," the old nun cried." Oh, my darlin' Annie. I didn't know it was yourself until today and I've been sitting here praying for ye' now." Tiny tears trickled down her lined face.

"Please don't shed any tears for me Sister," she said. "And thank you for your prayers. I'm sure God has answered them, for He has sent a wonderful man to care for me. His name is Charles and he is the one who is taking me to the sanctuary the doctor has recommended." She sat down on the bench.

The old nun squinted at her through eyes that, although dulled by age, had suddenly acquired a twinkle of mischief. "So the stories of the wandering wraith they called Annie Bags, were true after all. Some claimed to have seen the spirit and were not believed and I was not at all surprised. Sure now, the story was after sounding like the legends that were spun of the little people, the leprechauns, from my own dear Ireland, but I included her in my prayers just in case. At the same time I was praying for my little sister Annie *mavourneen* too. I never thought for a single moment that I was praying for yourself twice over."

Annie was confused. *Mavourneen* was a word she'd heard before, but where?

"Charles is the brother of James, the man you were searching for. He is the one you were writing to in London, is he not?"

"Yes he was the..." Annie's face turned ashen and she studied the elderly woman thoughtfully. "...Oh my *dear* Sarah; my beloved, - *my mavourneen?*" She threw her arms around her old friend and held her frail body close to her.

"Aye, it is indeed myself, Annie, my love. It is the very same Sarah Quinlan who was once blessed to be your companion in Ballarat at a time when the two of us were left lamenting for the want of an ear to listen to us and an arm to support us, each in our own particular wretchedness, but I'm now known as Sister Mary Gerardus since I made my vows, as is our custom, and I've had a happy and rewarding life serving God since we parted ways, but it has saddened me to discover that you did not delight in the contentment that I also desired so much for you."

Sarah listened intently while Annie told her the story of her heartache and after she had finished she took Annie's hand in hers. "God works in mysterious ways, my dear Annie, and you must accept that what has transpired may have been His special way of protecting you. I recall that you told me, in your darkest hour in Ballarat, that when you were growing up you promised your father and our God, that you would only ever give your love to one man, as your mother had, - and you believed that James was that man. Well now, I myself believe that God has released you from that promise because the man was not at all worthy of your love. If you feel in your heart that a penance had to be done, however, then the last twenty years of your life must surely be sufficient to expiate any sins of which you think you may be guilty. Annie, mavourneen, He has reunited you with the man who has *truly* loved you and remained dedicated to that love for twenty-five years. You must now decide, with a clear conscience and with no regret, whether you can return that love."

"Thank you for your reassuring words Sarah, my great friend. I feel that my life is complete now, knowing that you are here and you have had such a happy life. Charles is taking me to Herberton for the sake of my health, but I shall visit you as often as I can."

"That would not be a good idea, my dear Annie. I shall pray that your health does improve in your mountain retreat, and I hope that you will write to me often and tell me of your happiness with Charles. Peace be with both of you and I hope you will have a long and contented life together, as you truly deserve."

Charles and Annie left Townsville in a privately chartered coach and travelled to Ravenswood Junction where Charles introduced himself to Sergeant Kennedy and Constable Dan, not as Lord Pottingley but simply as Annie's friend, Charles. The police officers were both almost moved to tears when they saw Annie alight from the coach, resplendent in her fine clothes and with a radiant smile on her face.

Charles insisted on paying the constable who had cared for Annie's dogs so well in her absence that they had become quite attached to him, and he accepted eagerly the option put to him to keep them as his own. That was, of course, except for old Andrew who wouldn't leave her side and happily took his place aboard the coach. He was going to Herberton. The next stop was Mrs Ryan's small house where the old woman was dressed and ready to go. Annie had contacted her several weeks previously and asked her to go to Herberton with her as her chaperone. Mrs Ryan had accepted the invitation gratefully as she had no living relatives, and she too happily boarded the coach.

As they waved goodbye and the horses moved off in a cloud of dust, Sergeant Kennedy turned to his constable. "Dan," he said. "If I never accomplish another good thing in my whole career, I'll remember with pride the day we brought those two fine people together again."

"I couldn't agree more, Sergeant." The constable nodded. "It sure enough makes our job worthwhile." He backed out of reach before adding, with a cheeky grin. "I still can't believe she's the same age as you, Sergeant. Maybe you'd scrub up okay too if you paid a bit more attention to yourself."

Chapter 33: Return to Herberton

Charles, Annie and Mrs Ryan moved into a large house on the outskirts of Herberton. It had belonged to a successful tin miner who had sold his investment and retired to the coast and it came well equipped with a resident gardener, who was a retired man himself. He, along with many of the older residents and even some younger ones that she had taught as children, remembered Annie fondly and both she and Charles were received warmly into the town that had grown by several thousand in the twenty years since she had seen it last.

Charles hired extra staff from the local community to help Mrs Ryan care for Annie and although he took every precaution to ensure that the consumptive disease was not transmitted to the staff, he soon realised to his great satisfaction that the hardy mountain people of Herberton appeared to have a natural immunity to the infection, probably, he suspected, due to the bracing climate.

Soon after their arrival, Mr Vincent Robinson, a solicitor representing the Public Trustee for the district, contacted Annie. He told her that the Caledonian Hotel had been bequeathed to her by Andrew and Jane Gordon and had legally been in her possession since Jane had passed away twenty years ago. Annie was astounded. The lawyer explained that the hotel had been leased to keep it operating on her behalf as they tried in vain to track her down and it had been steadily making a modest profit, quite enough to pay the trustee administration costs and afford the leaseholders a comfortable margin. The current joint lessees had been there for the past year, he said, and had become popular members of the community. They would be keen to meet her to extend the terms of the annual lease. He offered to arrange a meeting at the hotel to introduce her and to initiate discussions if that was what she desired.

Annie felt pangs of nostalgia when she saw the polished brass knocker in the shape of a Scottish thistle on the side entrance door of the hotel. She waited while the solicitor knocked several times, and then they were ushered into the foyer of the place she had called home for several years. It was just as she'd remembered it, with the ledger book resting on the high desk. She sighed as she thought of the first time she'd walked into this room and saw the look of surprise on dear old Mrs. Gordon's face and then, with an alarming sense of history repeating itself, she realised that the woman who had been waiting to greet her had been smiling as she entered the foyer, but suddenly her expression had changed and she clapped her hands over her open mouth, her eyes widening in disbelief. "Annie," she cried, "Dear heavens, it's our Annie Bags. Don't ye' know me lass? It's myself, - Mary Johnson. My late husband George and I had the hotel at the Gilbert River." She pointed towards a small wizened old man with skin like tanned leather. He was smartly dressed in a pinstriped suit, but looked as if he would have been more at ease in an old red miner's shirt and a cabbage tree hat. "And, heaven help us, ye' must surely remember Frank. He was always there wi' us doing odd jobs around the yard."

Frank's face too was a mask of astonishment. "Miss Ferdinand - Annie, it's Frank. I, - I fixed your cart." He managed to mumble.

Annie stared at him for a moment, confused, and then her eyes lit up in recognition. "Oh yes, Frank, – Half-pint? You did fix my cart. - and Mrs Johnson, - I do remember you. You sang to me and combed my hair. You looked after me so well."

"Annie, ye' always asked me to sing my Scottish songs to ye' while I combed yer hair. Naebody else had ever asked me to sing to them before an' I could never understand why ye' did, because my voice is not the best, as Half-Pint will attest to." She laughed and held out her arms to Annie and they embraced, but although Annie laughed too she still felt the tears begin to well up in her eyes.

"How wonderful to see you both here in Mr. and Mrs. Gordon's hotel," she whispered.

"But it's *your* hotel, Annie." It was Mary's turn to be confused.

The bemused solicitor had been standing behind Annie quietly taking in the unusual conversation and now he spoke up. "Miss Ferdinand was a very dear friend of Mr. and Mrs. Gordon and they bequeathed this hotel to her many years ago, Mrs. Johnson. Like you, the Gordons were Scottish people."

"Annie, ye' always called me Mrs. Gordon, an' I always wondered why that was so; well now, I'm just this very minute, beginning to understand."

Frank's face still showed his surprise. "An' ye' called *me* Mr. Gordon," he added, "but now I think I understand why too."

The solicitor looked at the two women and then turned questioningly to Frank, but he was wiping tears from his eyes with the sleeve of his suit. "I see there's no need for an introduction. You seem to know each other quite well," he said.

Frank nodded. "That's true, Mr. Robinson. We've known - Miss Ferdinand - for a long time. She used to stay at the Gilbert River Hotel sometimes. Mary had to close it down an' walk away when George passed on – God bless the big man. Nobody wanted to buy it." He looked fondly at the two women still locked in an embrace. "We only knew Miss Ferdinand as Annie Bags then, an' we always wondered what would happen to her because Gilberton became another of North Queensland's ghost towns after that. George an' I used to drink a toast to her. It was a kind of a ritual, I suppose. We always hoped she'd find what she was looking for." He wiped his eyes with his other sleeve and then grinned. "Looks like she did, mate. Tiny would've been very happy."

Annie contacted Mr Robinson the very next day and asked him to draw up a contract to have the hotel transferred to Mary and Frank at no cost to them. The lawyer explained to her that, under common law, a legal contract required that both sides provide consideration. In other words, such a contract would not be binding and couldn't be enforced in court if it did not specify that each party gives something of value to the other.

Annie was aghast. "Do you mean that I can't even give the hotel to my hard working friends?"

"No, it doesn't mean that at all," the solicitor assured her. "I'll have to draw up a *peppercorn* contract."

She looked puzzled, so he went on. "It's a system that's been used for hundreds of years. You see, although each party must give something, the courts will not inquire into the relative value to either party of the consideration, so if a contract calls for one party to give up something of great value while the other gives up something of far lesser value, the contract is still valid. Peppercorn trees were in plentiful supply and so one peppercorn became the standard means of transfer to satisfy the law. You can legally sell the hotel to them for sixpence or a shilling, or for one peppercorn, to be paid on demand."

Within a month Annie had signed the Caledonian Hotel over to Mary and Frank. She thought that Jane and Andrew Gordon would have approved and Charles insisted they had no need of any money from the transaction.

Annie's health improved dramatically in the clean cool air of the mountains so that within a few months the colour had returned to her face and she looked and felt refreshed and in good health. Charles was ecstatic. He loved the open spaces of Herberton and the surrounding countryside, but of course, most of all he loved just being with Annie. One fine evening they sat together on the veranda overlooking the town. It was July, a beautiful winter month in North Queensland and the last of their friends had just left after a successful afternoon garden party. They could see them in the distance, the carriages making their way down the hill to the town.

Annie regarded Charles fondly across the small table that separated them. He appeared to be engrossed in his thoughts with a slight frown on his face. "Charles," she said, "you look troubled. Did you have a good afternoon?"

He turned to face her, "Annie my love," he said, "there is no man alive who could be happier than I am here with you, but there is a topic that I must raise with you and I am unsure of how you may react."

"I believe I do know what that is about Charles," she responded with a smile.

"Do you really Annie?" he said, surprised.

"Yes my dear, it is not difficult to fathom. Our friends have just taken their leave of us. It is about them, Charles, is it not? They seem confused. We live in the same house and even though we have Mrs Ryan and the other staff with us, we are not married. They are all so dignified and they love us too much to comment, but I frequently have the impression that the ladies are concerned for my reputation."

Charles sighed, "Isn't that quite the normal way of things?" he said. "While the ladies are circumspect on the subject the gentlemen are more forthright, perhaps an effect rendered more so by the good brandy we provided. One of our closest friends has even proposed, in his usual jovial way, of course, that it's about time I ceased dithering around and ended any idle chatter about the sanctity of our relationship before it works up into a galloping scandal."

"It's certainly a quaint way to put it, Charles, but I do agree with his sentiment." Annie laughed. Her face was flushed.

Charles was speechless, not knowing what to say or do. At last, after a long silence he jumped to his feet. "Annie, do you really mean it? Would you consider marrying me?"

He dropped to his knees in front of her chair, and looked into her eyes. "I hadn't dared to hope that you would."

"Yes, Charles," she said. "Of course I will marry you, but it is not for the sake of my reputation. I want to marry you because I love you with all my heart."

Charles, Lord Pottingley and Countess Anna Maria Ferdinand were duly married in what was considered a lavish ceremony for the little town of Herberton. The reception was held at the Caledonian Hotel of course, with Mary and Frank in attendance, and people came from far and wide to congratulate and toast the happy couple.

Mr and Mrs Mowbray had travelled from Maytown, but when Annie asked about Christie Palmerston, she was saddened to learn that the great pathfinder had died about ten years before. He had settled in Townsville for a while and had even got married, but eventually, bored with life in the city he had travelled to New Guinea. The official line was that he had died after contracting a fever, but there were some who still claimed that he had been murdered and eaten by cannibals.

James Venture Mulligan, who was now sixty-six years old and the proprietor of a hotel at Mount Molloy, had ridden over a hundred miles to be there. He told Annie that he couldn't afford to miss the wedding of the only woman who had ever dented his substantial pride by not knowing who he was, although, he said, that paled into insignificance when he considered who *she* was. '*And I'm not talking about you being a Countess. I'm talking about you being the famous Annie Bags.*' Sadly, a year later, the great explorer met an ignominious end. While trying to break up a fight at his hotel he was felled by a single cowardly blow from a much younger man.

When the festivities were over, Charles and Annie retired to their mountain retreat where they lived an idyllic lifestyle, surrounded by their many friends. They were inseparable and could often be seen riding in a two-horse carriage through the main street of Herberton, or attending the Sunday church service and mingling with the other parishioners afterwards for tea and scones in the church grounds.

Annie's health had stabilised. There were few episodes of fever or night sweats. Her weight had increased to a healthy level, and she felt so invigorated that she began to get involved in community affairs. This of course made her more popular than ever, but more importantly, it gave her a sense of purpose and helped her to overcome the niggling fear that, one day, the disease would return.

Each year after the wet season, when the lower temperatures on the coast made it bearable, they would travel to Cairns, which, after the construction of the railway, had prospered at the expense of Port Douglas, or they would go to Townsville to holiday on the nearby Magnetic Island. On one such holiday they relaxed, side by side, on the wide veranda of their hotel suite overlooking Cleveland Bay. It was a clear, calm evening and the sky above was filled with twinkling stars. The lights of Townsville, across the bay, were reflected in the dark water and the only sound was the lapping of tiny waves on the rocks below, punctuated occasionally by the mournful call of an invisible seabird.

Charles was in an effusive mood and spoke enthusiastically about his day. "I met a learned fellow on my morning walk who told me that Captain Cook named this island, Magnetical Isle, because his ship's compass was affected strangely as they passed through the bay; some kind of ironstone no doubt." He suddenly realised that Annie didn't seem to be in her usual happy and contented frame of mind.

It was cool but not cold and he became concerned when he took her hand in his and discovered that she was trembling. He went inside and returned with a shawl, which he placed around her shoulders. Annie confessed that she had not been feeling well all day and in fact, had coughed up a small amount of blood earlier that morning. During that night she developed a fever and by the next morning she had again coughed up some blood. Later that day she was transferred to Townsville General Hospital and Charles sat by her bedside, holding her hand as she drifted into an exhausted sleep. They were alone in the room and he kissed her on the forehead. Her eyes flickered, half open.

"Charles?" she cried.

"Yes I'm here Annie," he said, soothing her. "Try to rest my love."

"I don't think I have long to go on this earth, Charles," she said, "I feel so weak."

Charles wiped away some flecks of blood from the side of her mouth. "Let us not talk of such things my love. The doctors…"

"…I *am* dying Charles. I know it, but I am not sad. I am going to join my papa and my mama and we will all be together *im paradies*. I love you," she whispered.

"Annie!" he cried. "The doctors will do whatever they can…" He paused in mid-sentence as she coughed again several times and closed her eyes. Her head was turned slightly towards him and a tiny stream of blood trickled from the side of her mouth.

Alarmed, he reached for the bell to summon the nurse, but it was too late. Annie opened her eyes wide and smiled serenely at him, and then slowly her smile faded, her eyes glazed over and she sighed deeply. It was her last breath.

Chapter 34: A Time to Reflect

Charles Pottingley sat on the veranda of the house he'd shared with Annie on the outskirts of Herberton. It had been three months since his beautiful Annie had been taken from him for a second time and he was quite alone, the few loyal staff he'd retained out and about in the town on various errands. Occasionally he laid his head back on the headrest of his chair and smiled silently, for he could still feel Annie's presence with him as he sat surrounded by all the familiar and modest little things that she'd bought to make it their home. He would have provided her with any luxuries she cared to have and turned it into a mansion the equal of Topsham Manor, but Annie had never craved the furnishings and fashions that were to be found in the best homes in London and Berlin. She'd had no perception of self-importance and had remained a humble creature of the bush to the end, *going about her business and harming no-one.*

Charles also found it somewhat amusing that a young red-haired Mr Potts would one day, perhaps unknowingly, be the rightful Lord Pottingley. But that was not a burden that he would have wished on anyone and he felt it was best to leave it in the past. The Pottingley dynasty was at an end and the future did not concern him, but as it happened he was not to spend his remaining years in the comfort of the small town on the Atherton Tablelands.

The first decade of the Twentieth Century had seen a continuation of the tensions that had dominated politics in Europe and Asia for the previous fifty years. By 1910, the year of Annie's passing, the great powers of Europe had already come close to war several times due to the Balkan, Moroccan and Albanian disputes and Charles was advised that he needed to return to England to settle his affairs regarding the sale of Topsham Manor before things got any worse. And so it was with a heavy heart that he said goodbye to Mrs. Ryan and his loyal staff and headed south to catch the steamer from Townsville to London via Hong Kong, leaving instructions for the dissolution of his estate in Herberton should he fail to return within the year.

He stood alone at the foot of Annie's grave in Townsville's German Gardens Cemetery, immersed in his thoughts, letting the pain of his loss wash over him once more. *'I shall return, my beautiful Annie,'* he said aloud, *'and when I do I shall have the most impressive tombstone erected over your grave...'* He stopped short, for he knew that something so ostentatious wouldn't have mattered to Annie and it would have been her wish for him to simply cherish the memories and the happiness of their last few years together in love and peace; then, staring down at the barren ground without really seeing it, his shoulders heaved as he leant over his cane and shed silent tears of regret.

Epilogue

Annie Ferdinand died on Sunday 17th April 1910 and was buried the following day in the cemetery in the Townsville suburb of German Gardens. The suburb (and the cemetery) name was changed to Belgian Gardens due to the nationalism that gripped Australia after the outbreak of the First World War.

Albert Calmette and Camille Guerin accomplished the first genuine success in immunising against tuberculosis the following year. The vaccine was called 'BCG' (Bacillus of Calmette and Guerin), but it was not used on humans until 1921 in France. Whether Charles Pottingley lived long enough to see its success is uncertain, for he may have been another casualty of the *'Great War'* that engulfed the nations of the world from 1914 to 1918, killed millions of civilians and military personnel, and changed the lives of those who survived it forever. Whatever the case may be, Charles never returned to Australia and Annie Ferdinand's grave lay forgotten and unmarked for more than a century. It is located in

Section 2F, Grave number 200, Belgian Gardens Cemetery.

A brass plaque was unveiled at a simple ceremony at Annie's grave site on 17th April 2019 (the 109th anniversary of her death). Its purchase and dedication had been organised through the fund-raising efforts of some committed members of the North Queensland community, (led by Mr. Rod Jones of Raven Tours, Townsville), who became fascinated with Annie's story of courage and resilience in the challenges she faced alone in Australia's rugged outback.

Rest in Peace, *Annie Bags.*

Ghost Warrior
Jimmy Morrill
ISBN 978-0-9923046-2-1

Ghost Warrior, - Jimmy Morrill
is also available as an Ebook.
ISBN 978-0-9923046-3-8

The barque Peruvian was lost in a gale off the east coast of Australia in February 1846. When it was found wrecked on the Great Barrier Reef several months later there was evidence that some of the passengers and crew may have constructed a raft and abandoned ship. Nothing further was heard, however, and it was assumed all on board had perished.

A shipping agent based in Sydney in the Colony of New South Wales, Clem Ross, had contracted a young sailor James Murrells, (also known as Jimmy Morrill) for the voyage, and he became obsessed with the possibility that Jimmy, and perhaps others may have survived. Seventeen years later a man claiming to be a sailor from the Peruvian made contact with shepherds at an outstation on the Burdekin River near Cleveland Bay in North Queensland telling the astonished men that he had been living with an Australian Aboriginal tribe. The man was Jimmy Morrill and this is his story.

The Sound of Liberty

ISBN 978-0-9923046-5-2

The Sound of Liberty
is also available as an Ebook.

Felix Reitano arrived in Sydney, Australia from Naples, Italy in 1896 as a young teenager. He quickly learned to speak English after a chance meeting with an equally young aristocrat from England. Felix travelled to Queensland, first to the sugar cane town of Mossman and then to Halifax, a small cane farming settlement about 100km north of Townsville. In Halifax he met and fell in love with a Scottish lass, Sarah Livingstone.

Sarah's journey to Australia at the age of nineteen, having grown up in a small poverty-stricken village in Scotland with limited knowledge to prepare her for what lay ahead, was also truly remarkable and was only matched in true pioneering spirit by the man she married.

Felix and Sarah's story would have been similar to that of many pioneering families and therefore tremendously admirable, but not independently productive in the retelling. What set them apart, however, was their unusual (at that time) inter-racial marriage and the unique complications they were confronted with due to the rise of Mussolini's Fascism and the effects of Italy's entry into the Second World War on the side of the Axis powers.